Praise for The Book of Life

'Nadler seems to know his characters inside-out and spins out their foibles and frailties in a leisurely fashion . . . a writer's writer, a fine observer of the nuances and idiosyncrasies of character.'
Kirkus

'A moving debut story collection . . . a searing heartbreaker.'
Tablet

'Poignant, insightful, and beautifully written.'
Publishers Weekly

'A descendant of Cheever, Stuart Nadler traces evolving relationships with delicate, precise prose.'
Rumpus

'Nadler's work celebrates the complexity hidden in ordinary-seeming lives and makes you eager to read whatever he writes next.'
Taylor Antrim, *Daily Beast*

'Stuart Nadler will end up being compared to people you've heard of. Bellow, I'm guessing; Nathan Englander, probably Malamud, I. B. Singer. Heavy hitters. This is both apt and not. Nadler's great, and those guys are all great—so it makes sense. Sort of. But Nadler (like each of the others) is great in his own way. He addresses tradition, but he captures the right-now as well as anyone I know of. He's heart-breaking, yet he's funny. He writes beautifully, but his prose is lean—fat-free, even. He's really worth reading, so please do.'
Darin Strauss, author of *Half a Life*,
winner of the National Book Critics Circle Award

'Stuart Nadler has written seven of the most gorgeous, poignant, intricately crafted, and compulsively readable stories I have read in a long time. His flawed protagonists tend to be forever on the brink of heartbreak, yet the unlikely effect of Nadler's fiction is that life is continually reaffirmed.'

Frederick Reiken, author of *Day for Night* and
The Lost Legends of New Jersey

'Stuart Nadler is an artist of secrets. Line after line of clear, revealing prose turns out to be incendiary. These are stories that expand without warning. A striking, rousing collection of people waking up fast. Nothing in *The Book of Life* is without consequence.'

Rosecrans Baldwin, author of *You Lost Me There*

'Stuart Nadler treats his characters like people. *The Book of Life* is a fitting title for this collection—that's what it's about: life. Here's a Chekovian fascination with the human condition—the pleasures and tortures of family, love, sex, money, work, religion. These are stories about fathers, mothers, sons, daughters, wives, husbands, friends, lovers—people with complex lives, troubled souls, deep hearts, and messy desires. Nadler is a writer, who, like Alice Munro, John Cheever, or Bernard Malamud, does not write about "ordinary people" because he knows there's no such thing as an ordinary person. Each of these carefully wrought stories is as moving and masterful as a Chopin sonata; the notes and the silences between them will resonate with the reader for a very long time after they're done.'

Benjamin Hale, author of *The Evolution of Bruno Littlemore*

Stuart Nadler

The Book of Life

PICADOR

For Shamis

First published 2011 by Reagan Arthur / Back Bay Books,
imprints of Little, Brown and Company, New York.

First published in Great Britain 2012 by Picador
an imprint of Pan Macmillan, a division of Macmillan Publishers Limited
Pan Macmillan, 20 New Wharf Road, London N1 9RR
Basingstoke and Oxford
Associated companies throughout the world
www.panmacmillan.com

ISBN 978-1-4472-0242-4

This book is a work of fiction. Names, characters, places, organizations, and incidents are
either products of the author's imagination or used fictitiously. Any resemblance to actual
events, places, organizations, or persons, living or dead, is entirely coincidental.

Portions of this book have appeared previously, in slightly different form, in *Atlantic*
("Visiting" and "In the Book of Life") and *Avery* ("Beyond Any Blessing").

1 3 5 7 9 8 6 4 2

A CIP catalogue record for this book is available from
the British Library.

Printed and bound byCPI Group (UK) Ltd, Croydon, CR0 4YY

Visit **www.picador.com** to read more about all our books
and to buy them. You will also find features, author interviews and
news of any author events, and you can sign up for e-newsletters
so that you're always first to hear about our new releases.

Contents

The Book of Life

In the Book of Life

She appeared first to Abe in the parlor, carrying a platter of dates, each wrapped delicately in a thin ribbon of bacon. It was Rosh Hashanah. This was the sort of house his friend Larry Reinstein ran. It was a calculated bit of brashness that made him popular among those he wished to impress, and repulsed those whom he felt obliged to invite, like the rabbi who was milling around, still in his tallith and kippah. Under the lights, the bacon glistened. She held the tray to the side of his body and leaned forward to whisper into his ear, *"L'shanah tovah,"* her lips brushing against his skin. She was Larry's daughter.

"You have no earlobes," she said, stepping back and then rubbing the skin of his ear between her fingers. "I've never noticed that before. How strange."

"Maybe you weren't looking close enough," he said.

She smiled and then turned her bare right shoulder toward him. Her blouse seemed designed to fall off her this way. "Oh, I think I've looked close enough," she said.

"Have you, now?"

"Once or twice," she said. "Or perhaps three times."

Her laughter sounded very much like her father's. It was a husky sound, a gust of wind caught within her. She wore a low-cut black blouse and a short black skirt that ended two inches above her knees. He couldn't look away. Shoshanna, his wife, allowed this sort of behavior, but little else. They held to the old adage, looking but not touching.

"Have you seen my wife?" he asked.

"I haven't. Isn't that funny?" She smiled and ran her free hand along the length of his necktie. "I adore silk."

"Maybe she's in the yard with the girls," he said.

"Yes, maybe," she said, letting go of his tie, her hand brushing the buckle of his belt. "She's quite the woman, your wife."

"She is."

"My mother and my father speak of her often."

"I'm blessed," he said.

"Give thanks to God for that," she answered.

He felt himself flush with color. Behind them, one of the children at the party changed the music on the stereo. The new song was too loud for Rosh Hashanah, and someone immediately rushed toward the radio dials. She put the platter of dates down on a table and stepped slowly out of her heels. For the girl she'd been, she was an improbably sophisticated young woman. He saw no sign of Shoshanna or his girls in the yard. She stepped closer to him. Without her heels, she rose only to his chin.

"Tell me something," she said.

"As far as Rosh Hashanah parties go, this one's swinging," he said.

"You're not very funny, are you?"

4

He touched his ear. "You know, they say that not having any earlobes is a sign of hereditary brilliance."

"So you have no sense of humor, but you think you're brilliant?"

"Your father and I have made a living selling mediocre food," he said. "That means one of us is brilliant."

"I think the jury's still out," she said, looking away, her eyes narrowing. "Either way, I like your strange ears."

"Where's the booze?" he whispered. "I haven't seen any."

"My mother's trying to quit," she said, winking. "We're trying to be accommodating."

"That's understandable," Abe said. Jackie Reinstein was a famous, if not a gentle, drunk. "You wouldn't have a secret stash somewhere, college girl?"

"As a matter of fact, Mr. Rivkin, I might," she said. "Follow me."

Abe had seen little of her over the years. As a girl, she'd been awkward, bucktoothed, clad in orthodontics from the day after her bat mitzvah until the day she graduated high school. He was glad to see she'd changed. She walked in front of him. He held onto the banister as he made his way down the stairs. She carried her heels in her hand. It began quickly. She stepped toward him, put one hand on his shoulder, the other on his belt buckle, and as if she were a physician about to anesthetize him, she whispered, "Just relax." After a moment, he backed her up against the pool table.

He was not the sort of man to do such a thing. This was something he knew, unquestionably, deep in his heart. If ever he was to turn into one of these men, he would not do it with the daughter of his best friend, however terrific she looked in her skirt and blouse, and then, later, without her skirt and blouse. He had always admired his friend's pool table, but he had never wished to use it this way. In fact, he thought to do so might violate some deeply crass cliché. And this was a holiday. He would most certainly never commit such a sin during the High Holy Days. In all of Westchester County, he was perhaps the poorest and least observant of Jews, but he knew, at least, when to give respect to God. All of this aside, he knew he shouldn't expect this ever to happen again. A repeat performance, an encore, or some subsequent rendezvous would certainly be a catastrophically foolish thing to do. Abe Rivkin, for all of his flaws, was not a man who liked to do wrong. He was, after all, a man of business, and this, he knew, was bad business.

Her name was Jane Reinstein.

The next day, she appeared on the sidewalk outside the office, standing in the wind on lower Broadway. She was beautiful. This he couldn't argue with, even if, in the course of the preceding day, he'd hoped otherwise, wishing away the lust he'd felt in Larry's basement. He'd never met a man who hadn't been ruined by his mistress. One way or another, something went to hell when a man's cock ended up where it wasn't allowed. If there was ever a maxim to live by, this was it.

He paused in the lobby to watch her. She wore a black raincoat that she'd tied loosely at the waist. It was the sort of coat—cut at the knee, open at the chest—that allowed the thought that nothing else was on underneath. The thought was a pleasant one. Her face possessed no lines, only a trace of makeup, and, most important, none of the signs of mischief he took pride in recognizing. This was a skill of paramount importance for any half-decent businessman: a man needed to know when someone was trying to take something from him. In one hand she was holding a black-and-white leather handbag, and in the other she clutched a yellow umbrella. He hadn't been anxious in the presence of a woman in years.

"What a nice surprise," he said, a hand on her shoulder. He thought this was a suitable nod to what had happened. "Are you here to see your father?"

"I'm not," she said, pulling his elbow. "Let's go for a walk, Abe."

They turned the corner onto Spring Street. He and Larry had picked SoHo for the headquarters of their business because of the status it afforded them. They'd been nearly destitute as children, and they'd never tired of the accoutrements of good fortune. The rent was exorbitant, but, as Larry liked to joke, it wasn't as if either of them kept a mistress. It wasn't just the woman that presented the trouble, but the money a man spent to keep her happy—using the company card at Le Cirque, renting a Carrera soft-top for the day trip to Montauk, booking the honeymoon suite at the St. Regis—that could sink a company's free capital.

"First thing," she said. "If we're going to keep doing this, you're going to need to get an apartment in the city. I'm not schlepping all the way to Westchester to see you."

"Do you want to keep doing this?" Abe asked.

"Oh, Abraham," she said, a hand on his cheek. "Don't be foolish."

She pushed him against a wall and kissed him. Her eyes were closed. His were open. In the reflection of a store window, he caught sight of himself. He was good-looking enough. However dubious he was of Jane's intentions, he allowed himself the benefit of the doubt. He was funny, he knew, and he was successful, and, on a good day, he looked decent in a blazer and slacks.

"I don't know if I can spring for an apartment, darling," he said. "New York's quite an expensive city for a pied-à-terre."

"Oh, please," she said, smirking. "You're lying."

"I certainly can't write a check on your behalf."

"I'm not asking you to write a check," she said.

"Then what are you asking?"

"Just pinch a little off the top," she said, pinching him on the stomach.

"Your dad's a hawk with the books," he said. "You know that."

"Don't lie to me, Abraham," she said. "I know you control the purse strings. Everyone knows that."

"They do?"

"Yes, darling," she said. "You're the good Jew. My dad's the bad Jew. This has been established."

He paused to consider her, standing here with him in the middle of the afternoon. In the light, he thought, she seemed like she might be someone entirely new. She touched the back of his palm gently.

"What do you say?" she asked.

"If I were to do this, however unlikely the possibility," he said, "where should this apartment be?"

"Wherever," she said. "Brooklyn is good."

"I love Brooklyn," he said.

She pulled him close to her, bringing his head toward the folds of her raincoat. "Look," she said, pulling the fabric at her chest away to reveal a body unaffected by gravity or childbirth.

"You're trouble," he said. "You're certainly trouble."

"Tell me I'm sweet."

"That would be a lie."

He brought her to Hotel Paulette, a small boutique hotel hidden away in the intricate crosshatch of the West Village. A year ago, he'd taken Shoshanna there to celebrate their twentieth wedding anniversary. Just a day earlier, he might not have considered ever doing such things, but he found the arrangement—the furtive lurking, the promise of an afternoon in a hotel room, the temptation beneath her raincoat—so foolish that it thrilled him. At his core, he considered himself a serious, intelligent man. He had always thought himself capable of anything he desired. Even this most explicitly forbidden of trysts felt to him somehow manageable. All of life came down on two sides, he believed: that which was within his control, and that which was not.

He looked into the eyes of the receptionist, the same woman who had, twelve months earlier, complimented Shoshanna on her earrings. It felt brazen to do this. His marriage had become an arrangement bereft of such boldness. There was a saucer filled with mints resting on the reception counter. He took one, and put another in his mouth. He wanted to taste good. In the room, Jane was naked within moments.

He picked Brooklyn Heights not simply because it was gorgeous, but because, when he was a boy, the neighborhood had seemed so outlandishly extravagant, an exclusive province of the wealthy, the subway stop at which every rich-looking man, wearing a cashmere overcoat and carrying the *Times* under his arm, left the train with his head high. His mother once made the claim that any random dog plucked indiscriminately off the sidewalk in Brooklyn Heights was apt to be wearing more expensive jewelry than she. As he walked to meet a real-estate broker, he thought of this, and of his poor mother, dead now for half his lifetime. She would be proud of the money he'd made, but she would undoubtedly be ashamed by what he was about to do. The streets weren't crowded, but they weren't empty, and in the face of every stranger that passed him he thought he detected an implicit knowledge of his wrongdoing. He stopped to take in the view, leaning against a lamppost near the broker's office. He lit a cigar. Smoking allowed him time and the proper rush of blood to the brain to think well. A good cigar also helped to stanch the guilt.

He took great pleasure in surveying the riches before him: the row houses on Pierrepont Street, the bare cherry trees near the river promenade, the garden planters blooming with chrysanthemums, the patisseries on Montague blowing sugar and nutmeg and cinnamon into the wind. If there was ever a place to make love to a beautiful young woman, this was it. It seemed a far more profitable experience to think of this private triumph than to think of the wrong he was committing.

When his broker, an older woman with white hair, long fingers, and short, chewed fingernails, asked why he wanted to live in Brooklyn Heights, he cracked his knuckles.

"My wife's leaving me," he said. "And she hates the city."

"I'm sorry to hear that," the broker said.

"It happens," he said. "Such is life."

He felt terrible saying such a thing. He and Shoshanna had long since stopped making love, as she put it, but they hadn't stopped, as far as he knew, actually loving each other. Theirs was a love that transcended displays of physical affection. She'd been his girlfriend when he was a boy, his next-door neighbor on Division Street. No one alive knew him better than she did. If they wanted to make love, they could remember how it had been when their bodies were young. It was like a song they'd adored since childhood, learned by heart, replayable in their memories at any time.

"How much are you willing to spend?" the broker asked.

"However much I have to," he said, reaching into his briefcase. He put an envelope of money onto the desk. Doing such a thing felt absurd, but he couldn't deny the pleasure. The experience was the sort of thing he'd have told Larry if the circumstances had allowed it.

She showed him a studio near the river. It had a small galley kitchen, and a window that looked out at the downtown skyline. The view possessed none of the famous buildings, but merely the lumped, anonymous cluster of steel and glass that now sat at the foot of the island. He stood there for a moment watching the early autumn chop on the East River, and the cars stuck in traffic on the bridge. An oak tree rose from a garden across the street, its branches poking through the steel grates of a fire escape. The broker stood near the doorway, scribbling onto a pad of paper, chewing her fingernails. He imagined leading Jane through the door here, taking off her raincoat, fucking her on the floor. He'd buy a small stereo and a television. She'd smoke her cigarettes here, stub them out into the houseplants she'd put on the windowsill. The beginning of his own marriage had looked something like this: a small Brooklyn studio, a mattress on the floor, cold dinners eaten by the television. Shoshanna wasn't the sort of woman who'd become angry at his infidelity, he knew. She was the sort of woman who'd crumple and dissolve and shut down.

"It's not the Taj Mahal," the broker said. "But it has fresh paint."

"It's fine," he said. "Draw up a lease."

He stayed behind for a few moments. The place was clean, but it seemed, in the marks he found on the walls, and in the scuffs on the hardwood, so very ordinary, and so clearly possessed by the life of its previous tenants, that he couldn't help but feel disappointed. The complexity of this affair was beginning to feel underwhelming. He felt foolish that he might have expected otherwise. An old studio in Brooklyn Heights was the same as its counterpart seven miles south in Bensonhurst. Somewhere, a few miles from here, a young couple was living in the apartment where he and Shoshanna had lived and fought and where they'd conceived their first daughter. He'd never imagined that he would be in such a position. His mother had always warned him against turning into a fool. It was three in the afternoon. His wife, he knew, was about to pick their girls up from school.

Shoshanna had dinner waiting when he came through the door. When they'd met, she'd had aspirations of working in public service. Her life in Westchester had dispossessed her of the boundless energy Abe remembered from their youth. There was now a permanent expression of disappointment on her face, and most days Abe believed it existed there as the result of some judgment she'd made of his character, one that he hadn't yet been made aware of. On the coffee table, she'd splayed a collection of her recent reading material. She was a policy wonk, and because of it she enjoyed lecturing him. The topics were numerous, and uniformly beyond Abe's interests. She could speak as easily about energy conservation or about the imminent consequences of Chinese ownership in American T-bills as she could about the various teenage boys who doted on their daughters. He was far less intelligent than she, but it was something he was used to. He gave her a small kiss. She grabbed onto him.

"I just received the most disturbing telephone call," she said, leading him by the arm into the kitchen.

His two daughters, Leah and Rose, were already at the dinner table. They were eleven and thirteen, and had begun to openly disdain him for the utter ignorance he maintained of the popular culture they found to be so important. He took his place at the head of the table. She'd cooked lamb. He could smell the rosemary and the fresh mint.

"Larry called," she said.

"He did? What did he want?" he said.

He thought of Jane, and of her body, the bitter and salty taste of her skin, the way she'd closed her eyes when she kissed him on Spring Street—so eager and trustworthy, like a young girl. Shoshanna, if she were to discover him, would be one thing, but Larry Reinstein might actually try to put a bullet in him.

"He's having quite the problem with Jane," she said.

"Really?" he said.

"You might want to call him."

"I have my own daughters to worry about."

"I still think you should call him."

"I see the guy every goddamned day. I'll talk to him tomorrow."

"She's getting into all sorts of trouble. She's hard up for money. It's that wife of his. If Jackie wasn't so drunk all the time, she might have raised her daughter right."

"How hard up?" he asked.

"She's run up some exorbitant amount of debt," she said. "Something ridiculous. Fifty thousand or something."

He smiled at his girls. They rolled their eyes at him. This was the greeting he received. He loved his children. They were beautiful and bright and sarcastic and would one day make great, tough women. They took no shit, not from him or their mother. This, he thought, was the most important lesson he could ever give his children.

"Jane Reinstein is a tramp," Rose said. She was his older daughter. "Did you see her outfit at Rosh Hashanah? Rabbi Scheinman couldn't take his eyes off of her. Go figure."

"Watch that mouth," Shoshanna said.

"I think she's pretty," Leah said. "I think she looks like a Jewish Barbie doll."

"She does not," Rose said. "You know who looks like a Jewish Barbie doll?"

"Yes, I do," Leah said. She was sweet and smarter than her sister. "Jane Reinstein does."

"You annoy me," Rose said.

"Just because you want to be Jane Reinstein's best friend doesn't mean you have to be so mean to me," Leah said.

He felt diminished by the thought that Jane might be after him for his money. The idea, however, seemed terribly transparent and obvious, and because of this, he considered it implausible. He had just spent ten thousand dollars in cash on an apartment for the two of them. This was what two months' rent and a security deposit ran these days. He'd made countless business deals in his life that, in their way, felt riskier than this. This was something he prided himself on, a barometric aversion to bullshit he'd honed since childhood. If he'd learned anything over the years, it was how to deal with his money. Should Jane Reinstein want his wallet, he was confident he could fend for himself.

Very little about life, he believed, was beyond his means to handle.

"Are you going to call him back and talk about this?" Shoshanna asked.

He leaned back in his chair. He needed to seem nonchalant about all things that concerned Jane Reinstein. He took a bite of the lamb. His wife was a good cook, not great, but she was better than his mother. Good cooking was all a man could ask for.

"About what?"

"About Jane Reinstein, Dad," Leah said.

"Right," he said.

"Don't you think she's pretty?" Leah asked. "I do. She has straight hair. Do you think she could teach me how to have straight hair?"

"What do you want me to do?" he said to Shoshanna. "She seems like a sweet kid."

"Well," his wife said. "Larry's worried. He called to ask our advice. You should help him. He's been such a good friend to you."

"Advice?" he said, yelling. "How about he lets her do whatever she wants to do? She's a goddamned grown-up, for Christ's sake. If she wants to run up some debt, then let her."

He'd silenced the table. His daughters looked down at their plates. He knew, from the heat he felt from his body, that his face had turned red. This was a problem he was going to have to fix.

The following afternoon, Abe arrived at the apartment in Brooklyn Heights some time before he'd agreed to meet Jane. He stood by the front windows, looking out on his new beautiful street, all red-and-black brick and ivy and sugar maple. It was raining. He lit a cigar, rolled up the windows, and let in the cool air. He usually smoked only when he was nervous, or when he was about to finalize a business deal. He wasn't sure now which was which. Clinton Street was pocked with puddles. Across the river, the buildings were shrouded in mist, the tops of the skyscrapers emerging from the weather. He checked his watch, and a few minutes before she was to arrive, he stubbed out his cigar, checked himself in the mirror, and put a hand through his hair.

He watched her cab arrive. She stepped out onto the street, holding her black-and-white leather handbag and her yellow umbrella. He listened to her footsteps in the stairwell as she climbed the two flights. She came in smoking a cigarette, wearing her raincoat, dripping wet. Again, it seemed that the raincoat was all she wore. There was the small ball of her kneecap below the hem, and the wet skin on her chest, glistening between the lapels. He wondered if she ever wore clothing. She looked around and smiled at the mattress he'd had delivered earlier in the day. There was music playing from a small stereo he'd brought with him. He'd had no idea what to play for her. A clerk in a record shop had made suggestions. He found the music awful.

"How many months' rent did you pay up front?" she asked.

"Come again?"

"I just wanted to know how long you thought this would last," she said, placing her bag and her umbrella down on the hardwood.

He fiddled with his cigar stub and wondered if the truth would sound adequate. "Two months," he said.

"That's it?" she said, frowning. She thrust her hands to her chest. "I'm hurt."

"I thought two months was sufficient."

"Listen to you," she said, pushing him toward the mattress, sitting him down on it. *"Sufficient."*

"Do you like it?" he asked. He put his hands on her hips.

"Sure," she said. "It's great. It's cold."

"I thought you might like it," he said. "Do you need anything else?"

"Like what? Like jewelry?"

"Do you want jewelry?" he said. He wasn't prepared to do such a thing, and he hoped she wouldn't demand gold or diamonds.

"Never buy your mistress something your wife doesn't already own," she said. "It's bad karma."

"How would you know?" he said. "You've never had a wife."

"But I know Shoshanna," she said. "And she wouldn't take kindly to it."

At this, he attempted to laugh, but failed. He removed his hands from her hips.

"So, how're you feeling, you big cheater?" she asked.

She turned away from him, kicked her heels across the room, and walked barefoot toward the windows.

"I feel fine."

"Really? How was it sleeping next to your wife last night?"

"It was fine," he said. "I have quite a bit of practice at it."

"But you haven't done this before," she said.

"How do you know?"

"You have it all over you," she said, smiling, walking toward him.

She touched the crest of his upper lip with the point of her finger. He closed his eyes.

"I do?"

She laughed and gently took hold of his hands. "Yes, darling."

"Maybe you're wrong about me."

"So you're saying you don't feel guilty?"

"Well," he said, "I suppose I feel somewhat surprised by how easily it happened. But I'm older than you, remember, and I'm generally in control of my emotions."

"You know what they say," she said.

"No. What do they say?"

"If an affair is that easy, then something else is going on at home."

"Is that so?" he said. "I've never heard that."

He found her delightful and stunning and utterly full of shit.

"Then you don't feel like hell?"

"You need to stop asking me that. Do *you* feel like hell?" he asked.

"I like to feel like shit every once in a while," she said, smiling.

The sight of her white teeth, straight, perfectly aligned, brought back the memory of her as a girl. This was not, he felt, an opportune time for this sort of recollection.

"Besides," she said. "I was raised to feel guilty. Weren't you? Isn't that the way we're made? This is, after all, the High Holiday season. We need something to atone for."

"If you say so."

She smiled. "You know, I really do like you, Abraham. I really do."

She pretended to be tough, but he saw the gentleness in her.

"Here," she said. She placed his hands on the ties to her raincoat. "Pull."

He wanted to go slowly, to take it all in, but he finished too quickly. She made him feel like a teenager. Afterward, she lit another cigarette. They were side by side on the mattress. He'd forgotten to bring fresh linens. He began to run his finger along her skin.

"I want to live here," she said.

"I bet you do," he said.

She grabbed his finger and squeezed and started to bend it backward. He was stronger than she was, capable of resisting her, but he was amused to see her do this. Her father had done the very same thing to him when they were children, the two of them on the stoops of their tenement, listening to the Dodgers game on the radio.

"Did you hear me?" she asked.

"I know," he said. "You want to live here. The place is great. The area is great. Do you want to go for a walk?"

"No," she said, laughing, rolling over on top of him. She put her fingers through the hair on his chest. "I really want to live here. I'm going to move my things in."

"I don't know about that," he said.

"I don't know what my father told you about me," she said.

"Let's not talk about Larry," he said. "Not while I'm without my underwear."

"I'm a smart girl."

"Of course you are," he said.

"I'm smarter than you are," she said.

"You think so?" he said, picking her up, kissing her mouth. She didn't kiss him back. He was sure he possessed the greater mind, but she was able, with the simple act of refusing him, to deprive him of his confidence. She got off the bed and walked to the open windows. His scarf and coat were folded over a chair. She took the scarf and wrapped it around her neck; she wore nothing but her eye makeup, her earrings, and his scarf. A fire engine drove by, its red-and-white lights flashing into the apartment, across her flat stomach and her thighs.

"I should get some curtains," he said.

"No," she said. "I like it like this. It's like anyone could see us if they knew we were here."

She was exciting, in her way. He put on his pants and walked over to his coat. He took a fresh cigar from his jacket. He liked to make a show of clipping his cigars. Years ago, Red Auerbach, the old basketball genius, lit his cigar when he knew his team had sealed a victory. For this very reason, Abe had always considered Red one of his personal heroes. He found an irrefutable brilliance in that sort of psychological gamesmanship, in the bravado involved in that one tiny act. Gamesmanship and bravado were valuable currency in the business world. Abe put the cigar into the teeth of the clipper and brought the blade down loudly.

"You're a cute kid," he said, speaking from the corner of his mouth, wagging the cigar over the flame of his lighter.

"I'm moving in tomorrow, Abraham," Jane said.

Larry came to his desk the next afternoon, an hour before lunch.

"We need to talk, Rivkin," Larry said. "Get your car keys."

Larry turned around and headed for the staircase. For a moment, Abe sat still at his desk, alternately trying to catch his breath and wondering about how many punches he might be able to take. It seemed foolish that he might have kept this going without getting caught. Their families were too tightly entwined to escape unscathed. Larry turned around in the doorway and threw his hands up in the air.

"Let's go, Abe. Don't dillydally. I'm in a hurry."

"Okay," Abe said. "I'm coming."

He followed Larry out onto the sidewalk on Broadway. His hands were shaking, and he put them in his pockets. To appear calm seemed impossible. In the unseasonable warmth, he began to sweat through his shirt.

"I'm gonna fucking kill her," Larry said.

"Jackie?" Abe said. "What's she done now?"

"Not my wife," Larry said. "Jane."

"Jane your daughter?"

"What's the matter with you, Abe? Are you slowing down?" Larry struck the side of his head with his knuckles. "Of course Jane my daughter."

Larry put a hand on Abe's shoulder. He remembered how Jane had done this to him days ago in the basement. Larry fumbled with a cigarette.

"Is something wrong?" Abe said. He took his lighter from his pocket. "Talk to me."

"We need to go to Brooklyn," Larry said. "Give me your damn keys."

"What for?" Abe said.

"I just need to show you what my daughter is up to. I need to drive your car. She'll recognize my car."

They went in Abe's Mercedes. It was a good car, Larry said, as he drove across the Brooklyn Bridge. This was the shorthand Larry used, a false display of modesty, for they both knew that the car was far better than good. It pleased both of them to pretend that they were still the boys they had been decades ago in Brooklyn, shoplifting food on their way to school.

"Where are we going?" Abe asked.

"Brooklyn Heights. Clinton Street."

At this, Abe felt ill. "Why? I hate it there."

"I do, too. But my daughter and her boyfriend just moved into an apartment there."

"Her boyfriend?" Abe asked. He took a deep breath. "How come I haven't heard of this boyfriend? I see you every day."

"It's not serious. It's some *shaygets* she's been running around with for the past few months," Larry said.

"Come again?"

"She's dating a *shaygets*. A goy. Some Jew-hater."

"A Jew-hater? How lovely," Abe said. "How do you know this?"

Larry made a show of exhaling, throwing back his head and clenching his fists.

"I don't want to have to worry about you, too, Rivkin. What's happened to your head? I called your house the other day and talked to your wife about this."

"She told me that Jane was in debt. She didn't say anything about a boyfriend."

"She and her boyfriend are in some sort of trouble," Larry said. "Drugs or something. I don't know. No serious person runs up that much debt."

When they arrived at the apartment, Larry parked the Mercedes by the large oak tree that only yesterday Abe had stared at from the window. The street felt more illicit from the ground than it did from two stories in the air.

"How did you know she was here?" Abe asked.

"She came back to our house last night and picked up some

of her things. I asked where she was going. She wouldn't tell me. So I followed her here."

"Why would you need to do such a thing?"

"So, I get this call a few days ago," Larry says, his hands moving wildly. This was the way Larry Reinstein told a story, half narrative, half pantomime. "My daughter's calling me from a pay phone. Says she's in some trouble. Says she needs me to wire her money."

"Okay," Abe said.

"She says she needs fifty grand."

"That's quite a lot."

"Right. I tell her I love her. I tell her that I'll help her however I can, but that I can't give her that kind of money."

"That's the right thing to do, Larry."

"The next part is hard."

"Just say it."

"Don't think less of me," he said, his brows furrowing.

"I don't see how that's possible, old friend."

At this, Larry smiled. "She tells me she knows about this little affair I've been having."

"Oh, Larry," Abe said, trying to sound sufficiently disappointed. "Who is it?"

"I can't say."

Abe laughed. "If you can tell anyone! I can't believe you haven't told me until now!"

"It's Susie Mintz."

"The blintz lady?"

Abe laughed. Susie was a sales representative they did business with. She was a redhead, a classic Borscht Belt Jew, always performing her bad Jackie Mason imitations and bringing by her homemade grape blintzes on Friday afternoons.

"I'm ashamed to admit it," Larry said.

"I always liked Susie," Abe said.

"Yeah," Larry said. "Unfortunately, so have I."

Abe had never enjoyed playing poker; gambling had always seemed distasteful to him, but he knew enough not to show his hand. He took a breath, wiped his brow with his sleeve. He thought he needed to appear bewildered, and he did his best to act the part. He shrugged his shoulders and raised his eyebrows.

"So, what's your plan? What are we doing here?"

"I told her I needed a few days. I had to talk to you."

"Of course." Their business arrangement had always been that Abe controlled the checkbook while Larry maintained an eye on the quality of their food. If money was spent, Abe needed to sign off on the amount. Everybody knew this.

"And I just wanted to see the apartment for myself. I had this vision of going up there and making a scene. Now I don't know what I'm gonna do."

Abe saw her first. She was at the window, smoking a cigarette, looking out toward the water. A moment later, a man came up behind her. He was young, with black hair. In a way, Abe thought her boyfriend looked very much the way he had looked as a young man. He felt surprisingly jealous, an emotion he had not encountered in decades. She smiled down at the Mercedes, and then, blowing smoke against the glass, she waved.

Larry cursed as he sped away. Abe knew she wasn't waving at her father.

Over lunch that afternoon, Abe and Larry smoked compulsively. Abe feared that Jane might come for his money next, but he thought, sitting across from Larry, that perhaps he had become involved in a complicated rivalry between a father and a daughter. Although he had slept with Jane, had rented her an apartment, his loyalties were, and had always been, with his friend.

"I think we both know what you need to do," Abe said.

"Tell me," Larry said.

"Don't look so hopeless, old friend."

"Jackie is going to kill me."

"This is why I think that we both know what's necessary."

Abe leaned forward. They were eating at a pizza place. He spoke loudly.

"You have to give her the money. If not, then she's going to tell Jackie. If she tells Jackie, then Jackie's gonna leave you. If she leaves you . . ."

"Don't say it." Larry said, waving his hand. "This is why I came to you."

"If she leaves you, then she'll take you to the cleaners. We'll be out of business."

"How did I let this happen?" Larry said, looking up at the ceiling. "Forgive me, God."

"You know what I always used to say: don't stick it where it doesn't belong."

Larry leaned forward and whispered, "You've never fucked around?"

"On Shoshanna? Get out of here."

"I don't buy it for a second, Rivkin," Larry said. "You're full of it."

"How long have you known me? Our whole lives? If I tell you never, I mean never."

Larry smirked. "I still don't buy it."

Negotiations had always been Abe's favorite part of doing business. He was at his best when he was trying to convince someone to relinquish something he needed. If Abe needed to coax the jacket off a man's back, he went into the negotiations without a scintilla of doubt. He loved the rush he got from getting a deal done.

"Can we afford fifty grand?" Larry asked.

"Sure," Abe said, shrugging. "Is it gonna sting? Sure. Is it gonna sink us? No."

"You're sure?"

"Look at it this way," Abe said. "Fifty grand is a lot of money."

"I know."

"But fifty grand is a hell of a lot less than what your wife's gonna want."

Abe knew the look of defeat—the placidity in the face of his opponent, the stiffening of the upper lip, the resignation in the spine—but he had never felt so terrible to see this in the body and the face of his best friend.

The shame felt so much worse than he'd expected.

The following day, she was on the sidewalk outside the office. This time she wasn't in her raincoat, but in a pair of khaki pants and a sweater. Around her neck she wore a long white scarf. She looked beautiful, he thought, but she also seemed to him more severe and adult than she had before. He paused by the elevator bank and stopped in the lobby to watch her. It was a marvel to see how unaffected she appeared, standing there in the wind, the entire mess of her father's marriage, and of his own marriage, at her feet. He saw so much of Larry in Jane—the cut of her chin, the tiny bulb at the end of her nose, the laugh that started in her throat and whistled out through her teeth—that it troubled him to see that his friend could have created a girl like this. Although it discomfited him to think of her as a girl, he had known her when she was young, and in his memory she was kind and awkward, making paper jewelry for Shoshanna, gently petting their golden retriever.

He wanted very much to sneak out the back door onto Crosby Street, to avoid her until the payoff had been made, to vanish completely from her life, but as he stood by the elevators, she saw him, and she began to walk toward the office doors. He had no choice but to go to her. He wondered why he had only now begun to see the mischief in her. It was everywhere.

"Let's walk," he said, grabbing hold of her arm.

"I have an appointment later on," she said. "So we need to make this quick."

"Who would this appointment be with? Another one of your father's friends?"

They turned the corner. At midday on Spring Street, the sidewalk was mobbed. He grabbed her arm tighter.

"If you must know," she said, "I have to see my waxing lady. A good Jewish girl doesn't look like this naturally. But you're so smart, Abraham. You must know that already."

He stopped. She smelled lovely, a mix of cigarettes and citrus and lavender. The scent, he knew, was one he would need to work to forget.

"I came by simply to thank you," she said. "For the apartment, and, of course, for helping to convince my father to do the right thing."

"You know, the rent's going to run out on that place," he said.

"You know, for a *businessman,* you're about as dim as they come."

"Am I, now?"

"The landlord's not going to call me," she said. "I'm sure you know that to default on a lease in this city can lead to terrible trouble. It can wreak havoc on a businessman's credit."

"Don't be a fool," he said. "Any idiot can get out of a lease."

She smiled, reached into her purse, and removed a long cigarette.

"I was pleased to see you and my father the other day," she said. "Christopher sends his regards."

"Christopher."

"My fiancé."

"Of course."

"He looks quite a lot like you when you were young," she said. "Don't you think?"

"I didn't get a good enough look," he said.

"The similarity isn't a coincidence. But I hated for you to see him like that. I really do like you, Abraham. I've always had something for you in here," she said, her hand on her heart. "I did when I was young, and I still do."

"Why would you do such a thing to your father?" he asked.

"I suppose I'm more of a mommy's girl," she said. "And either way, I don't think you know too much about my father."

"I don't? I knew him when he was seven years old. You're telling me I don't know my best friend?"

"Are you familiar with the word *covetousness?*"

"What happened to you? You were so sweet when you were young."

"You should look it up. *Covetousness.* Go home and look it

up and show it to my father. It's in the dictionary. It's even in the Torah, I believe."

"Your father has always been good to you. He gave you everything you wanted."

"Of course he has. *Everything*," she said, grinning. "And of course you know that he's refusing to pay for my wedding."

"I didn't know that," Abe said.

"There's a great many things you don't know."

"Is he angry because Christopher is a Christian?"

"No. My father doesn't care about religion. He's as godless as they come."

"Then why?"

"Because Christopher said something about Israel once that my father didn't especially care for."

"Are you kidding me? This is why you've done all of this? Over your father's *politics*? Larry hasn't read the paper since the Dodgers left Brooklyn."

"You're both idiots. Neither of you is immune from that, fortunately for me. I want a wedding, Abraham. I'm a traditional girl. I want the dress and the flowers. And as much as I like you, and I do, you weren't going to pay for it, were you?"

He laughed at this. "I suppose the definition of *tradition* has been changed. Should I look that up as well? Let me ask you, though: does your little boyfriend know about me?"

She smirked, bit her lip, and turned away. He'd evidently hit a sore spot.

"Cheating's a bitch, huh? How about I keep your secret, and you keep my secret," he said.

"He's a free spirit," she said.

"I'm sure he is."

Two little girls in matching yellow rain slickers and white

hats walked by just then and he caught her staring at them with a certain amount of wistfulness in her eyes. He saw here what he had seen earlier in the apartment on Clinton Street, a particular, buried benevolence that she tried to suppress.

"I told you earlier," she said, turning back to him. "I really do like you. I'm very sorry that you were caught up in this." She took his hand, brought it to her mouth, and kissed his fingers. "I'm going to go now."

He watched her walk away down the street, her scarf caught in the wind, so white against the gray city that he could still see her minutes later, blocks away.

At the end of the Days of Awe, Abe threw a party. Many of his friends came with their families. Larry arrived with Jackie. The rabbi arrived alone. Abe stood in the kitchen, one hand on the dining table, the other on his belt, looking out through the doorway into the living room, where his daughters and his wife greeted company. He was thankful that Jane had not come. Rose and Leah, nearly always competitors when it was just the two of them, looked like sisters here amid a houseful of the congregants of Temple Beth Elohim. They sat politely on the living-room sofa, side by side, refusing offers of food until sundown. He rarely saw them this way. Larry made a deliberate effort, every few moments, to wink in Abe's direction, a nod, surely, to confirm the payoff had been made. Shoshanna, elegant tonight in a shawl and a skirt, stood in a slant of sunlight that had within it the wetness of a recent storm, but also the gold wane of a Yom Kippur fast about to break. She was laughing at a joke Larry was telling. Abe loved his family and his friends. Family, his father had told him, was the only thing that mattered in the end.

Twin crystal candlesticks awaited the holiday blessing. Every year the Reinsteins and Rivkins alternated hosting the party for Rosh Hashanah and hosting the break-the-fast celebration following Yom Kippur. Shoshanna, in preparation for this year's party, had spared no expense.

"Honey," she called to him. "I have to run up to use the ladies' room. Could you go down and get the food ready?"

"Of course," he said, smiling.

To prevent anyone from pilfering one of her knishes, or swiping their fingers through the stalagmites of her lemon meringue, she stored the food in a refrigerator they kept in the garage. He started for the garage, but, deciding that he wanted a cigar, doubled back into the kitchen and saw, at the foot of the back staircase that led to their bedroom, a secluded space empty of partygoers, Larry and Shoshanna, inches from one another. They were whispering. Abe stood silent in the hall. After a moment, Shoshanna took Larry's hand in hers, smiled, and brought it to her mouth.

Abe rushed to the garage. He lit a cigar. He felt his blood rush to his cheeks. He stood alone in the garage for a moment, smoke billowing to the ceiling. Hooked onto the door handle of the refrigerator was a yellow umbrella. Suddenly, he found himself quite unsure of what to think. A window was at his back, and he turned to look through it, half expecting to see Jane as he had seen her so often recently, standing in the wind, wearing her black coat. He was grateful to see only the familiar bark of his backyard oak tree. No one could enter this garage without going through the house. She must have come and gone while he was in the shower. He took the umbrella in his hands. As he did, a piece of paper fluttered down to the floor from the folds of the canopy. He bent to pick it up. The note had one sentence. It read: "My father's lover isn't Susie." Above him, in his house, he could hear the children singing along to something on the radio.

He considered the very first Yom Kippur the two families had spent together: a rainy weekend in October, eighteen years earlier. Everyone had huddled in a small apartment on the Upper West Side, a place too expensive for Abe, but a place he'd bought anyway, a place with a view of Central Park, a place he felt proud to arrive home to, a place where they had just one tiny sofa upholstered in rough cotton pushed up against the wall, on which they all sat—Larry and he and Shoshanna and Jackie and Jane. She was a little girl then, always at her mother's side. They spoke through the night of their childhoods and their poverty and their parents, all of whom had died too young and too poor, none of whom would have believed how successful their children had become. Jackie was quickly drunk, and Larry told jokes to Shoshanna. Abe had done nothing but call toasts to their good fortune, to their luck, and, of course, to the love he felt for everyone in the room. Everyone stopped for a moment to hoist their glasses, even Jane, her lips marked with a ring of grape juice. Abe drank first. The wine was the most expensive he had ever bought. *I adore all of you,* he said. *All of you.*

Then Larry hoisted his glass. *To my friends,* he said. *May we live like family.*

Winter on the Sawtooth

At the train station in Back Bay he emerges from the rear of the crowd, the tallest one, his hair clipped short, wearing a gray overcoat, a man. "My son," I say aloud. A station guard standing near me, older, white at the temples, grins at me kindly. The terminal becomes for a moment temporarily crowded. I wave, get up on my toes, shout for Josh. At ten past three in the morning, I'm the loudest thing for miles, louder even than the baritone of the recorded public-address announcer. Josh comes to me with his head lowered, so serious now after only a season away. I clap him on the shoulders, take his bags, hug him tightly, try to lift him. He's been a head taller than me since the sixth grade. "Jay-Jay," I say, a nickname from infancy.

"Dad," Josh says.

I've squeezed him too hard, too eagerly, and he squirms beneath my grip.

"Easy," he says. "I'm exhausted. I've been traveling all day. Give me some space."

He leads me outside, blocks the wind with his body, stops for a moment on Dartmouth Street to look at the sky, the pink swirl of weather atop the city, the faint hanging sliver of the moon. Winter in Boston has deposited ankle-deep gullies of iced rain along the curb where I've parked, and both of us, without looking, plunk ourselves wetly into the mess. Josh bristles at the cold, flips his collar up, curses. Four months in San Francisco, I think. It might as well have been a decade. Soon, his mother worries, his visits will fail to happen at all.

His flight, originally headed for Boston, was diverted to New York because of the weather, and he's made the last four hours by rail. He is thin, his face squaring off with age, his chin marked with a two-day beard. All the sun, the warm Palo Alto air, the beaches and outdoor sports—everything that lured him away from a scholarship here in town—seems to have been cast aside. Below the streetlamps, his complexion betrays a semester spent indoors. What was the point, I think, except to escape, to flee to the corner of the country farthest from us.

At the car, he peers into the front seat, making a show of it, and allows his disappointment to breathe out of him—a big white cloud of a sigh.

"Mom stayed at home, huh? Couldn't be troubled to spend a half hour with you in the car?"

"It's a bit late for her," I say.

"She told me she'd come," he says.

I hesitate a moment before getting inside. Four months ago he was my boy. Now here he is, in an overcoat and a collared shirt, trying to level with me.

"You know her," I say. "Driving at night makes her anxious."

"You and her just can't figure out how to get along, can you?"

I hear him clearly. He's asked me the same question over the telephone. Nothing is as easy as lying over the telephone, however.

"The road home will be empty," I say. As we pull away, snow begins to fall. "This looks lovely," I say. "Winter."

His first four months away in California have been dominated most pressingly by the quiet in our house. A big Tudor, bricks and stucco, dark at noon, enshrouded by Wichita Blue Juniper, it is, at its best, loudly beset by creaks, moans, the whine and whinny of century-old pine slats, and our beast of a furnace singing to us in the evenings. Most nights, my wife, Peggy, claims the head of the dining table, where, in place of the charger and china, she installs her slate-gray laptop and writes to Josh. Sometimes they write to one another simultaneously, a feat of technology that dizzies me. I am a Luddite, and prefer to write to him the way my father wrote to me, on ecru-colored correspondence cards, my initials engraved at the top in a handsome navy-blue Roman font. My letters to him are short, full of the sort of paternal wisdom I wish my father had known enough to give me. *Study earlier in the day,* I write, *so that you have time to unwind in the evening. Don't mix your liquors, but if you must, stick with the clear stuff. Find a woman who loves English novels, but don't forget to take her to the movies.* I feel insubstantial sending such trivia to him, especially when his mother seems to do little else but write to him, and because his attention has always seemed sharper on her than on me. The true sound of his time away, I often think, has been the sound of Peggy's computer when another of Josh's short notes drops into her in-box—that jazzed-up, liquid drooping. Nothing—not the painful fissure of our marriage, our arguments, not the deaths of our parents, nothing, I think—has bothered her more than having her son away at college. Theirs is a constant conversation, a correspondence without beginnings or endings, the written version of the Himalayas, streaming from one end of the year to the other, everything in short ungrammatical crags.

In the car, it's obvious that she's told him of our plans to divorce. His posture is stiff, and he fiddles with the radio dials, bouncing across genres, from Mozart's *Turkish March* to a coarse discussion over some disputed public-works project. In one form or another, Peggy has had this plan for a year. Now he wants to know all the details.

"How long?" he asks, silencing the music. So suddenly, there is the whoosh of the wipers, and the slow, steady rain against the glass. "How long has all of this been in the works, Dad?"

We are in Concord, passing the cold white face of the Old Manse, lit now in the early morning with twin flickering bulbs. My car hums in the darkness, a hitch somewhere in the heating system. Tuition at Stanford means that the hitch will grow louder.

"Oh, I don't know, Josh. It's not important, is it?"

"Do you have separate bedrooms?" he asks.

"That's really not something I want to talk about," I say.

"What about Phil?" he says. "Do you know about Phil?"

That Josh knows about Phil is a shock to me, but, as always, I do my best to keep my composure. Phil is Philip Osgood, Peggy's lover. On two occasions, I've found Osgood loitering in my kitchen in the middle of the evening, wearing his slippers and robe. I have little else to say about him, and so, to Josh's question, I shrug. "I know lots of things, son. Phil is just one of those things."

"Doesn't it bother you? Doesn't it just"—he is seething, searching for the words—"doesn't it just piss you off? She's your wife!"

I let his question hang between us. Anger is easy at his age, especially over a woman, and I don't have much interest in entertaining his youthful sense of marital propriety and moral righteousness. His mother and I were college lovers. I met her two days before my own first trip back from Thanksgiving, standing in the rain on Broadway waiting for the city bus to take me south to Penn Station. She was wearing a slick green mackintosh and pink Wellingtons, and she was smoking a cigarette with her hand cupped over and atop the paper like a sailor. Who wouldn't fall for a girl like that?

"I love your mother," I say. "I always will."

"Clearly not enough."

"Nothing is clear, Josh," I say. "You should know that by now."

"But she's sleeping with another man," he yells just as we arrive, and just as the headlights from my car track across the lawn to reveal his mother, fresh-faced, neatly wrapped in a wool blanket, standing at the front window, jumping for joy.

The trouble began with a course in which Peggy enrolled herself at our local adult learning center. It was a class in the memoir, a genre for which my wife has always figured herself especially well suited, owing mostly to the peripatetic childhood her family forced her to endure. Her father was an oilman, and because of this my wife spent most of her childhood bouncing around the world's various petroleum capitals: Houston, Caracas, Riyadh, Lagos. There are photographs in our home of my wife as a small girl taken in each of these cities. In them, she is always smiling, wearing a broad-brimmed hat, and clutching her daddy's hand.

The class is where she met Phil Osgood, who was leading the whole ordeal, and who, I suppose, saw some vulnerability in my wife's prose that led him to pursue her as doggedly as he did. The exact details have always been a bit of a mystery to me, but what is important is what happened later, which is to say that their relationship did not end, and neither did my marriage. The common wisdom, of course, is that divorce is bad for the children involved, something that Peggy offered up very soon after Osgood came into our lives and that I, hoping to keep my marriage together, agreed to wholeheartedly. It's not as if I disagreed entirely with the premise, but my judgment at the time was clouded. At first, she made promises to stop seeing him, and I accepted her infidelity as a one-time transgression, an error that she hoped I might forgive. I thought I'd simply wait her out. I don't wish to go on about this. She didn't stop seeing him, and although I became angry and made hollow promises to take a lover myself, she convinced me that what was happening to her was not a case of misdirected boredom or simple lust. It was love: she and Osgood were in love, and it would be good of me, decent, in fact, to allow their relationship to develop.

All of this started a little less than a year ago now, when Josh was just about to mail off his applications to college. I can remember coming home from a particularly heated argument with Peggy—we used to drive around Concord in her tiny silver Mazda screaming at one another—to find my boy at our kitchen table, finishing up his essays to the Ivy League. I wonder sometimes what would have happened if Josh had stayed East. There were offers, of course. He seems made to be a student, in a way that I never was. If he'd stuck around, his presence may have weakened her resolve to leave me. Or maybe this is wishful thinking, but, nevertheless, it's an idea I believe Josh shares. An hour after we return home, I catch him standing alone in our kitchen, in very much the same position I last discovered Osgood lurking around in his stolen Hyatt hotel robe. There is something in his expression, a certain bewilderment at the small changes in our house, which I remember feeling myself at his age, and it makes me believe he is feeling for the first time the terrible strain of regret. It's the worst part of adulthood, I think to tell him, because it's an emotion that accompanies every one of our important decisions.

His back is to me, but he sees my reflection looming in the window beside him.

"Should I go see him?" he asks into the dark.

"Who?"

"Osgood. I think I should just go tell him to back off. You think he'd listen to me?"

"Lord, no," I say. "He's not that sort of guy."

He turns to me then and shakes his head. "I really hope the Lord has nothing to do with this."

At breakfast the next morning, he announces just what Peggy has feared: he won't be coming back East in December. Hanukkah, he claims, is not a serious enough holiday for him to consider the trip again. And he won't be part of some half-baked Christmas celebration, either. We had for years combined the two—with clumsy results. Evidently, he has become something of a devout Jew over the last four months. It's the influence of his professors, or his roommate, an Orthodox Philadelphian who arrived with a separate kosher dorm fridge. Or it's simply the result of a semester's worth of introductory religion wreaking havoc on his conscience. I haven't yet figured out which is the truth. Peggy is a lapsed Catholic, and I haven't been to synagogue since my bar mitzvah, almost forty years ago. Each of us is plainly surprised by his newfound faith, even though neither of us says so.

"I'll have work to do," he says. "Maybe for Passover I'll come home."

"Passover?" Peggy says. "What's that mean? We've never done a Passover."

"It's not the holiday that matters, it's seeing family," I offer.

"Is Osgood family yet?" he asks.

This makes his mother blush with embarrassment, and then well with tears. In a moment, she's gone to her bedroom. The door slamming above us is a stark reminder for me of how badly she had wanted this day to arrive. There was a countdown, even, tacked to the pantry door. The fact of his flight's delay had caused her to weep over her breakfast cereal. Now this:

"On the Friday after Thanksgiving," he tells me, talking to me as though I'm his employee, "I'll be going to Sabbath services. Just so you know."

Peggy's sadness is a boulder I cannot budge. I try. I sit on the edge of her bed, where, on the nightstand, beside a handsome photo of Josh, there is a photo of Phil Osgood, looking stocky and hairy and smiling like a jackal. My bedroom down the hall is empty of photographs. I put my hand in her big nest of red hair. Josh is right. I do hate Osgood. He does enrage me.

"Oh, Peg," I say.

"What now?" she mutters into her pillow. A slant of light has edged a diamond across her breastbone. "Does he want to be a rabbi?"

"He's been away for four months. He's just experimenting."

I help her sit up. Since Osgood arrived in her life she has seemed more beautiful to me, a predictable consequence, I know, of another man taking her to bed, and of her attention officially being transferred from me to him. But this new beauty is honest in a way that reminds me of her years ago, at nineteen, shoeless, running through the weeds behind her mother's house in Riverdale.

"He won't be home for another year, then," she says. "I know it. He'll want to stay there during the summer. Being a Jew."

This makes me laugh, it is so ridiculous, and then it makes Peggy laugh; for the briefest instant we're in concert again. For the first time in months. Somewhere below us, I believe Josh has heard us, because a moment later the front door slams loudly. Peggy collapses into the bed again.

"I'll go get him," I say.

I close the bedroom door behind me, and as I do, I hear the loud pulsing of her dialing a telephone. It's Osgood.

"Phil," I hear her say into the receiver. "Oh, it's awful. It's worse than I imagined!"

My first fall without my son seemed to be the most colorful. Every goddamned falling leaf seemed to announce itself to me as it landed on the toes of my shoes. All the old, trite romantic symbolism seemed to me for those six weeks to be an artifact of inarguable truth. The decay of a sugar maple, its slow photosynthetic bleeding from green to burgundy, seemed an apt, if rather blatant, metaphor for my marriage, and for my new empty house. It's always been my favorite season, and when Josh was a boy, it was the season that seemed to allow us the most time out in the yard together, throwing around a football or raking leaves or building a wooden house for the wrens Peggy likes to feed. Even when he was in high school, he often roused himself late on a weekend day to come meet me in the yard, or to join me on a walk into town, where we always shopped for pumpkins on the lawn of the Unitarian church. Without him, and with Osgood suddenly feeling so comfortable in my home that he'd begun to bring his slippers with him, I often went out on these same walks alone. A good walk on a brisk night is, I've found, a decent way to be respectably lonely.

Now the town is bare. Winter denudes the village, strips the paint from the houses, the fence posts, the lindens; wields itself like a sanding brush prepping the town for the first coat of snow. But what happened overnight was just a dusting, a haphazard cover of whiteness, far from the real wintry artifact. The house is a few blocks from the center of town, and I go there on foot, positive that Josh has taken up at one of the coffee shops. Without a car, there is nowhere else to go. So different from San Francisco.

At the crest of the town center—nothing but a trio of Protestant churches, a manicured Revolutionary War battle green, and a string of novelty stores—I decide to check Josh's old favorite coffee shop. He liked the Steamer, which is the kind of coffee shop they're always trying to recreate in the movies. Cozy, filled with overstuffed, plush armchairs. Board games stacked up on old Shaker bookshelves. Jangly slacker rock on the stereo. He worked here a few nights a week when he was in high school, and I'd come to see him, order a tall cup of decaf, tip him with a twenty. On weekends the owner books folk acts who come play on kitchen stools and sing songs while their cats hunt around for rodents; the musicians linger around afterward sipping fair-trade espresso, and all of them know the owner by name. Her name is Kristen, and I suppose that when I'm officially divorced from Peggy, I might try to get to know her, but this is simply a possibility I keep at the back of my mind. This is foolish, I know, because my marriage is over, and has been over for some time, and my reluctance toward Kristen is based on nothing but fear. We make polite conversation sometimes. Mostly, she talks to me and I nod eagerly. When all of this business with Osgood started, I think Peggy might have been relieved if I'd found myself another woman. But even after this long, I can't seem to allow myself to talk freely to a woman who isn't my wife.

At the window, I see her behind the counter frothing milk. She's my age exactly. Fifty-one. A good age, she told me. It's quite possible, she thinks, that fifty-one might be a plausible halfway mark, that in this new day the common man might eclipse the century mark. Heartbreak, I think, must shorten one's life span, however. She's in black, a style she holds in common with Phil Osgood, who for whatever reason is always dressed this way. His is the face I see first. Before Kristen can look up, before I can find Josh, Osgood is calling my name.

"Lewis," he calls out, clapping me on the shoulder. He is out on the sidewalk, his cheeks flushed in the cold. "What in the fuck is going on up at that old castle of yours? Your son cause a scene or something?"

This is the way he talks. He teaches high school English here in town and his speech seems to be a strenuous attempt to sound contemporary. I shuffle my feet on the sidewalk. I've gone out in my winter boots. They are big, bulky, insulated to the point that, purportedly, my toes could survive a cold night in the Arctic. But I like them most because they give me a few extra inches, and in them I am almost at eye level with Osgood.

"The boy's just angry," I say. "I'm out looking for him."

At this Osgood shakes his head. "Kids that age," he says, and then he doesn't finish. This is something I'm glad for.

"Peggy'll be okay," I offer.

I think I catch him simpering at me. I can't be sure. Everyone in town is wise to what's happening in my house. Osgood was the first one to use the words "open marriage," and not even a day later one of Kristen's employees said, apropos of nothing, that she was the product of such a union. By now, Kristen has noticed me, and twice she's waved from behind the counter, trying to catch my attention. She has beautiful blond hair that goes halfway to her hips, and it's not terribly difficult, or unpleasant, to imagine taking her to bed. My back is to her, but I can see this in the reflection of a Volvo wagon parked outside the shop.

"Hey," Osgood says. "I want to bring over something nice. Cheer her up. Get her looking at the sunny side. What do you think?"

The moon is still out. It's noon, and still the fat, waxing belly of the moon. How in the hell, I wonder.

"Get her some red grapes," I say. "The kind with the seeds.

She pretends they're too extravagant. But they always make her happy when she's sad."

Before Josh left for California, Peggy admitted to me that she feared she'd lose some part of him forever once he landed in Palo Alto. "He'll be different when he comes back. I know it. He'll have changed into somebody else." She said this to me one evening as we were sitting on the porch. To our neighbors, I suppose it might have seemed that we were out enjoying a nice warm evening, when in actuality we were sitting and discussing how Peggy had fallen in love with Phil, how he understood her in ways I didn't, and how she loved to sit in his Pontiac Firebird as he drove her along the Shawsheen River, the two of them listening to French pop music, or whatever the hell Osgood listens to. Hers was a sentimental notion, that Josh's very essence might be erased simply because he was moving to the Pacific time zone, and I believe I told her so, although I can't be entirely sure what I said and what I merely thought to myself. This was at the beginning of their affair, when I was convinced that it would merely peter out slowly, and that I would have my wife and my family back.

This is why, in those last few months before Josh went away, when both Peggy and I were dreading the date we'd have to fly him to Stanford, she took him off every Sunday evening to cultural events in the city, events she figured I wouldn't enjoy very much—the symphony, an exhibit of Cézanne's landscapes, a German theater troupe performing some souped-up version of *The Magic Flute*. When she did this, I stayed behind and did what I used to do when I was a boy when my mother went off with my sisters to do some of the same things, which was to sit out on the porch and listen to the Red Sox game on the radio. To insert myself would have been inappropriate in Peggy's eyes, even if I would have very much liked the symphony. She claimed that I already spent a good deal of time with Josh, with our walks into town and my dropping in on him at the Steamer.

Now Josh calls every Friday afternoon to talk to me. Our conversations are notable only for his newfound reticence, a quality that, when I complained about it recently, led him to suggest that we begin to communicate by text message. He promises me that he is far more voluble in this medium. Of course, I know that people do really speak to one another this way, and I've even seen Peggy receive communiqués from Osgood in this fashion. If I know him at all, his messages are likely vulgar and stupid, but Peggy seems to enjoy the soft trilling of her phone as it calls to her. Still, I refuse to speak with my own son this way, and when I told him so, he didn't call me for two weeks.

I suppose it was this feeling of frustration that led me to steal my wife's computer a few nights back. She saves all of these conversations she has with Josh, a fact I knew before I made my theft. So much of the future, it seems, is obsessed with record-keeping in a way that seems foreign to me, or overly indulgent. Peggy was out with Osgood when I made the theft, and simply to sit in her chair, at her exact station at the table, with the rings of tea stains on the oak, felt so risky to me. It gave me a glimpse, however fractional, of what she must have felt when she began to sleep with him.

At the beginning, I found the whole trove of these letters unremarkable. At best, they were rather ordinary, and I found most of them to be painfully mundane. *I ate waffles for break-fast,* he said in one, dated Saturday, September 4. In another, dated Friday, September 17, he wrote, *Going out with friends to see a Giants game.* But then, because I'd gone backward, moving from the most recent conversations to the oldest, I found one of the first messages he sent. *I guess this is my first complete week on my own,* Josh wrote rather wistfully, to which my wife responded, *You can always come home. Any time you want. You know that, right?* This was her way of saying she missed him, and as I read this I remembered that particular weekend and how positively strange it felt to have our house empty of our son. Peggy had wept when she closed the clamshell of her computer. *I'm good out here, Mom,* he wrote. *Stop worrying and just let me be.*

Eventually, I find Josh standing outside the closed storefront of our town's bookshop. Over the autumn, the shop had closed, which didn't come as much of a surprise, even though its shuttering was met with a collective wail of disappointment. All of us in town had quietly, if not shamefully, taken to the internet for our shopping, and old Mac Weingarten had to pack up all those lovely leather journals and his collection of first editions. I must have forgotten to mention this to Josh, because he is beside himself, sitting by the shop window.

"Have some urgent shopping to do, buddy?" I call out.

"Maybe," he says. He is dressed up like a young professor, in tweed and another collared shirt. Eight months ago, his favorite thing in the world was a faded, paper-thin Lemonheads concert T-shirt.

"You come to buy yourself a copy of the Hebrew Bible?" I ask.

He turns quickly. "That's not funny."

"It's a little funny," I say.

"Only you would think so."

"It's not as if you grew up in the most pious house."

He seems to think about this for a moment before looking back to me. "Maybe that was part of the problem."

"How so?" I ask.

"I just saw Phil Osgood walking across Dey Street. Cocky as hell. Going to see my mother. So yeah, I think maybe that's the problem. Everywhere else that's a sin, don't you think?"

His sarcasm is a hair's breadth away from a sobbing fit. This is something he shares with his mother. Behind me, at the only intersection in town, I can hear a car spinning its wheels in the gathered slush.

"What are you going to do? You can't just sulk around this way," I say. "Your mom's been looking forward to this."

"I don't know. I can't be around that guy. This isn't what I thought it would be."

"What isn't?"

"Coming back."

What I want to say is that you've been away four months, and before that our life wasn't much different, just more secretive. Instead, I clear my throat. "You want to grab a beer, Josh?" I ask.

This is something he hasn't considered. "I don't think I can get served," he says, meekly.

"We can take a couple of cans down to the mill," I say. "That's what the teenagers do, isn't it?"

After a moment he smiles at me. "You'd *do* that?"

The effect of sitting in the woods with a laptop—the same woods where, when I was a boy, I used to hike every week, using for balance a sturdy branch from an alder my father

48

trimmed for kindling—is so odd that for a moment I don't seem capable of using my fingers to do what Josh is asking of me. He has pictures of his friends up on the screen. So many happy faces, everyone out in the San Francisco evening. When a photograph pops up in which someone is holding a cigarette, or is visibly bleary, he skips ahead quickly, hoping I haven't noticed. At the beginning, San Francisco is clearly the star in many of the photos. My boy has an evident passion for architecture. For ten minutes he talks to me about the Victorian row house, the strength of the redwood roof beam, the subtle nuance of the Coit Tower.

After a beer, Josh is drunk. Or close to drunk. Like me, he can't hold much of anything. I read once that many Jewish men lack the enzyme to digest the proteins in alcohol, a medical anomaly that renders us a cheap date. It's good, though, in a surprising way, to see him like this: he is looser, slower, more passionate. It's one-thirty in the afternoon. The snow is melting. There are beaver tracks near us. Up in the trees, there are birds' nests. One beer in me, and I'm sensitive to every rush of noise in the woods, every odd, wet crunch. We're sitting on a dampened, rotted log. A storm recently toppled some trees here in the town forest. But trees are always falling here. Storms come through and make a mess and nobody comes to clean. Down a small slope, there is the millstream. Centuries ago it made paper pulp. The towns nearby were cut clear of everything, and they brought the timber here. The original mill, though, is dead, just a badly dilapidated relic infested with animals and rot and graffiti from when the structure was sound. This is a mile into the forest. There is nothing to mark its prominence. A model has been erected in town, fresh with gilded plaques, and the children go on field trips to take pictures. For a while, I tell him about all of this. He's a history major now, officially, and while I talk, he is patient, if not politely bored. That's when I notice that many of his most recent photographs feature a certain girl. He's taken the computer from me and has been flipping through his albums. She's a brunette. A big, even smile. The easy, round cheeks, the kissable mouth, oak-brown eyes. She is plainly Jewish to me, and this, I realize, is the reason for his new piety.

When I ask about her, he hesitates.

"Let's not talk about me," he says. "What about you?"

"It's not like I didn't fight," I offer. "I did. You should know that."

"I don't get it," he said. "Phil?"

What I want to say is that her taking a lover is, in my opinion, a reaction to Josh going away, first the fear of it, and then the actuality of his absence. This is her way of filling an empty nest she wants nothing to do with, a crazy way of complicating her life. I may be wrong, of course. Peggy once told me that my being wrong was a skill at which I was particularly gifted. But I can't say any of this to my son.

"He's very tall," I say instead. "That's not something I can offer her."

"She could do much better," he says, and then, seeing my reaction, he laughs to himself. "Or she could go back to you."

"Listen," I say. "I didn't mean to make you feel bad about feeling religious."

"Being religious," he says. "Not just feeling it."

I sigh. "You know what I mean."

I look to see if he understands that this means I'm perfectly fine with him becoming a devout Jew, a rabbi, a cantor, or simply someone, so unlike myself, who feels it possible to believe in something larger than himself. I'm not really prepared to say much more about this. This is the first conversation we've ever had about God. A beer is one thing, I think.

"Sarah," he says. "That's her name."

I nod. "The wife of Abraham," I say.

"Good," he says, laughing.

"Six years of Sunday School," I say.

"I've been trying to get her to go out with me for weeks now."

"And she's not having any of it?"

He laughs, and then loudly groans. "There's hope," he says. "Let's put it that way. There's at least hope. She knows my telephone number by heart. That's good, isn't it?"

"And she lets you take her picture," I say. "That means something."

"I guess."

I take the liberty to flip through his pictures. Above us, a starling emerges out of nowhere. Lost in the season. Bounding from nest to nest. But so quickly, I'm fixated on these pictures. Not because they are well taken. Josh has a crude eye, and it's quickly evident that everyone, in nearly all of the photographs, is drunk, my son included. My interest is piqued because of the sheer volume. He has so many photographs of Sarah. Pictures in which she is the focus, in which she is posing, in which she is wearing black tights and patent leather shoes, wearing merino wool and a foolish pillbox hat, wearing Levi's and canvas shoes, wearing a loose green-and-white baseball-team ringer T-shirt. And there are pictures in which she exists by accident, as an incidental ornament in someone else's portrait, a blurry figure in the back of a Chinese restaurant. For the few minutes I look, and for days afterward, I'm left with a dark, discomfiting regret that, for all my effort, I can't seem to lose.

"Here," Josh says. "Let me show you a picture from the day I met her."

To have such a thing, I think.

There were letters on my wife's computer that I had written her. These were letters, I should say, that I'd written years ago, decades, even, when I was as young as Josh is now, and when my meeting Peggy on Seventy-sixth Street seemed to me to be as large a miracle as any on earth. Evidently she had scanned them into her computer, a process that I, predictably, find baffling. Either she did this to preserve the integrity of the old card stock, or because she wanted a better, easier, more discreet way to look at all those old envelopes I'd sent from my tiny dorm room to hers. I can still remember my father buying the stationery for me that last weekend I was home. He drove a 1960 Plymouth Fury, which is a perfectly fine car, neither a terrific representation of its era nor in its day a particularly wise choice for the money. But it was the car my father drove for ages, the first and last car he owned outright, and it was a rare thing to go out with him for a drive in it, the two of us going through town with the windows down. My father was a very difficult man to get along with, tough as hell, and unshakably quiet. But that afternoon, I don't think I'd ever seen him in happier spirits. He took great pleasure in buying me a fine set of correspondence cards, thinking, I realize now, that I would use them to write him. I suppose he envisioned that I might turn into a man with whom he could exchange deeply held thoughts on politics or society or even simply the pitching woes of the Red Sox. But at the time, I remember thinking that he was happy because I was leaving, and that he'd have his house back again, all that quiet, his big comfortable den unencumbered by my distractions. And although it is unbearably painful to remember, I said this to him, all of it, while the two of us were standing at the counter at Waldblum's Stationers.

These are the cards Peggy has scanned into her computer. There are hundreds of them, so many that I am momentarily surprised that I wrote her as often as I did. My handwriting is nearly identical to the way it is now: messy, excited, spiked with unsightly marks. I can only get through one before I walk away, one in which I'd drawn in the lower left-hand corner of the card a terrible likeness of a pineapple.

Do you realize what I did yesterday, Peggy? I walked all over Manhattan searching for that perfect pineapple you've been craving, just like the ones you said you ate as a girl in Africa. I report back to you a failure. I hope you will accept in place of a perfect piece of fruit this drawing.
~ Sincerely yours, Lewis.

Later, when I go to find Peggy in bed, I see that she has her computer open to these letters. Osgood is gone, she tells me, closing the screen slowly.

"Really," I say.

"He brought me seeded red grapes," she says. "Do you believe that?"

Her pillow is still wet from her crying. She can weep all day long, and when she starts there is little to stop her.

"I've told him a thousand times that I'm allergic to grapes, but he doesn't listen. He comes over with like five pounds of grapes. Who can eat five pounds of grapes? What kind of idiot does that? Says he wants to feed them to me. Like I'm Elizabeth goddamned Taylor and this is *Cleopatra*."

"What a jerk," I say. I get into bed beside her. She is warm beneath my hands. "Jeez."

"Lewis?" she asks. "What are you doing?"

"I'm getting into bed with my wife."

She is rigid beside me. "Lewis, are you okay?"

"I don't like Osgood," I say.

At this, she is quiet.

"He's an ass. I don't understand what you see in him. Even Josh agrees with me."

"You're going to make me cry again," she says.

She has the ceiling fan going. Menopause has made her warm even in the most bitter cold. For a while, both of us seem to watch the blades spin. It feels nice to be beside my wife again.

"Do you remember what I was wearing when you first met me?" I ask.

"What sort of stupid question is that?"

"Well, do you?"

"No," she says. "What a thing to ask. I don't even remember what I'm wearing right now. And I got dressed five hours ago."

"You had your boots on," I said. "And your raincoat. At the beginning, you were always wearing that coat."

For a moment, she's quiet. I put my hand flat against her stomach. When she was pregnant, we'd thought of taking a photograph of her belly at each month. But nothing came of the project. I save nothing, I realize. I can feel her tense for a moment, and then I can feel her soften, warm to me. My father, I remember, shook her hand the very first time he'd met her. This was in our house, not even a mile from here. He'd tell me later that he thought she was a perfectly swell girl. High praise from a man who failed at finding much in life worthy of praise. I'd driven us up from the city, through Connecticut, trying my best to give her a tour of what we were passing, even though I knew nothing of what I was saying. Then I felt the need to impress her. Peggy always had impressive men saying impressive things to her. I began to lie halfway into the trip, when we were outside Hartford. This is the Sawtooth River, I said. George Washington famously lost his artificial teeth here, while his men had camped out for the night. He'd been washing them in the river and the current swept them away. Many books have been written about this particular river, I told her. Crews of archaeologists have come for years hoping to find the smile of the first president. She turned then, and asked if we could stop. She wanted to go down into the woods and root around herself. She had on her boots and her green coat. And because she wanted to, I parked the car on the shoulder of I-84, and we walked into the woods together.

"I liked that coat," I say.

"It wouldn't fit me anymore. I was tiny then. I could eat a whole birthday cake for lunch and I could drink beer. Do you remember?"

"We have no pictures," I say.

"We had no money for a camera," she says. "And besides, I look stupid in pictures. I always worry that the flash will make me blink."

"We have letters, though, I guess." I nod with my chin at her computer.

She grips at my hands, her fingers locked into mine. Osgood's picture is gone, I notice.

"You were always trying so hard to win my affection," she says, finally. "I liked that about you."

"That's something that hasn't changed," I say.

She flips around in bed so that we are facing one another. Her nose is cold. For a moment, I'm sure she is going to kiss me, and I close my eyes in anticipation. Two beers have made me foolish.

"Is Osgood gone forever?"

"Yes," she says, nodding. "I think so."

"That's good. Because if I caught him again in our kitchen I was going to pop him," I say.

"Pop him?" she asks. This makes her howl with laughter. "Did Josh tell you to say that?"

"He's far too pious for that now," I say.

Her laughter grows louder, although I notice a twinge of bitterness in the sound of her voice, just a flickering of it, before she relaxes in my hands.

In a way, I have always had faith in my wife. That may sound funny, but it's the truth.

Then: "Is he at least going to stay for dinner, Lewis? Or is he off praying somewhere? Can't we at least feed him before he runs off again?"

The Moon Landing

My mother was the first to die. It was, as she suspected it might be, cancer of the liver. She was of an older generation of drinkers, always in her bathrobe after six in the evening, a connoisseur of Scotch, that most gentlemanly of drinks, and I have only the rare childhood memory that does not include her in the basement, walking barefoot across the carpet, clutching an empty tumbler in her elegant, thin fingers, three melting cubes of ice rattling in the glass. She passed away inside a private room at Beth Israel two hours after midnight. My father followed her days later, in a pattern I suspected he might, for it only made sense that he would go in death as he had in life, behind my mother, at her beck and call as always.

My father taught poetry for years at a small university near our home. His era was the Moderns, and while he did not maintain quite the same stomach for Scotch that my mother did, when I try to picture my dad, his starched flannel button-downs paired with black slacks—half lumberjack, half banker—it is always with a glass of Scotch that I see him, too, reclining in his imitation Eames chair, a book of verse propped on his lap. That is my dad.

His books are the first things I find in the house, using the same key that I've had hanging from my key chain for twenty-five years, despite the thousands of miles between my home and my parents' home. There are books in the living room—*Red Roses for Bronze*—the fold open against the arm of the sofa, scribbled notes tucked into the pages. There are books in the bedroom—*Paterson*—a photograph of my father as a young man standing beside the great waterfall in that town, used as a bookmark, slipped into the pages. There are books in the kitchen—*Harmonium*—a spectacular splattering of tomato sauce obscuring an open page.

My dad, at the end, told me that he was making my mother her favorite dishes, the foods that, for years, she had been forbidden to eat, the rich custards, the roast pork loins, the ragu that he began with a greasy panful of pancetta and oil. I take the book, close the fold, rub my hands across its cover. He took such care of these books, finding pristine first editions, traveling to New York, riding the freight elevator to the fourth floor of the Strand, paying far too much money. He shook at the end, from the elbow, and it is terrible to imagine that he might have caused the splattering inside this book, and how he must have felt seeing that red splotch across the text.

There are dishes in the sink, flatware with my dad's fingerprints, tumblers with the imprint of my mother's lips. She wanted to wear her lipstick at the end. My father told me how he sat on the bed, applying it for her as best he could. Alone in the kitchen, where for years it was my responsibility to wash the dishes, I allow myself a small laugh. "Chores," I say. There are bills stacked in piles, and upon them, a note written in my father's handwriting. It is addressed simply: *Son.*

I was in the air when he died, flying home from my mother's funeral. At the moment that I believe he passed, the plane shook. I'm not one to believe in that sort of thing— evidence of divinity, the existence of the soul—but still, I was overcome with the desire to close my eyes amid the turbu- lence, and as I did, I smelled, passing under my nose, the distinct sweet cologne of my father. Out of the nine people on the red-eye back to California, I was the only man, and it was not my cologne.

I take the note, fold it, put it into my pocket, and for the first time in years, feel the strong desire to have a drink.

Then my brother arrives.

One month after the Apollo 11 astronauts arrived home from the moon, the city of New York threw a parade along lower Broadway. My mother had the idea to take me to New York that day so that the two of us could see these spacemen as they rode through the falling ticker tape. At the time, I fig- ured that afternoon was an act of spontaneity on my mother's part, a simple case of her reading in the paper that a parade was happening. "I've got this great idea for a fun trip today, Charles," I remember her saying that morning. We left my brother, a toddler at the time, with a neighbor, and rode the four hours from Chestnut Hill to New York on a late-morning Greyhound, my mother dressed in the outfit she wore to work at the Lord & Taylor near our home. She always looked nice in her uniform. I don't remember this exactly, but I'd like to. Her clothing must have been unfashionable for the times— black stockings, patent leather Mary Janes, a striped French blouse, a wool skirt. This was August 1969. She made peanut-butter-and-banana sandwiches for the ride, and I remember that we ate them on the interstate between Hartford and New Haven.

It was my first time in the city, and I remember very little of how it all appeared to me, the buildings, the bridges along the East River, the constant stench rising up from the sewers. What I do remember is standing on the corner of Chambers Street and Broadway as the Apollo astronauts rode slowly by us, the three of them, Buzz, Neil, and, my mother's favorite, Michael Collins, all sitting atop the backseat of a Chrysler Imperial Parade Phaeton. When the men passed by, people began to chase the car, my mother among them, and for a block, I ran with her. I was eleven and normally could do quite well for myself on foot. Earlier that year, I'd run the mile in under ten minutes. At a certain point, as the Chrysler crossed Duane Street, I stopped. I was surrounded by people, everyone running and hollering. Ticker tape came down from the sky, a weatherstorm of small paper slips. Secret Service agents ran beside me, their pistols in their hands. My mother kept running after I stopped, and despite how loudly I tried to yell for her, she did not turn around.

She didn't find me for hours. I sat on a bench in City Hall Park until dark, rebuffing the few strangers who stopped to ask whether I was all right. "I'm just sitting," I told two old women who, for most of the afternoon, sat watching me fidget and cry silently to myself. When all of the oil lanterns in the park were turned on, I crossed my arms against my chest for warmth. My mother arrived at some point during the early evening, stumbling into the park on the arm of a man I had never met. He was dressed in uniform. My mother was smiling.

"There you are," she said, as if we'd simply become separated inside the Woolworth in our town. She tried to balance in her shoes. "Wasn't it something? Wasn't it? All of that!"

I sat stiff on the bench.

"Don't be rude, Charles," my mother said. "Say hello to my friend."

My mother's stockings were rumpled at the knee. The man had his hat cocked to the side. He wore an unlit cigarette in his smile.

"Hello."

He saluted me, his right arm rising like an ax to his head. "Reporting for duty," he said.

"Are we going home?" I asked my mother.

"Home?" my mother said, grabbing onto the man's arm for balance. "Do you know who this man is? He's someone very special. Do you want to meet someone special? This man here, this is Michael Collins. Michael Collins the astronaut. He's been to space!"

"From the parade?" I asked.

"Yep," he said, nodding. "From the parade."

He grinned at me, pretended to pull a quarter from my ear. I smiled reluctantly at him.

"How was it landing on the moon?" I asked.

"It was really something to be up there," he said, pointing up into the sky. "Walking around and everything."

"I bet. Wow."

"I got to jump up and down," he said, pantomiming the effects of zero gravity to my mother's giggling delight.

I looked up at my mother. "Can we go home now?"

My mother let go of the man's arm, took two steps toward me, and crouched so that she was at my eye level. She always did this, so that she and I were the same size. I put my small hand on her shoulder and whispered to her. "I want to go home." She kissed the tip of my nose. "We'll go home in a little bit," she said. "Just a little longer in the city, all right? I don't want to go back yet. Just another hour or two. That's all. Just a little bit. Okay?"

David enters through the front door, calls my name. He is tall, the better-looking brother, the owner of a silver Mercedes, which he's parked in the long driveway that we used, as boys, for a street-hockey court. This is suburban Boston, and when we were children we both wanted to play professional hockey for the Bruins. He wanted to be Bobby Orr. I wanted to be Derek Sanderson, the one who liked to fight.

It's a relief to see him here, ducking through the door frame, standing on the old linoleum tile, the original peel-and-stick kitchen flooring that now, after forty years of footsteps and spilled Scotch, is worn to the plywood in places. David is nine years my junior, a litigator at a firm in the city, where for seventy-five hours a week he harangues and browbeats other lawyers just like himself. For years before this, he worked at City Hall as a prosecutor. He is an ornery fellow, as my mom would have said, capable of shaking the most hidden, repressed secrets from the toughest motherfuckers. Unlike every other man in our family, David has a head full of hair and a thick Boston accent. In his voice, my name is not Charlie, but *Chaaahlie,* as if some invisible sprite is shoving a tongue depressor into his mouth every time he tries to speak. He is the one Isaacson without a taste for liquor.

We hug. As a child, he was always small for his age, the shortest boy in every one of his class photographs, but now he's bigger than me, and he never misses an opportunity to threaten me with a punch to the gut. He's a good kid, tough as nails, all business all the time, and the smartest, by far, of every Isaacson man before him.

"So I had the will read," he says, straightening his posture, leaning against the Formica counter. "In probate court, downtown."

"I don't want to hear about it," I say, waving my hands in the air. "I don't want anything. You can have it all."

"It didn't say much," he says, ignoring me, taking a piece of paper from his pocket. "They had some retirement annuities. Life insurance for one another. And the house and everything inside it. Dad wants his books given to some colleague of his I've never heard of. Mom wants one of us to save her scrapbook of the moon landing. I didn't know she had such a thing. Did you? We're supposed to save it for her *unborn grandchildren*. That's what she wrote."

"Is that her idea of a joke?"

David shrugs. "We can do what we want with the rest of the belongings," he says, reading from the piece of paper in his hands.

"Like I said, I don't want any of it," I say. "It's all yours."

He looks at me with the same judicious measure of disappointment and familial tolerance that my father, when I was young, used to give me whenever I interrupted his reading. I've never been especially good at looking people in the eyes, and rather than meet David's stare, I look at the floor beneath his feet. He folds the piece of paper, puts it back into his pocket.

"Fine," he says, shrugging. "Let's do this, then."

"I'm not sure I can," I say. "I'm not sure I can even be in here. Let's call someone to do this."

"Think of it as a job," he says, using a phrase from my father's mouth, slapping me on the back. "Look, bud. The truck's coming at five tomorrow. So let's get going. What do you say?"

"This is going to take more than one day?"

I haven't planned for this. I've planned to be back in California by nightfall, in and out of Massachusetts as quickly as I can manage, simply to avoid having to confront everything in this house. I feel foolish for thinking David would ever allow this to happen.

"They lived here for forty years," my brother says, rolling up the sleeves of his button-down. "You think you can clean it out in a day? Go for it."

Five years ago, I wrote a movie about monsters, beginning it one rainy afternoon in a coffee shop in Hollywood and finishing it nine days later in that same coffee shop beside a man who happened to be a film producer. I was struck with the inspiration for the movie while witnessing the armed robbery of a nearby bank. The robbers, a pair of drug addicts, weren't successful. They were using at the time, and, as a result, moving quite slowly. I came away from the experience with an idea. The robbers became monsters, and the monsters became a movie.

It was a terrible picture, in and out of the theaters in two weeks, but it sold, and I went, in one month, from living in a dark one-room apartment on Sunset and Vine to a small stucco bungalow in the Hollywood Hills. It was a house that boasted a pair of tall picture windows, which looked out onto the conifers and cliffs of Laurel Canyon. I bought furniture with the money I had left, and made for myself a small office in the corner of the house. I bought some of the books of poetry I remembered my father treasuring and an actual black leather Eames chair. When my father came to visit, I told myself, he would be impressed with that piece of furniture. In that room, against a small window, I began to work in the mornings.

Besides the picture about the monsters, I sold two other movies. One was almost the same picture as my first, but rather than monsters, there were pirates. I'd been told that pirates were in fashion at the time. Hollywood can be easy like that. And the second, more recent picture was about my mother and my father. It gave me no particular pleasure to write this story, however necessary or cathartic I found the process. It was not a conscious decision of mine to write their story—their drinking, their silence—but sometimes our deepest, most hidden instincts find their way out into the open in the most mysterious fashion.

I imagine it would have pleased my parents to know that one of their favorite movie stars purchased the screenplay. He wants to play me, even though he is closer in age to my father. Before I came to Boston for my mother's funeral, his assistant called me over to his office for a meeting. I dressed in my only suit. I bought it years ago, when I wasn't sober, and now it's too large for me. His assistant led me into a small office with a pair of oval windows that looked out upon the ocean. I love California, but I've always preferred the ocean in New England to the Pacific. There is something in the ragged coast off Massachusetts, its messiness and its cold spirit, that I feel closer to. I stood for a while at the window while a pair of small finches flew close to the glass. When the movie star came to see me, he had the screenplay in his hand, having rolled it into a baton. I had the feeling, shaking his hand, that I had arrived. It was a small moment, like smelling a hint of spring on a day in February. He asked me if I'd based the story on my own life, or whether it was fiction. I thought for a moment about how to answer the question. He cleared his throat. The only thing I suppose I knew for sure right then was that I wanted my mother and father to see how far I'd come. I didn't yet know that my mother was gone.

"You know what?" he said. "You don't have to tell me. It doesn't matter. If you want to keep it to yourself, keep it to yourself."

Then he took a bottle of Scotch from a liquor cabinet and asked if I wanted a drink.

I'm not positive of the correct word for what we do. It's not packing. The way I take the sheets from my parents' bed, ripping them from the mattress, stuffing them into large, industrial-strength trash bags, is done with little care for how these linens might appear at the other end of the process. These are the same plastic bags, David tells me with pronounced morbidity, that the Mafia prefers to use when they dispose of bodies. I don't fold or crease the pillowcases, the mattress cover, the bed skirt. My mother loved Egyptian cotton. Like my dad's fondness for first-edition poetry, fine linen was, besides Scotch, her great extravagance, and the single thing for which she enjoyed saving her money. I shove all of it into the bags.

It's not disassembly, despite how David and I unscrew the shelves from the walls in the living room, or the way we take apart the kitchen table. Nor is it appraisal, for we don't stop to inspect the tchotchkes on display around the house, the Venetian glass bowls, a collection of Hummel figurines, a series of African masks, the framed snapshot of my dad standing beside Saul Bellow. Decades ago, he ate dinner in the same restaurant as him. He never missed an opportunity to talk about this.

Everything goes into the bags, or else into sturdy cardboard boxes. It's remarkable how quickly David works. I feel the need to examine everything I touch. This is a symptom, I imagine, of the distance I've kept.

"Should we keep any of this?" I ask, holding a framed winning lottery ticket. My mother played my birth date, and that of my brother, and won two thousand dollars. I was living then in a month-to-month studio apartment on Hollywood Boulevard. She wired me the money.

"Maybe," he says, putting into a bag a set of throw pillows, hand-embroidered by my mother. "But maybe not."

"But maybe," I say.

He looks up at me. His eyes are red. This may be an allergic reaction to the thick layers of dust covering nearly everything in the house, or this may be genuine emotion. I've been waiting for some emotion out of him. At our mother's funeral, he gave the eulogy with the sort of practiced ease that comes to those who speak publicly for a living. It bothered me that he didn't cry, not even when we closed the casket for the last time.

"I have to stop," I say, sitting on the arm of the green sofa, trying to breathe.

"What's the matter, Charlie?"

"Doesn't this bother you?"

"Charlie," he says, a heavy, sagging bag in his hand. "You know, it's different for me. I was here. Every weekend, I was here with them. With Mom. I wasn't in California doing whatever the fuck you do out there."

"I do things," I say.

"I'm sure you do," he says. "Lots of things."

I turn away from him. The stacks of boxes and plastic bags fill every open space of the hardwood. The utilities have been turned off, and, without the heat, I've begun to catch a chill. I've lived in the warmth of Southern California for so long that I've lost my ability to withstand even the tepid early spring of New England.

"The quicker we do this, the quicker we leave," David says, going back to work.

I have to stand to the side as he packs my mother's tumblers into a cardboard box. This, for predictable reasons, is a bitter sight to witness. When I was younger, I always assumed that I would inherit these glasses, as if they were the family silver. I haven't had a drink in five or six years. At this point, I've lost the exact count, a fact that I consider a minor triumph. For years, I counted each day, in a reversal of the way, when I was young, that I used to count down the days until summer vacation, or until Hanukkah.

I stand against the wall, try to catch my breath; David brushes by me. He never stops working. He is well built, toned by a membership to an expensive gym. He is determined and steady and, despite his protests to the contrary, he is largely incapable of sentimentality. It's as if, as a little kid, he watched the drunken faces of our parents as they tried their hardest to appear serious and composed, and, thinking this to be the actual way adults went through the world, he co-opted their attitudes for himself.

We speak on the telephone once every year. They're short conversations. He tells me about the women he's currently sleeping with, or planning to sleep with, or of the women he's stopped sleeping with, but who, of course, still want to sleep with him. I tell him as little about me as I can without seeming impolite. It's always been like this with my family, with them over here, on the rocky, cold East Coast, and with me over there, in California, in my stucco house in the canyon. It wasn't that I disliked my parents, or David. I always intended to come back here when I had my life together, so that they could see that I was not just the balding mess calling from a pay phone on Hollywood Boulevard, begging once again for that final installment of their money. The reunion just didn't happen the way I planned.

David wheels the liquor cabinet out into the garage. That piece of furniture, four feet tall, two feet deep, made from Swedish teak and decorated with twin mirrored panels on the doors, was for my entire childhood and adolescence the center of this house, our own Ark of the Covenant. As I watch it go, a sound escapes my body. It's a grunt, or a wail, or simply the sound of stress releasing from my muscles. The sound stops David, who turns in the doorway and frowns at me.

"It's because you didn't say good-bye," he says. "That's it, isn't it?"

I haven't been alone these last five years. At first, there was Elise. She liked to read to me at night. She had a passion for the confessional poets—Robert Lowell, Anne Sexton, Sylvia Plath—and I often wondered, while she read to me, whether she was trying to confess something to me all those nights that we stayed awake with her books. I'd heard most of the poems already, having listened to my father read after dinner when I was young, sitting in his imitation Eames chair by the fireplace. Elise had a great reading voice, an accent from the South, a warmth in the aspirations of her vowels that comforted me those first few times I tried and failed to stop drinking. My sense of time suffered during that relationship; the conflation of months upon drunken months. Ultimately, she moved away from California. She wanted to travel. Once in a while, I'll get a postcard from her, from Hong Kong or Tahiti. Her handwriting is perfectly neat, as if she's part machine. The last letter I got from her read: "Charlie, I hope you're well. I really do. I'm in the South Pacific. I miss you sometimes. The feeling comes on so strong, just like you're squeezing me the way you used to in the old apartment in Silver Lake."

Then there was Allison, who taught composition at Santa Monica College. She was younger than me by twenty years, but even at twenty-six, she possessed such a strong sense of purpose that I attached myself to her, as if she were filled with helium, because I believed at the time that she was my ticket up and up and up. She was the last girlfriend I had before I began writing. Then, I was employed marginally, doing the occasional odd bit of construction. At the end, when I'd first begun to get sober, she taught me what she taught her students. We'd sit at the small kitchen table in my apartment on La Brea with a ninety-nine-cent composition book and a box of ballpoints. She gave me writing prompts. In the end, she rose faster than I did, and I couldn't catch up, or hold on to her tight enough, and when she moved away to New York to pursue her PhD, I stood outside her apartment in Toluca Lake, right in the middle of the road as her moving van drove away, and for the first time in my adult life, I felt what it was to lose someone I loved. I was sober by then.

And then there was Robin, who was the assistant to my

agent. She hid her addictions from me, even when I told her that I knew she was a drunk the first time I saw her. "You don't understand," I told her. "I can see it in the way you breathe." When I think of Robin, I see her cooking me eggs in the morning, wearing my T-shirt and boxers, smoking French cigarettes in the backyard beneath the lemon trees. She was trying to get ahead in the industry, and saw in me, I think, some semblance of a meal ticket. It was a telling turn of events, finding myself on the opposite side of a table I'd forever been struggling to set.

I mention these women because, at the time that I knew them, their existence provided an excuse for me not to visit my parents. Without fail, my mother called twice a month, on alternating Saturdays, her hoarse voice crackling across the line, a product of a bad telephone connection and a lifetime of bad living. She wanted to buy me a ticket home, or else wanted to come and visit me, something I never allowed her to do. I always told her that I was busy with a girl, a fact that I would like to believe made her happy. My father always came on the phone at the end of the conversation and asked, in his deep, professorial voice, if I was sure that I didn't want to come home. "Are you angry with us? You can tell me. It won't hurt my feelings."

Now there is Audrey. She is my age, also a former drinker, but, in truth, we haven't sat down to hash out the details of our respective war stories. There is a certain distance behind her stare, which I know quite well; things are hidden there behind her proud resolve, and I'm comfortable enough now in my life to let them be. Every few minutes she holds her right hand up by her face and checks to see if she's shaking. In California, I tell myself often, the sun seems able to absolve even the most painful transgressions from people like her and me. This is just a guess, or a wish, but we spend most of our time out in my backyard, in the sun, feeling warm. I know we'll talk one day. She reminds me of my mother. Not in an unsettling, oedipal sort of way, but in a very subtle way, as if the way she moves her head when she drinks coffee from a paper cup, or the way she twirls pasta around a fork when the two of us eat in a restaurant, is the same way my mother might have done those things.

If I'm being honest, I'm not sure I remember the way my mother did those things, or any things, except, of course, how she drank.

Later in the afternoon, while David talks on the telephone to a colleague, I do the clothes, and it's awful. Into the bags go my father's terribly unfashionable sweaters, which for years were the targets of his students' teasing. Into the bags go my mom's underwear. It's something I do with my eyes closed, upturning the dresser drawer, dumping everything at once. Into the bags go my dad's slacks, his flannel button-downs, every pair of his shoes. His feet grew over the years as his arches flattened. He told me this on the telephone. For a time, when I needed them, he sent me his old shoes in the mail. Into the bags go all my mom's dresses, the black cocktail knee-length, the long blue gown she wore to the university Christmas party, where every year she overdid it. Into the bags go all my dad's sweatshirts, his unused exercise clothing, the awkward bow ties that, for a period in his forties, he wore when he taught.

I listen to my brother speak on the phone. He's ruthless. "Don't buy a word that piece of shit says. Everything that comes out of that asshole's mouth is a lie." His shirt is pulled up around his arm, and a vein in his biceps pulses, as does a corresponding vein in his forehead. The color of his skin changes, reddens. He flashes me a smile. It's the sort of smile—vindictive and arrogant—that for years I saw in bars, at the end of the evening, in the dark half-hour between last call and closing.

"Take it easy, Dave," I say to him, but I'm rebuffed by his open hand, held to my face as if he's a crossing guard. He ends the conversation by uttering the words "bullshit, bull-shit, bullshit" into the receiver. He flips shut his tiny silver mobile phone and looks at me. "Defense attorneys are all ass-holes," he says. Without a moment to regain his composure, he opens a dresser drawer, and continues with what he was doing, grabbing one of my mother's old sweaters. I recognize in this shifting of his moods, from anger to calm, the evidence of a childhood spent perfecting the art of psychological cam-ouflage. These were the sort of survival skills we learned in this house.

"Hey, look," David says, grabbing from the pile of clothing the Santa cap my dad used to wear on Christmas Day. We were, by birth, all Jews, however unobservant or unfaithful, but on Christmas, with the entire state of Massachusetts closed down for business, we celebrated with a big family din-ner.

"He liked that," I say, trying not to look.

"He was probably shit-faced," he says.

"Even still," I say. "He still liked it. Shit-faced or not. Peo-ple who are shit-faced still enjoy things."

"You would know, big brother," he says.

"I would know."

"They drank rum on Christmas," he says. "It made them very loving."

"It made them loud."

"Hey," David says, tapping my shoulder. "Look at me."

My little brother has my dad's Santa cap atop his head. He stands beside the bare bedroom window. We dismantled the vertical blinds earlier. In the light, he is both my mother—the hair, the nose, the brow—and, pretending to drunkenly sway with the cap crooked on his head, he is my dad.

"Merry Christmas, Charlie," he says, replicating exactly my dad's Jersey accent. "How about you and me go out and throw the football around, kid? The old pigskin. What do you say?"

"Don't be an asshole," I say, turning, walking into the hall.

It's unnerving the way his voice sounds.

"Charlie," he calls after me. "It's just a little fucking joke. Relax."

We always sang in the car. My father had a terrible singing voice and awful pitch but he loved Italian opera, and it wasn't uncommon for him to make the four-mile drive from our house to the liquor store with the windows down and Verdi blaring. My brother was sixteen then, and was breezing through school with perfect marks, on his way to Harvard. He stayed out of trouble, never drank, never snuck out of the house at two in the morning to steal our parents' cars. I was back from California, hoping to parlay my visit into some money to take back West; I was half a year late on my rent. This was November, days before Thanksgiving. We went to the liquor store on a Monday afternoon. My brother tagged along, sitting in the backseat, a tattered paperback in his coat pocket. He was always reading. We sang in the car. My brother didn't know the words, and couldn't join in. He tried to read. I'd been drunk the entire time I was home, as was my father: we drank and he read to me from some of his new poems and we drank more and he performed those same poems for me with a new, impassioned fervor. At the liquor store, my brother found a bottle of fake absinthe that they were selling, van Gogh's face painted onto the glass in imitation of his self-portrait. David held up the bottle for my father. He'd always loved the Expressionists.

"Look, Dad," he said, the bottle in his hand. "Van Gogh."

"You know who drank the real stuff?" he said to David, and then to me. He took the bottle into his hand, held it up, looked into the liquid as if he were searching for the answer to his own question. "Rimbaud."

"I don't know who that is," my brother said.

Then my father began to recite some Rimbaud. I came into the aisle, carrying two jugs of bad cognac. I stood beside him and joined in. I still don't know where my memory of that poem came from. Even now, if prompted, I couldn't recite a line. Perhaps my father had performed it for me years earlier in our house and it had simply stuck to the inside of me. Regardless, I joined in with the recitation, the memory of the text returning from some hidden place, and the both of us stood in the aisle saying and then shouting and then singing the words while my brother stood, unable to join in, his tattered paperback nearly falling from his coat pocket.

When we were done, my father slapped David on the back gently. "Maybe when you're older. Maybe when you're older."

* * *

After we're done for the evening, I sit shotgun while David takes the Mass Pike into the city. He plays loud music as we drive. We cross the Charles River and I put my hand on his shoulder and say, "It's good to see you," but the music is too loud, a cacophony of guitars and crashing cymbals. My brother, looking alternately like some more handsome version of myself and, with his expensive Cartier watch, like a complete stranger, doesn't respond to what I say. Instead, he looks straight ahead at the string of snaking red brake lights along the Southeast Expressway. "Fucking traffic," he says.

As we approach the city, we drive underground in the new gleaming system of tunnels, emerging near Boston Harbor. When I was young, the harbor was one of America's most polluted bodies of water. In an act of political protest, the Museum of Science sold murky bottles of the harbor water. I owned for a time a bottle that contained the severed head of a Barbie doll, a novelty that provided me endless amounts of amusement. I liked to shake the thing as though it were a Magic 8 Ball, asking it existential questions—Will I *ever* get laid?—and receiving for an answer Barbie's peaceful, decapitated head emerging from the muck. I have been told that the harbor is clean now, so clean that if I were struck with the desire, I could take a dive into the water from the rocks at Rowes Wharf without fear of contracting tetanus. I think about this, about swimming in Boston Harbor, as David cuts the music. We take an exit toward what must be his building, a gleaming forty-story glass tower. He says to me, "It's good to see you, too," but I pretend not to hear him. Out in the harbor I act as if I've seen a dolphin. I point and say, "Did you see that? Was that a dolphin? Could the harbor be that clean?"

David's apartment—two bedrooms, two bathrooms, one

zebra-print carpet by the balcony—stands high above the water and has a view of the airport. I've never visited him, but I've seen pictures. In person, the view is more impressive. We stand on the balcony, the wind in my brother's hair and across my bare scalp. Shellfish trawlers motor in and out of the harbor, coming and going from the islands. There is the distinct smell of Boston: fish and ocean and brine and wind.

He tells me that the girls like the view. I can imagine David pointing to East Boston, to the planes taking off from Logan, and saying, "Now, *that's* just something, huh?" He has a way about him, a persuasive intelligence and a cockiness that yields an unlikely charisma. Whether or not he's in control of this— the way a musician is in control of her violin—or whether this is an unconscious product of his upbringing, another skill that he accrued and that I didn't, it is, I'm sure, what makes him a successful attorney.

We stay out on the balcony for an hour. It's a cool night. This is late April. My brother used to smoke cigarettes but now smokes gigantic Panamanian cigars. The stench is thick and sour.

"I used to have some Cubans," he says, puffing and then looking at the burning end. "But I ran out. I know some guy in Miami, but he's out, too. Everyone's waiting for Castro to die."

"Really," I say.

"Yeah," he says. "Castro might die."

"I didn't know that."

"You need to read the paper."

"I live in Los Angeles," I say.

"Touché."

"You can come out to visit me," I say. "Anytime. I have a nice house. It's not as nice as this, but it's all right."

"Yeah," he says. "I could do that."

"It's in a canyon."

"A canyon," he says. "How about that."

We sit in silence for most of the time. A lighthouse in the bay throws light around in a circle. After a long while, my brother asks, "Do you miss them?"

"I don't know," I say. "I hadn't seen them in a while. It doesn't feel much different."

"Yet," he says.

"What?"

"It doesn't feel much different *yet*."

"I guess."

"It's like they're on vacation," he says. "That's what I'm telling myself."

The last conversation I had with my father occurred only miles from here, inside one of the terminals at Logan. This was two days after my mother's funeral, a rainy Thursday, and the airport was relatively empty. He was dressed in his beige trench coat and carried a black umbrella that he tapped against the floor. At the security checkpoint, where he couldn't accompany me any longer, we hugged good-bye.

"Do you have to go?" he said to me. "Can you stay with me for a few days? Just a few more?"

"I wish I could," I said. "I have work to do back home."

"Home," he said, laughing, still hugging me. "I guess it is home for you, huh?"

"Yeah," I said.

And then my father whispered something into my ear. It

was a line from a poem, although I'm still unsure who wrote it. He said to me, *But one man loved the pilgrim soul in you.*

After I went through security, I turned to see him still standing at the glass security barricade. He met my eyes, and raised his open hand in the air. I did the same.

That was it.

Late at night, David pours himself a glass of Scotch from a bottle that I know he took from our parents' liquor cabinet. This is the last of their stash and it seems only fitting that one of us polishes it off. From a chair on his balcony, I watch as he drinks alone at his kitchen table. He sits beneath a hanging blue light fixture that shines brightly over him, revealing a few strands of gray in his hair.

David turns his back to me as he drinks, fearing, I imagine, that if I were to see him, then some alcoholic urge might overtake me. That he drinks at all is news to me, and for a few moments, it's fascinating to watch him. I wonder whether he's inherited the small idiosyncrasies that accompanied all of our habits, such as my father's comic way of hissing at the day's first sip of Scotch, as if the bitterness were new to him. I wonder whether David swoons the way my mother did when she used to lower her nose into the glass to sniff the stuff from a new bottle. For reasons that I'm still unsure about, I used to swish the first few sips around my mouth as if it were mouthwash.

Despite my brother's fears, I'm quite comfortable around liquor these days, and so rarely afflicted with the desire for a drink that my proximity to the stuff achieves not so much as a rise in those parts of me that matter, my tongue, my stomach, the certain section of my brain that corresponds to vodka.

Maybe this is just something I tell myself, hoping it might be true. Regardless, I stay on the balcony, watching.

The lights of the airport don't change, but remain consistently and rhythmically blinking atop an air traffic control tower and on the wings of the airplanes that come in and go out. I close my eyes, and this is when I smell my mother—peonies, talcum powder, Glenlivet—rising up from the harbor. I don't have good hearing, or good eyesight, so, in some way, I find it fitting that the ghosts of my parents come to me in wafts of the perfumes they used. A doctor friend of mine in California, when I mentioned smelling my father's cologne on the airplane the other day, suggested, somewhat insensitively, that I might be suffering from a brain tumor. Olfactory hallucinations, he claimed, are a symptom of such cancers.

"That's nonsense," Audrey says to me after I call her and relay my fears.

"Where are you right now?" I ask.

"I'm in the backyard," she says. She's staying at my house while I'm in Massachusetts. "It's sunny and I wanted to be outside. Is it sunny there?"

"It's dark here," I say. "It's night."

"I keep forgetting about the time difference," she says.

"I'm coming home tomorrow night."

"I can't wait," she says.

"It's been horrible," I say. "All of it."

"Which direction are you looking?"

"What do you mean?"

"West? East? Which direction?"

It takes me a moment to orient myself. I'm used to having the ocean to the west of me, rather than to the east. "East," I say. "I'm facing the water."

"Turn around," she says. "So it's like we're talking to each other."

"Are you going to give me a hug?" I ask. "A cross-country hug?"

"No," she says, laughing at me in her deep, husky voice, a result of thirty years of smoking. Even though she's supposed to have quit, I believe that I hear the flicking of a cigarette lighter across the line. We have known one another for six weeks, and these small things—her boyish laughter, a surreptitious cigarette—are still new to me. "You've been watching too many movies."

"It's my job," I say.

"I just don't want to talk to the back of your head."

"He's drinking," I say. "My brother."

"What an asshole," she says. "What a dick."

"It's okay," I say, watching the way he leans back in his seat as he sips, the way his head tilts back as the Scotch goes down.

"If you say so," Audrey says.

"I keep smelling my mother's perfume," I say, as another gust of wind carries by me the smell of Glenlivet and ice.

"Maybe she's visiting you," Audrey says. She got sober in twelve steps, many of which necessitate the belief in a power higher than one's self, something I could never agree to. "I wish my mother visited me. She always liked my sisters better. Those spoiled brats."

"Maybe I have a brain tumor," I say.

"Maybe you do. Maybe you're in God's hands."

"I thought that God always has me in his hands."

"Maybe God gave you a brain tumor."

"This isn't helping."

"I'm sorry," she says. "Do you want me to say that I love you? Will that make you feel better?"

This is a joke from the night we met, when we both admitted that, in our past lives, each of us had suffered from the drunken tendency to say those words to strangers in bars.

"We haven't gotten there yet," I say, laughing.

"You could say it to your brother," she says. "That might make both of you feel better."

"I don't know how he'd take that," I say.

"Oh, please," she says. "Everyone likes to hear those words."

"Do you think that's true?"

"You just to need to let go," she said.

I say good-bye and I hang up the phone and put my feet up on the balcony and look out at the city. I take from my pocket the note my father left in the kitchen. With my fingers I trace his hasty longhand, the arc of the *S* of the word *son*. I love my parents. *Let go.* I say it aloud, let the words echo into the cool air. I say it again. I hold the note in my hands. I say it again. Let go. Let go. Let go.

The doctors who cared for my father at the end claimed no apparent cause of death, other than the obvious. "This happens," the doctor told me. This was a conversation on the telephone. I was in the airport in Los Angeles. I had seen my father eight hours earlier.

"Broken heart," the man said.

"Don't fucking bullshit me," I said.

"Excuse me, sir?" the doctor said.

"I want a real reason," I said. "Not some sentimental crap."

"There may have been some underlying reasons, but some-times people just surrender themselves to a higher power."

"Are you fucking kidding me?" I said, before proceeding to yell some more.

By the time I was finished, the doctor had gone.

In the morning David and I drive back to the suburbs. We leave his apartment on the harbor before the sun rises, and as he maneuvers the Mercedes through the green streets of Chestnut Hill and Newton, the sun emerges through the budding maple trees in Upper Falls. David drives with his left hand while rubbing the ball of his right palm into the skin below his eyes. He's not used to drinking, he tells me, and as he says this, I think of telling him that I love him, and I wonder, watching the way his mouth twists as the car sinks in and out of potholes, whether the sentiment is true or not. He was only a boy when I left home. We've never really known one another, and I'm not sure if what we share as brothers could possibly be called love.

"I can't get a fucking break," he says, after his telephone rings for the third time in fifteen minutes. "You tell people that you have to clean out your dead parents' house and you'd think they'll stop calling."

"Do you have to be so callous?" I say. " 'Clean out.' What a terrible thing to say."

"Callous," he says. "Look at you using such a fancy word."

"I'm a writer now," I say.

"Is that just some sort of thing you can call yourself, or does it actually entail any real work?"

"Do they surgically implant something up your ass when you become an attorney, or does that happen in law school?"

"It's a hot poker," he says, straight-faced. "It hurts more than you think it would."

I smile and lean back in the seat as we take the turn onto our old street. David watches me as he drives. He's traveled back and forth from his house to our parents' house so often that he can do the drive without looking. David's eyes are large, brown like my mother's, and the way he holds them on me, on my face, is intended to make me feel nervous and conciliatory. This is a prosecutor's trick, a way to get me to speak. I've faced this look before, from him, from others.

"So," he says. "What're you writing now?"

"I don't think I should say."

"Why's that?"

"Because you'll get angry."

"How do you know?"

"Because I know you."

David laughs to himself as he pulls the Mercedes into the driveway of our old house. He leaves the engine running as he turns to me again. "You *know* me," he says. "Did you really say that?"

"You know what I mean."

David keeps his eyes trained on me and with a flicker of his eyebrows, he says, "I guess I don't."

Rather than face my brother's cross-examination, I get out of the car. My father loved to work on his yard but now the long slope of grass in the front yard is pocked with early-season weeds. There are buttercups and dandelions and large patches of clover and a whole host of plants and flowers for which I don't have names. I don't have an eye for botany, unlike my father, who could name, with ease, the genus and species of any plant he came across. This skill, I assumed, was a prerequisite for his love of poetry. I get out of the car and walk into the grass. High up in the branches of the lone oak in the yard is an old bird feeder that I made as a Boy Scout. I'd forgotten about this.

"So," David says, coming up beside me, placing his hand on my shoulder.

"That's it, David. I have nothing more to say."

"Don't be a dick," he says. "I'm your baby brother."

"It's about Mom and Dad," I say, finally.

"What is?" he asks.

"It's about Mom and Dad. I wrote a movie about our parents."

"You didn't."

"I had to," I said.

My movie is called, for now, *The Two Moons of Massachusetts*, and it begins during the parade for the three Apollo astronauts. As the credits roll, the Chrysler phaeton passes by the camera. A young child, Charles, becomes visible amid the crowd. He is eleven years old, dressed in an orange plaid shirt, khaki shorts, and high white tube socks. A pesky cowlick bobs whenever his head moves. In the mild August wind, his cheeks are flushed. His mother is beside him, wearing large Jackie Onassis sunglasses, a striped white-and-black blouse, and fashionable blue bell-bottom dungarees. She is tall, and with that same August wind in her hair, she is beautiful.

When they've finished chasing the car, and Charles has been left alone in City Hall Park, the camera moves slowly, framing him as he sits on the park bench. The oil lanterns in the park begin to ignite, one by one, as the camera continues to track, moving closer to his face until just his eyes remain in the frame, blue and watering, reflecting in their dark pupils the flickering of the oil lantern closest to him. The shot then dissolves to another, older pair of eyes, those of the adult Charles.

I hoped that Hollywood would be quite fond of that little trick. When I wrote it, I assumed that I, and I alone, was the one writer to think of it, until of course the man who bought the movie, the star, frowned at me and said, "You know, I think I've been in at least five pictures where they've done this sort of gimmick. Try to think of something else, Charlie. You're a fine writer, but this scene's just not cutting it for me right now."

"Okay," I said. I had a notebook in my lap. I was taking notes.

We were in his office. He leaned back in his chair and smiled at me. "Charlie," he said, and he sounded for one terrible, strange moment just like my father. "I believe in you. I know you'll do something great."

After the meeting, I called Audrey from the parking lot. She'd been pursuing her master's in English when she began to drink too much to study. She was proofing my rewrites for me, something she was quite good at.

"Weren't you scared?" she asked. "Waiting there in that park for your mother?"

"No," I said, sitting in my car in a lot in Santa Monica. A sign on a nearby bank displayed a temperature with three digits. I was sweating through my clothes. "I was always the brave little boy."

"That can't be true. You must have been scared. Anyone would have been scared. She left you all alone."

I fiddled with my car keys. I'd never told anyone about that afternoon. My mother and I never spoke of it. "What do you want me to say? That I was frightened?"

"You can tell me whatever you want. Whatever you're comfortable telling me."

I waited for a moment to speak. The windows in my car were fogging up. I tried once to sweat out my drinking habit; I joined a health club with a sauna and went every day. For a week or two, it worked.

"Of course I was scared," I said. "I was eleven, and all of a sudden she comes stumbling into the park with this man."

"With Michael Collins?"

"It wasn't Michael Collins. The guy with my mother was a blonde. Collins had black hair. I knew that then, but I didn't say anything."

I waited for Audrey to speak. She believed in the healing properties of talk therapy.

"And you know what else? I tested him. I asked him how it was on the moon. And he said it was great up there, that he jumped around. I asked him that on purpose because I knew that of the three Apollo astronauts, Michael Collins was the one who never set foot on the moon. That guy with my mother, he was just some guy. He was probably just some young soldier in the city for a weekend."

We put the bags of linens, bath towels, and washrags in the driveway. We stack the boxes on the grass. David does most of the work. He hauls two boxes at a time, grabs three bags in each hand. It takes him an hour to do the books. They sit in the yard, the word POEMS written with marker on the cardboard. He seems full of energy, and says to me, "We're going to be done early. I called the movers."

"Good," I say. "I want to go home."

Whenever I exercise, or exert myself for a long period of time, I can feel the effects of my years of drinking. Although I'm healthy now—along with alcohol, I've disavowed meat, dairy, sugar, cigarettes—my body isn't immune from the damage I've inflicted upon it. So, while my brother works, I sit on the grass beside the liquor cabinet. I absently open and close the mirrored doors. The sound of this—a clicking, followed by a pop and a rusty squeak—is so familiar, like the opening measures of a favorite song heard for the first time in ages, that in some way it's as if the intervening twenty-five years have been nothing but an afternoon away. Inside, along the shelves, there is the dusty residue of liquor bottles, and the evidence of spilled Scotch. Although it feels foolish to do, I stick my head inside the cabinet and breathe.

"Hey, dickhead," David says, kicking me in the ass, toppling both me and the liquor cabinet. "If you didn't want to help, why'd you come at all? I'm killing myself out here."

I stand up quickly, get in my brother's face. For years, I fought in bars, on the street, in empty parking lots. This is my instinct. Liquor made my dad thoughtful and woozy, as it did my mom. It made me belligerent. My brother's impatient and unfazed. He tilts his head to one shoulder.

"What now, Charlie?" he says. "You want to hit me? Is that it? Go for it, fuckhead."

I look away at the grass, where one of the doors of the cabinet has broken off, the mirror shattered. My superstitious mother would have shrieked at this most unholy of transgressions.

"You broke it," I say.

"So I broke it," he says, turning away from me. "They're

dead, now, Charlie. That's the whole point. That's why we're here. Why else would you be here? To get some more material for your *movie?*"

"What's wrong with you? Why'd you make me come and do this?"

"You're here on your own, Charlie," he says. "And besides, Dad told me to bring you here so you could see the house again one last time."

That's when I hit him. His head is turned when I do it, and my fist hits the side of his ear, momentarily bringing him to his knees. I'm good with my fists when I need to be. When he stands and turns to me, I feel the sort of fear that in the years of drunken bar fights I never felt. This, I suspect, is one possible downside of sobriety.

"What is it with you?" he says. "I've seen you two times in twenty-five years, right? And you punch me in the goddamned head?"

"How can you be so casual about this?" I ask, trying to ignore the pain in my fist. "About all of this? About breaking that?"

"When was the last time you saw both of them alive? Can you even remember? What about all the times Mom called and asked you to come home? You were too busy with your *work*. Finally, fucked-up Charlie does something with himself, right? Charlie has a girlfriend. Charlie has a job. That's the truth, right? Or was it because you were afraid of what they might think of you?"

"Please David, don't," I say, raising my hands above my head to surrender. "Please don't."

"You don't have to tell me," he says. "I know that's the truth."

"Fuck you," I say, turning around. I am stopped by my brother's hands. He grabs my chin, grips me until it hurts. I'm ready to be hit.

"Twenty-five years. That was the last time. You know how I know? Do you know, Charlie? Ask me."

"How do you know?"

"Because she told me. Mom told me. That's how I know."

I'm the one who realizes that we've forgotten the refrigerator. Inside, I find all of the food my dad was making for my mother, the Bolognese sauce, the roast pork, a pepperoni pizza, two apple pies. Nothing has been touched. The dishes are stored in their entirety, packed tightly into Tupperware containers. I take the food out, place the dishes on the counter. My dad told me that my mother was having trouble with her appetite, and this was the reason why he decided to cook the dishes he remembered her loving. I never had such a problem. Drinking kept me thin. In Los Angeles, people asked for my secret. I laughed, said I was on a liquid diet. For a time, I believed it.

Most of the house is empty, and as I try to find a bag to dump all of the food into, on top of the counter I find my mother's scrapbook of the moon landing. My brother must have uncovered it and left it out for me to take. As I suspected, it's filled with pages of newspaper clippings about the landing of Apollo 11. It's only as I get to the last page that I discover a photograph of my mother as a young woman, dressed in a pilot's uniform. Her hair is curled around her ears. She looks happy and sober. If not for a man lingering in the background dressed as a cowboy, I might not have realized that this is a picture taken at a costume party, and not, as I first assumed, an actual photograph of my mother dressed as a pilot, evidence of some secret life I wasn't aware of. The picture is glued down to the page, but it's not difficult to pull it away from the paper. Written on the back, in the longhand script I recognize as my mother's, is the date October 31, 1942. This would make her sixteen. The rest of the inscription reads: "When I am older I want to become a pilot and eventually fly a rocket into space."

When the truck comes, I stand alone in the empty living room and look out through the large picture window. I expected the emptiness of this room to feel haunting, as if by removing the wide oak coffee table, and my father's books, and the liquor cabinet, I'd find something revealed to me in the emptiness we made, some secret pattern I could decipher from the stains of spilled liquor on the hardwood. But I've moved enough in my life to know that an empty room is an empty room, and this empty room looks no different than any of the others from my past, despite the familiar view out the window, the linden tree, the slope of weedy grass going down to the street. We've left the Eames chair in my father's study. I asked my brother if he wanted it; I have my own. It looks inviting, resting in the corner as if it's awaiting my father's return.

The house has been sold. I've been told by the real-estate agent, a sunny blonde in a short skirt, that the young couple who purchased it will likely do a tear-down. All of this, I think, is for the best. Through the window, I watch my brother speak to the team of movers. David, I'm sure, doesn't want me around right now. In a few hours, we'll reassume our respective positions on the coasts, me on one side, him on the other.

The movers have taken the large pieces of furniture—the

couch, the bed frame, the large television—the things we were too tired to lift. We've wrapped the furniture in clear plastic sheets. David stands in the yard, looks up and down the street. He has showered, changed his clothes, is wearing a suit and loafers. Movers grunt under the weight of my dad's bookshelves.

When the men are finished, I'm summoned to the front yard. I don't look as the truck pulls away. The calendar says that it's April, but I'm not sure if it's the end of winter or the beginning of spring. The trees along our street have not begun to bud, but the air is warm. Children are riding their bicycles on the street. The neighborhood seems to have aged well. David rubs the back of his head.

"Are you okay?" I ask.

He shrugs his shoulders and drops a set of keys into my hand. "For the storage locker."

The truck is still on the street, turning onto the main road. I watch it go.

"Storage locker?"

He smiles at me and wiggles his eyebrows. "You're lucky I didn't punch you," he says as his telephone rings. "I work out. I could do some real damage."

"Wait," I say, watching him answer his call. "You got a storage locker?"

He speaks into the telephone. "We don't want that judge," he says. Then he turns to me. "Took you long enough to ask, Charlie. You didn't think I was throwing all of this away, did you? What kind of person do you think I am?"

I'm not sure what is appropriate—a hug, a handshake, a thank you. "I'm going," David says to me. He throws a fake punch at my gut, stops inches away. It's a phantom punch, but

I feel it anyway. As he gets into his car, I take the note from my pocket. It wasn't for me. I realize this now. *Son, please take care of this. I love you.*

"Dave," I yell as he pulls out of the driveway. He's on his telephone, and no matter how loud I scream, or how many times I yell, he doesn't turn in my direction. I think of running into the street after him.

I fold the letter and put it back into my pocket and then, looking across the grass as my brother drives away, I can, for a moment, see all of us, my mom and my dad and David and me, all of us in the yard on a warm night in July standing beneath the large oak in the yard while the lightning bugs circle around us. I am eleven. My mother hands me her glass of Scotch as she bends to take my brother up into her arms. I take my first sip of alcohol and then we all look up at the moon. My brother, new to speaking, shouts the word over and over—Moon! Moon!—his baby voice so exuberant and happy that soon all of us are smiling. I take another sip, and then another, before my father, laughing, wearing a checkered red flannel shirt and gray slacks, takes the glass from me. "Taking up the family pastime at an early age," he says. Our neighbors are in their yards, everyone looking up at the sky. My father grabs my mother at the waist, kisses her cheek. She yells, to no one in particular, to the neighbors, to me and David, to the sky and the astronauts and the lightning bugs. "There are men up there! On the moon! In space! Isn't that something!"

Catherine and Henry

Catherine laughs when her friend first mentions the idea.

"He'll never actually act on it, even if it's true," Catherine says.

This is in a corner booth at the Palm Court. Even though Catherine is relatively new to the city, she knows the place is no longer popular, or at all fashionable, something that Minnie, she worries, has yet to discover.

"I'm not saying I think he will. I'm just saying that I think he might," Minnie says. At thirty-seven she is ten years older than Catherine, and has, when she speaks, the husky, rusted voice of a longtime smoker.

"Why is that?" Catherine asks. "How can you be so sure?"

"Every man I know would do it," she says. "That's excellent empirical data."

"You see?" Catherine says, allowing herself a smile. "You're a cynic. You have no choice but to think like this. It's how you're wired."

"I'm realistic," Minnie says. "There's a difference."

Against her better judgment, Catherine is drinking a seven-dollar iced tea, fiddling with a plastic straw, and when she complains about this, Minnie scoffs at her and then slides a copy of *Cosmopolitan* across the table. Inside, there is an article with the title "Is He Telling You the Truth?" To accompany the text, there is a photo of a beautiful young brunette wearing nothing but a striped scarf, her skin airbrushed and unblemished. This brings a smile to Catherine's face. As if any normal woman might ever have a leg like this, without hair or cellulite or freckles. Below the picture is a caption: *Is this what he really wants?* Catherine takes the magazine and thinks immediately of her father, who had, when she was young, fallen in love with a woman he'd once known as a teenager. The affair had, for the six months it lasted, caused her mother to lose her sanity slowly: a gradual trickling of envy that upended her.

"Honestly," Catherine says, reading quickly. "This is quite low. Even for you."

"Did you get to the part where we get someone to seduce him?" Minnie asks.

"Yes, I did," she says, placing the magazine on the table, her eyes catching the heading on that very page. "That's a joke, though," she says, pointing to the text. "They've written it as a joke. You know that, right?"

She has never liked fashion magazines, the subtle way they degrade her, the hopeful way they offer suggestions on how to feel better: moisturizing creams, mud baths, diet pills, weekends away at expensive spas, tawdry photographs of half-dressed eighteen-year-old boys. Minnie lives on them, carries two in her purse wherever she goes.

"It's only a joke if you want it to be a joke," Minnie says.

"Can we please drop this?" Catherine says.

After a moment, Minnie takes back the magazine. "Aren't you going to marry him?" she asks.

"Oh," Catherine says, shaking her head. "I don't know. That's far off."

"It would be different if there were any attractive women in Wisconsin," Minnie says. "Then you'd know what I'm talking about. Then you'd be worried."

"This is upsetting me," Catherine says.

"I'm *kidding* you," Minnie says then, falling back into her seat, her teacup raised.

"Why don't you play this awful game on Paul?" Catherine says, thinking of Minnie's husband. He seems to her to be the perfect Deerfield-Harvard-Wharton-McKinsey money man, possessed with a careful dirty-blond side part and at least a little bit of mischief. The few times they've met she has always found his attention uncomfortable.

"Because I already know what Paul would do," Minnie says. "He'd go home with her. He'd brag about it to his friends. And I'm okay with that."

"No you're not. That's why you want to meddle in my life," Catherine says.

"How do you know he's not out there right now messing around?" Minnie asks.

"I don't."

"Exactly."

"That's what trust is," Catherine says.

Minnie brushes this aside with her hands, as if a fly has crossed the air near her teacup. "Trust is just some concept psychologists give to women whose boyfriends cheat too much."

The Plaza is always Minnie's idea. Catherine usually

protests, relents, and arrives on time, while Minnie, habitually, saunters in twenty minutes late. Sometimes Catherine waits outside on Fifty-ninth Street, where the edge of Central Park stands against the city like a green curtain. She likes the hansom cans that line the curb. It's funny, she thinks, that when the wind is right the sidewalks outside the Plaza smell like horses.

"So," Minnie says, "We're doing it."

"What are you going to do? Try to seduce him? He won't sleep with you, Minnie. You're not his type."

"Not me," she says.

She can see now the quality in Minnie that has always made her worried.

"I know someone. It'll take one quick call."

Henry smells her perfume before she comes through the door. It's rose water, talcum, and at least a trace of Ivory soap. He's painting in the kitchen. A mason jar filled with wet brushes and a filthy paper towel sits atop the table. His lunch dishes are still in the sink: a corner of a turkey sandwich, the rind from a hunk of Gruyère, an untouched dollop of applesauce. He is filthy, paint up and down his arm, splattered on the waistband of his pants, streaked somehow in lateral bands across the skin of his neck; it's the only way he knows how to work. He takes off his smock. It's nothing but an old dress shirt. He wears it backward when he works, just the way he did when he was a small boy learning to paint with his fingers.

She comes through the door in her leather coat, the zipper down. He loves to watch her come into a room. It's something about her hair, the way it moves a moment after the rest of her body, the way the smell of her follows a moment after that. Or it's the searching way her eyes move. They are big, green, nearly always accompanied by blue eye shadow.

"You have no shirt on," she says. "It's freezing. You'll get a cold."

"I wanted to surprise you with my beautiful body," he says, flexing, going to kiss her.

"Don't touch me," she says, poking his chest with her finger. "You have paint all over you."

"So what?" He angles his head and lips toward a spot on her neck.

"So," she says, poking him harder, stepping away from his kiss, "this outfit was very expensive and I don't really care to have it ruined by your paint."

"Then why don't you take your outfit off?" he says.

"Oh, quit it," she says, turning back to the cabinet. She goes to their pantry. "I want wine. Do we have any wine?"

"It's still light out," he says. "Are we drinking before dark now?"

"I thought we had wine," she says, rustling through the cabinet. She takes a bottle of kosher wine from the pantry that he'd bought for the last Passover seder. He'd tried to show her what the holiday was like.

"You can drink that," he offers.

"Where the hell is the *real* wine? This isn't real wine. This is your wine."

He can tell that she's been at lunch with Minnie. Whenever they see each other, she comes home disappointed, in need of a drink. He has never liked Minnie. She is the sort of woman who has never had a job, who tips poorly in restaurants, the sort who pretends to love men but who never misses an opportunity to insult them. He watches Catherine go off to the hallway, stopping for a moment at a drawing on the wall. This is new, a picture of her he did early in the week; pencil and India ink.

"What's this?"

"A present," he says.

"You didn't ask me before you hung it up," she says. "You should have asked me."

"I didn't know I needed your permission," he says, calling out.

"Of course you need my permission," she says. "My name's on the lease."

"Smile for me," he says. "Cheer up."

"No," she says, walking out of the room, taking her coat off.

She has a great mess of a mouth, a mouth that has nearly always necessitated a dentist. He likes to think that in each of her misdirected teeth, there is an equal amount of personality. It took her a very long time to allow him to see her smile.

"Did I do something wrong?" he asks.

"I don't know," she says. "Did you do something wrong?"

She comes back toward him, drops her purse on the ground. It lands with a thud. He is always amused by how heavy her bag is, as if she feels the need to be prepared for any theoretical possibility. She's stopped now in the hallway once again, staring at the drawing. He'd done it of her, from memory, and put it up to try to entice her to pose for him, something she's refused to do.

"You're upset with me, aren't you?" he asks.

She lights a cigarette, exhales, the smoke collecting for a moment against the ceiling.

"I don't like you doing this," she says. "Trying to guilt me into doing something I don't want to do."

"Do you like it?" he asks.

"It's fine, Henry."

"That's it?"

"You didn't capture me," she says. "But otherwise, it's fine."

"Not as fine as you," he says. His own humor, however flimsy, makes him laugh. She claimed once that this was a sign of deep dysfunction, or an aggrandized sense of self: she was a psychology major in Madison.

"Henry, can I ask you something?"

"Shoot," he says, coming up behind her, rubbing her shoulders. The muscles in her back are tight and unresponsive. Massaging her feels impossible.

"When you have models come in to pose, do you ever find them attractive?"

He can tell she is paying close attention to the shape of his eyes while she asks this question. He is well acquainted with her belief that she maintains some intrinsic skill at discerning truth from fiction based solely on the subtle flickering of a person's eyelashes, the dilation of the pupils, the frequency of blinking.

"You need to stop worrying," he says to her, refusing to blink.

"So that's a no?" she asks.

"It's work. I'm not doing it for fun."

"But what if it was? What if it became fun?"

"What do you mean?"

"Would you fuck her?"

To hear her cuss so plainly is shocking to him, and he becomes instantly afraid that she might interpret his surprise, and whatever it's done to his eyes, as some evidence of his supposed guilt.

"You need to stop seeing Minnie," he says. "She's getting to you."

"This has nothing to do with Minnie." She grabs his wrist. He wonders if she is going to measure his pulse. "How do I know you're telling me the truth?"

"You don't," he says. "You just have to trust me."

"Sometimes," she says, laughing, raising her arms above her head, as if she is about to hug someone, "sometimes this place makes me crazy."

She walks away, hissing through her teeth, kicking her purse across the room. This sudden dissatisfaction of hers is new, as is a certain volatility he's noticed for weeks. He has lately found himself praying that she will somehow discover some hidden reservoir of trust, and that whatever suspicion she harbors will dissolve into a peaceable, livable calm. It's an endeavor he believes is useless, for he is sure that God doesn't work in quite that way, answering individual requests. Even at twenty-seven, he isn't sure he's learned the difference between wishing and praying.

Alone in their living room, he can hear the thumping of a car stereo somewhere outside his building. Far off, there is the bleating of a fire engine. He grew up on his father's apple orchard, surrounded by trees—so many acres of trees—but still he feels most comfortable in the city. His whole family, going back to the Ukraine, grew apples, and he is the first among them to break the tradition. Out the window he sees two elms moving in the river wind. Brooklyn is country enough for him.

When she comes back into the room, she stops to look at his newest painting.

"Do you recognize it?" he asks.

"It's the view out the window."

He stands beside her, rubs the skin on her arms with his hands.

"I like the little birds," she says, pointing at the small shrikes he's painted. "They're my favorite."

"Me, too," he says.

He made them by making tiny crosses with a pointed brush. It's the small effects of color, the illusions, the tricks, that have always thrilled him about painting.

"You know what I'd like?" he says.

The bridge of her sternum is visible in the right light. He puts his thumb on her chest and then places his entire hand at the curve between her hip and her waist. She is shaped perfectly for his hand.

"I can't read your mind," she says.

"I want to paint you."

"Oh God, Henry," she says. "You need to give it up. You're driving me crazy. That's twice in five minutes you've asked. Paint the Brooklyn Bridge. It's much more beautiful than me."

She turns, goes back to the pantry.

"I don't think a bottle of wine grew in there while you were in the bathroom," he says.

"Does the liquor store deliver?"

"Let me take your picture, at least," he says. "Take your clothes off and let me take your picture."

"Like hell," she says, turning sharply, toppling a canister of paint to the floor. "Like hell, Henry."

Although she would regret ever doing so, it was Catherine who had suggested to Henry that he abandon the work he was doing in order to focus on painting the figure. He was an amateur, she knew, and it was unfair to judge him, but she thought his paintings seemed very much like the art her kindergarten students made when they were angry. This was weeks after they'd met, when she was sure already that she loved him, and sure that she was going to ask him to move into her one-bedroom apartment just south of Prospect Park. She loved Henry, she had decided, in every way that she had felt herself previously incapable, and in ways that her own mother considered foolish. She had confessed over the telephone that she had no doubts as to his goodness, eliciting at first just a stunned silence, and then a quiet, if not suspicious, scoff across the line.

When they met, he was working for the city's parks and recreation department. Because he had grown up on an apple orchard, he possessed the requisite knowledge of trees and soil, and had a certain aptitude for manual labor that made him a natural for the job. It was a position she knew little about, but one from which he returned home exhausted and sore and covered in grime. This was when he usually preferred to paint, late in the evenings, when he was filthy already, using a space in the back of Catherine's apartment, where he'd put up an easel and where he used mason jars to mix his colors and store his turpentine and gesso and primer. He'd start usually after they'd made love, his mind suddenly clear. She would watch him as she fell asleep, turned on her side, the sheets tangled. She adored the sight of him at his easel, his hair untended, his eyeglasses on, paint everywhere, the furious way he attacked the canvas.

When she suggested to him that he paint the figure, hers was the one he wanted to try first. She was twenty-five then,

fresh to New York from Wisconsin, the daughter of a fire
chief and an amateur dressmaker, six feet tall in sneakers.
Like her mother, she was an ash blonde, possessed with a
diver's body: boyish hips and breasts. He said once that she
was a straight line of a woman. He'd asked while they were
in bed together and she was on top of him. Her refusal was
simple: they had not even been together long enough for
him to have discovered the flaws of her body—and she knew
they were there—on his own. To sit for him would mean to
submit in some way to him, to allow him to lock away some
image of her that might exist for years. And what would
that picture be? Her in the nude, surely. This, of course,
was what he really wanted: for her to sit naked for him for
hours, inert, obeying his commands to move. As if being
able to have her body—her actual body, in the flesh, in his
hands—was not enough.

The girls started to come a year later. A friend of his suggested he hire figure models to pose for him. At first she
thought nothing of it, until Minnie demanded she reconsider
her stance. Such an arrangement, Minnie told her, was rife
with trouble. After this, she began to look over his paintings
when he'd gone to work. Usually she did this on Saturdays.
They were stacked up in their bedroom, or in the kitchen, or,
when their apartment simply could not give up another inch,
in a storage locker in the basement of their building. Uniformly, they were paintings of women so different from her:
all of them with dark hair, wide hips, full breasts. He was able
to choose the models he wanted, and in his work, she discovered he had a type, and that she was anything but his type. It
was on one of those early Saturday mornings when she discovered a series of pictures of the same woman. There were

dozens of them, and in Henry's work she found a new sense of attentiveness that discomfited her. Part of this, surely, was that Catherine believed these new paintings to be his best work. She knew little about it, but she thought the light looked good, and that he'd captured some hint of mystery in this new girl. But also, the pictures grew explicitly more lustful. In one, the girl lay on the bed—on their bed—in a white dress shirt but without any pants, her legs spread. She'd found this last painting a week before Minnie had ever broached the subject of his possible infidelity.

Now, when Minnie tells her it took only a simple telephone call to Henry, all Catherine can think about is that girl, and the exacting detail Henry had used to paint her body. They are in a taxi headed downtown. Catherine has never liked cabs, their sticky vinyl backseats, the ticking meter like a bomb, the constant radio-rattle of a far-off cricket match. To make things worse, she is terribly susceptible to car sickness. Minnie seems to be aware of this, reaching into her purse, handing her a bottle of water.

"Don't panic," Minnie says. "Hydrate. Breathe. This will be over in an hour."

"What did she say?" Catherine wants to know.

"That she called him up, offered her services as a model, and that he said yes."

Catherine thinks of the painting. In a way, it was very much like the photograph embedded into that article from *Cosmo:* everything so smooth.

"You're a bad person," Catherine says.

"*I'm* a bad person? You're traveling with me," Minnie says. "What does that say about you?"

"That I'm frightened."

"No," Minnie says. "It says that you're curious. That you're suspicious."

"You're so certain that you know me, aren't you?" she says. "That you know Henry."

Minnie counts off each indictment with her fingers. "Jewish kid from Boston. Grew up with money. Doesn't want to follow Daddy's wishes. Tries to be an artist. Finds himself a hot little blond girl with cute little tits. After he's tired of being poor, he'll probably go to law school. Or at the very least, he'll just marry himself a nice Jewish girl. At the very least."

"Sometimes the things that come out of your mouth are really disgusting," Catherine says, shaking her head. She wraps her arms around her chest, either to warm her body or to protect herself from what she is about to do; she can't decide. The car goes south on Park Avenue, passing the restaurants below Grand Central where Henry likes to take her when he is fresh with cash. It happens infrequently, whenever his father wires money. They go crazy and eat oysters on the half shell, paella with king crab, braised rabbit in port. She presses her face to the window as the car drives south to Union Square.

"The thing is," Minnie says, "Jessica is a sweetheart. I know that sucks to hear."

"Who is Jessica?" Catherine asks.

"Oh," Minnie says. "That's the girl. My friend. The one who called Henry."

"Is she a whore?"

Minnie scoffs. "I don't know what she is. She's a graduate student, I think."

"A graduate student?"

"Look," Minnie says. "She needs the money. That's who she is. Okay? Just forget about it."

Minnie has a habit of not looking at her when she speaks. It is a disconcerting affectation that has forever fostered her distrust.

"A sweetheart, huh?" Catherine says.

"And knowing Henry, he'll probably rebuff her. So relax."

Catherine says nothing to this attempt at humility, which is a serious faux pas as far as Minnie is concerned. What follows—a harsh glance, a dismissive purse of the lips, the systematic, orderly cracking of each knuckle—is all an indiscreet call for Catherine to affirm Minnie's saintliness.

"Thank you for trying to cheer me up," she says, finally.

She doesn't recognize the sound of her voice as it escapes into the car. After three years in New York, her whole personality seems to have changed: a week earlier, she spent forty dollars on tacos. Minnie, she realizes now, makes her terribly homesick for Wisconsin. Her own constant acquiescence wounds her. There is no good reason for the two of them to be friends, except for the unbearable fact that without Minnie Catherine's only true friend would be Henry, and for a week now Henry has become inextricably linked in her mind with that woman without pants.

The car stops on the corner of Avenue B and Seventh Street. It's early, before noon, and the streets are mostly empty. Catherine gets out first, her heels on the pavement like tap shoes. There is wind in the trees in the park, a rustling, the smell of ginkgo and sugar maple, a waft of Nag Champa incense. She feels like sprinting away from Minnie. This part of Manhattan is unfamiliar to her. She looks north and south, trying to gain her bearings. In her fantasies she does this—

she runs the length of Central Park, she crosses the Brooklyn Bridge on foot—but Minnie is always faster, able to pounce on her like a lion on a hunt.

"What do we do now?" Catherine asks.

It occurs to her that they've come just to spy on Henry at a coffee shop, a situation she finds deeply uncomfortable. She wonders whether it's best not to know what Henry is about to do. If her mother had never known, Catherine thinks, then she may have saved herself so much grief.

"Look," Catherine says, finally. "I think this idea is foolish. I really do. I don't want to do it. Let's call it off."

"Call it off?" Minnie says. "I paid her days ago. She might have already gone through with it."

"You did?" she says. The panic comes so quickly. "Really? You're not being serious."

"Think about it this way," Minnie says. "Either he doesn't do it, or he does."

"I'm leaving," she says.

Minnie grabs her arm, tries to pull her back. "No you don't. I don't go around neighborhoods like this on my own."

She slaps Minnie in the face with her open palm. It's the first time she has ever tried to hurt another person. The ring on her index finger, the ring Henry gave her years ago, a simple silver band he cast himself, leaves a mark on Minnie's face. Before Minnie can say anything, Catherine has her other hand in the air ready to strike again. There are other rings on this hand, she feels like saying.

Minnie turns, wordless, and escapes into the bar, clutching her face. Catherine waits a moment before she peers through the window. The girl is, as Minnie claimed, easy enough to find. She is straddling a red Naugahyde stool, her elbows on the bar, her backside pointed up in the air—part target, part decoration.

All she can think as she looks this young girl over, her long pale legs, her smooth face, and her tousled blond hair, is that soon Henry will have his hands all over her.

He isn't at home when she comes through the door. She calls his name, opens the bathroom door, foolishly checks the closet. When she calls, his telephone goes straight to his voice mail—his curt voice, obscured by wind in the receiver. Just to hear it, and to think of the way Jessica had straddled that bar stool, causes Catherine to feel that peculiar emotion of weightlessness and terror, which she knows to be heartbreak.

She goes to the hallway, where Henry has hung that sketch he'd made of her. Everything is wrong, she thinks. Every inch of her body done in his hand is a wish—everything tauter, higher, smoother. She takes it and tears it into quarters, the paper fluttering to the ground.

The house is quiet without him. His most recent canvases are stacked against their one brick wall. She flips through each of the paintings that have consumed the past two years of his life, of their life together. She supposes that she is looking for paintings of other women, but this particular pile contains only pictures of the view from their window. To see New York on canvas this way reminds her of how, only a few years ago now, she'd dreamed about coming to live in this city. Then, the idea of her life here, an idea she'd mention to anyone who'd listen, was something to strive for: she'd waited tables at a Culver's to save the money. She was going to shop at Bergdorf's, have terrifically interesting friends, travel to the Hamptons on the weekends for parties at which she would wear white and go sailing and discuss good art or the films of Fassbinder. But here, in paint, Henry has seemed to capture so easily the actuality of what her life in New York has amounted to: the cluttered streets piled with snow and trash, the sky above Staten Island burned at the edges by petroleum, the men on the corner at Prospect Park West and Sixteenth who always tell her how beautiful her ass looks in jeans. She thinks of Lake Monona in February, dotted with ice fishers, her grandfather taking her by the hand across the surface, the way he would pull her by the arm and let her go, his raspy voice telling her that the ice was so thick they could park a school bus on top of it.

She goes into the bedroom, sits on the edge of the mattress, and looks out across the river at Manhattan. Fog and clouds obscure the sky. Only a sliver of the skyline is visible from their apartment, just a corner of some downtown buildings for which she does not know the names, even now, even after years in the city. This is a secret about her that Henry doesn't know, that she still carries in her purse a map of Manhattan, that she is constantly terrified of becoming lost in the grid of the island.

On the nightstand, her telephone taunts her. Her friends in Wisconsin have no patience for her stories of New York, of lunch in expensive restaurants in Williamsburg. Her mother will only gloat. On Henry's pillow, she finds strands of his hair. His scalp has only recently begun to show itself beneath the thicket of his brown curls, like a green patch of earth emerging after a thaw. She holds one hair against the light, and rubs it between her fingers before letting it go. She loses sight of it before it hits the ground. Her mother had once claimed that jealousy was just an extreme form of love, the way that a lethal influenza was just another form of the common cold.

She considers her first few months in the city. In the corner deli near her office, she was terrified to order a tuna on rye, afraid that the man who made the sandwiches, a Bengali no less, would ask her to repeat herself, and the entire place would fall quiet to hear her broad, flat Wisconsin accent. In those early days, her coworkers at the elementary school often asked her to say certain words for their amusement. The word *definitely,* which had apparently become a tic of hers, a way to agree forcefully with someone in order to seem kind, or a way simply to ingratiate herself with a new group of people, was one of their favorites. She had been so eager to make friends, she remembers now. This is what led her to Minnie. To think of her life before Henry seems like some prehistoric conversation with herself; to think of her life without him is terrifying. A whore! A real whore! She fears that everything she's gained in the past two years, her comfort, her furniture, her new urban fluency, her lack of fear, will vanish. Catherine's mother had been like this after she'd discovered her father's affair— every tiny movement of his drew scrutiny.

Her plan now is to make nothing of it. If Henry has slept with her, then she can forgive him. Women do this all the time, she reasons. She thinks of how her mother eventually forgave her father. She ruined his laundry, scolded him in front of company, even taunted him with the threat of taking a lover of her own. This seems like something Catherine is capable of doing. What she isn't sure she is capable of doing is negotiating her own envy. Absolution, she figures, is what comes after forgiveness.

In the mirror bolted to the bathroom door, she can't see

anything but the shame on her body, a creeping redness rising from her toes up through her thighs. It goes from her hips and then to her chest. And everywhere she sees that redness, she thinks of the red bar stool and that girl standing astride it.

His keys in the door are the first clue that he is home, followed by the heaviness of his steps. She hears him come into the kitchen before she sees him. He stands against the refrigerator, sighs, opens the door, grabs a beer.

This is the last peaceful moment.

He's in the studio when she calls. Her accent, that gorgeously flat bit of Wisconsin, has always seemed to him so honest, so bereft of sarcasm. It's a trick on his ears, he knows, her vowels stretched out, every word precisely measured and truthful. This is two years later. Suddenly he has an image of her in their old apartment, sitting alone at their kitchen table in a boy's baseball shirt, her elbows on the table, a cigarette in her knuckles. He isn't sure whether this is a real memory, or something he might have painted years ago. Over time, the two, the images he's made with his hands and the images of what their life had been together, have merged somehow into one.

"Henry," she says, her breath betraying to him her considerable nerves.

He sits at his kitchen table. "Catherine?"

"Are you busy?"

A screen door is open, wet with a recent rain. There is a wind over the hills, and from his seat he inhales the familiar smell: apples, dirt, trees. "No," he says, reaching for a piece of paper and a pencil. "I'm not busy at all." He thinks to make a list of conversation topics in case he becomes too nervous. First on the list is his house. Second is just the phrase *missed you,* scrawled out in pencil. He traces the words over and over, the pencil wearing grooves through the paper into the wood beneath. He has the idea of sketching a question mark beside these two words, not because the sentiment is untrue, but because he isn't sure that he can utter it.

"I'm going to be up in your neck of the woods, soon," Catherine says. "I'm visiting a friend in New Hampshire."

"A visit," he says. "You want to come and visit?"

She breathes across the line. "If it'd bother you," she says, but doesn't finish the thought.

"No," he says. "Why would it bother me?"

He still has friends in New York who knew him when he lived with Catherine, but the updates he receives from them are spare, purposefully oblique, and he knows very little about her life aside from the basics: she stills lives in the same apartment, and she still teaches at the same school. He's ignorant of everything else. There are ways now to know exactly what her life is like—the internet has made this easy, he knows—but he has been unable to think of Catherine without feeling that particular mark of shame he encountered when she caught him that afternoon.

"It'd just be one night," he hears her say. "Not even twenty-four hours."

He's unsure whether this is a good idea. The moment he ends the conversation he's filled with his old shame, an emotion he had tried to rid himself of, to pray away, and it lasts the week, right up until he steps onto the platform at the station in Westwood to meet her train. This is thirty miles west of Boston, very close to the orchard. He stands beneath a veranda. Water drips from a storm gutter. Small rainbows flicker in the rain puddles. For the first time in two weeks he's shaved. The cool air stings at his pores. His face feels nude and thin without a beard. It rained a half hour earlier, and he is soaked as he paces the platform, moving stiffly in his wet jeans. He leans over the edge of the tracks, hangs his head out into the imaginary path of the train. In the city, he knew when a train was coming by the gradual change of light on the station walls. As in a horror movie, the light would grow closer, the grime would become exposed, a rat would bolt into a wall, and then the train, gigantic and long and silver, would come into the station. Here, he can see Catherine's train a mile away, its one headlight bright in the trees.

Before the cars glide to a stop, Henry straightens his posture, runs a hand across his head. In two years he's lost much of his hair, but has gained in the process, he likes to think, a great forehead. He is bigger now than he was when she last saw him. He searches for her in the crowd, puts his collar up, wants a cigarette; he cannot catch his breath. He moves closer to the train, puts his hands in his pockets, takes his hands out of his pockets.

She comes out of her car carrying a small green bag, waving, shouting his name. It's a terrible feeling to see that she has not aged as poorly as he has. She wears jeans and tall black boots and kisses him on the cheek. The smell of the train's air conditioning comes off her hair like perfume. "I hate trains," she says by way of a greeting, kissing his other cheek. "There were children crying the whole time."

He kisses her again on the face, where her lips meet her cheek, catching her off guard. The moment has passed, the kiss is misplaced, and she flinches. She squints at him. He looks at her eyes and her lips. What he wants to say is, "I missed you." Instead, he points to the parking lot and says, "My car is the blue one."

In the car beside him, Catherine decides to be generous with his bad humor and his nerves, and whenever he looks out to the road, she turns to stare at him. He is larger. This she expected. It is the way men go. She wonders when the right time will present itself. A confession like hers must be done without liquor. She thinks for a moment, while he drives, about placing her hand flat against his thigh. She has missed his body as much as his company. He drives with the windows down. She can smell the country. It is October, the best month. Children are selling pumpkins on the side of the road. She loves autumn, the pageantry New Englanders give to the season, the farm stands of acorn squash and hay.

"So," she says. "I remember you telling me about this house. Years ago."

"It's strange to be living in the house where I grew up," he says.

"I think it would be nice," she says. "It must be comforting in a way."

"Do you think so?" he asks. "I wonder sometimes."

"I was sorry to hear about your dad," she says.

He nods and then raps at the steering wheel with his fingers. This is something he used to do years ago when he wanted to change the subject, and to see it now, after so long, this little thing that she has forgotten about, causes her chest to swell. She feels in her face as if she might cry at the prospect that he has been here this whole time, living and breathing and full of nervous tics, and that she has not been with him.

"We're picking the apples now," he says. "Some of the

neighborhood kids come in and pick the old ones off the ground and have apple fights."

"I can throw apples at you? This is allowed?" In order to sound bright and funny she's come off sounding cruel and sarcastic. This was, she remembers, one of his biggest complaints about her—that she'd become a cynic, that her humor was mean-spirited. And, as if on cue, she sees him frown. Just as it used to, it hurts her to see his disappointment.

"If you want," he says. "I guess you can throw an apple or two at me."

"You're so much older," she says, putting her hand on his forehead. She sees his skin blush. "You look like a French film-maker. Where did it all go? Your wonderful messy hair?"

"I got older," Henry says.

"Only two years," she says. "Two years is nothing."

After a moment, he turns to her and asks, "Are you living with a guy in New York?"

She watches him chew his fingernails. She looks out to the road, lets the silence build. This she cannot help but do. It's her insecurity, her fear that he's lost his love for her after so long. His thumb begins to bleed. He tries to hide this, but she sees him wipe the blood on his blue jeans, a swipe like a crescent moon. He is artful, even in the smallest moments. They drive by a paper mill. A wooden wheel churns on the river. There are six ducks standing around, doing nothing, looking at each other, being ducks.

"If you are," he says, "I'd rather know now, before I get drunk tonight and embarrass myself."

"No," she says, softly. "Unfortunately for me."

"Good," he says.

"Do you think so?"

"I shouldn't have said that."

"It's okay," she says, finally touching his thigh. She had been staring at it and daring herself. "What about you? Do you have some woman back at your country house waiting to meet me?"

"No," he says. "It's just me and my apples."

Just then, he turns onto an unmarked street crowded by overgrown conifers and sugar maple. He makes the turn too fast, and she slides in her seat, bumping into his shoulder, his chest. She smells him—cologne, cigarettes, fabric softener. The branches slap against the car window. From here, she can see his house high on the largest hill in the valley. The sun is about to set and the sky is big and purple and blue. His house looks like a toy from so far away.

Henry is glad to hear her gasp at the sight. His orchard spreads across a few hundred acres. It's his father's old land, which he inherited earlier this year when his dad died. It's a great sight, that many acres of apple trees, and he loves the way it looks in autumn, when the branches are bare and the ground is red with leaves. Despite this, he has no idea how to run the place. He and his father shared few things in common beside their love for Henry's mother. The least of these was an interest in growing apples, and he had, when he was younger, sworn that he would never find his way back to the orchard to run the business. He remembers the way his father used to smirk at hearing this, as if he knew something that Henry didn't, that there was some inherited sense of gravity that would pull him back.

He parks beside his house in a patch of dirt that he uses as a driveway. The tire swing his father hung when Henry was a boy is still strung from the oak closest to the barn. She steps out into mud and turns toward the hills and the apple trees and the house. He watches her take a big deep breath of the country.

"This is so very, very nice, Henry," she says, walking off toward the trees, stepping out of her boots, rolling up her jeans, sinking her bare feet into the mud. He watches her go. The ground is wet from the rain and the hills behind his house are rich and green. She ducks under branches. His dog, Smiddy, runs off the porch, barks twice, inspects her. She pulls an apple off a tree, tosses it up and down in her hand. Although it pains him to realize it, he can't seem to look at her without thinking of the girl, the model, the way he had slept with her, and the way Catherine had discovered.

"Look at this," she says, pulling on an apple. "I've been in the city too long. You forget that some food actually grows on trees."

"Maybe later we can go for a walk and pick some. We can make a pie."

She laughs, bends to pet Smiddy, rubbing his head with her small hands. He turns over on his back, asks with his paws to be scratched across his stomach.

"Okay," she says, standing up. "We'll go for a walk and you'll make me a pie. I don't cook, remember?"

"You cook fine."

"We've been apart too long," she says, moving close to him, close enough so that he can smell her skin. "You've forgotten things about me. That makes me sad."

Some wind blows across the orchard, blowing west across both his body and her body. He's tried to paint her for years, but now he sees that he's made errors with the smallest parts of her: her lips are not like a bell, as he'd thought, but like the letter *C*, stretched out and turned on its side. The dog barks beside him, wants to run or play. Henry takes the apple from her, throws it as far as he can. His dog gives chase.

They stand in the apple trees until the sun goes down in the sky, lowered into view like a theater prop. His father had welcomed him back without questions; they had never talked about Catherine. He follows as she goes from tree to tree comparing the apples. The older he gets, the more he feels himself turning into his father. The sun turns orange before it sets. There is little pollution this far north and the sunsets are not as good as in the city. When he can't remember what kind of apple she's holding—he is still learning, or relearning—he makes up names. "That's a Macadoo."

"Macadoo?" Catherine says. "Really?"

"No. But everything really does sound better in your cute Wisconsin accent."

"Shithead," she says. "How was that?"

She plays with her hair. He wants to kiss her.

They are walking back to the house when she says, "Do you have a lot of friends here?"

"Some guys from when I was a kid," he says.

"Buddies," she says, in a voice he remembers her using when she wanted to sound tough, everything pitched lower. He never met her brothers, but he always assumed this was what they sounded like.

He tries to think of something smart to say. "Do you still see that friend of yours?"

"Which friend?" Catherine asks.

"You know who I'm talking about," he says. The name has escaped him. He puts his palm to his forehead, and then snaps his fingers. "Your partner in crime? Very rich?"

"Minnie?"

"Minnie, that's right," he says, recalling clearly a New Year's Eve when someone had spilled wine on her chinchilla coat. "How is she? Is she still bullying you around?"

"She's fine," she says, turning around and facing the orchard.

Her skin turns red.

"And *no*," she says. "She doesn't do that anymore."

During those first months without Henry, her body shuddered, as if in withdrawal, and for a very long time she thought that she was not so much in love with Henry as she was addicted to him, his stink, his body, the paints on the kitchen counter, the small plates of food he left everywhere. Her body reacted at certain times; the circadian rhythm of her heartbreak was something she learned to read. At noon, when she always called from work to check on him, her chest ached. At seven, when she always came home, she needed something to divert her attention. Often, she went to the movies. It was not long after that afternoon when she'd told him to go—so firm, one hand in the air, her strongest tone of voice—that she heard that he had moved north to his father's house. She had never been to the orchard, had only heard Henry speak of it, but she began to imagine, in intricate detail, a life in which they lived together in the country. On the subway back to Brooklyn, she liked to place herself inside a typical morning. She had traveled as a girl to Giverny, and she imagined Henry's house to be like Monet's, a tiny cottage and a great garden. He would paint in his studio, and she would walk through the rows of apple trees, picking fruit, watching birds. In the evenings, they would drive together to a market thirty miles away. There would be decent markets closer, but they would like the drive together, the time in the car. He would play good music on the ride. They would buy fresh seafood and good white wine and lemons and capers and bring everything home, place the bags on the counter, eat olives from the plastic containers. A simple country life.

On the telephone she told him that she was traveling north to New Hampshire to visit a cousin who had moved from Wisconsin. It was a lie, and she wondered whether he could detect the dishonesty in her voice. She has no cousins outside of the Midwest, and knows not a single person in the entire state of New Hampshire. She has always been a terrible liar. She has come to see him so they can be together again. This much she knows. Her plan is murky. She wants to stay at the orchard a few days, try to fall in love again. If such a thing is even possible. Her reality always differed greatly from her fantasy, like a terrible game of chance, and just this once, she hopes her wishes might be granted.

While he prepares dinner, she stands in the small bathroom off the kitchen, staring into the tiny mirror, running a comb through her hair, trying to disguise her lack of sleep with makeup. She couldn't fall asleep the night before, thinking of this trip, of hugging Henry on the platform of the station.

The smell of his food seeps under the door. For a long while she just stands in the center of the small bathroom and listens to him move around the kitchen. This is him, she thinks. Beyond this door. That noise. Those are Henry's footsteps.

Two years: she says it quietly to herself.

* * *

He puts music on the stereo and pours her a glass of wine. She puckers her lips at the first sip. She has aged and he sees again how he painted everything wrong. There are creases that fall in small crescents from the corners of her eyes. When she was younger, she had bad teeth that she covered with her fingers when she laughed. Her old messy smile has been fixed; her teeth have been shaved down. He can smell her perfume, the old scent, rose water, talcum, Ivory soap. He remembers the way she applied it, the same way his grandmother had: five spritzes into the room, two steps into the wet mist, a quick twirl with her eyes closed. Every day, a tiny dance.

He stares at her neck, remembers being behind her in bed, his tongue on her skin. Even something ordinary from her mouth—*New Yorkers are nicer than I thought*—was charming to hear in her accent. At first, he liked her simply because of the way she spoke. It was a terribly shallow thing to remember, but it's the truth.

They finish four bottles of wine in three hours. Like any good Midwestern girl, she can drink, but as she stands from the table and goes into the living room to search for music, he believes he sees her sway. He remembered to put the Rod Stewart records at the top of the heap. "He is perfect," she'd said when they met, and he, because it was the beginning, had agreed. Even now, he isn't sure whether she was being ironic in a way that he wasn't hip enough to understand. He watches her go across the room. She saunters for him, shakes her ass, and his head feels warm and gauzy.

"I have a job teaching painting," he says. "Part-time."

"That's perfect for you."

"I teach drawing mostly," he says.

"I bet you enjoy that. All those pretty girls coming in and posing for you."

He winces. She is turned away, bent over the records, and can't have seen. There are cigarettes in his front pocket and he wants to smoke one. Catherine puts a record on his turntable, comes back into the kitchen, looks around. He has hidden all of the paintings he's made of her, all of his failed attempts at her face and body, upstairs in his studio. She'll look for them if she has the chance, he knows, and he doesn't want her to realize the extent to which he still thinks of her. He's made dozens of attempts to get her right.

"I hope you're still painting," she says. "Seriously. You had real talent. Don't wait until you're old and crazy and want to put a bullet in your belly."

"In my belly?"

"Like van Gogh," she says.

"You're drunk," he says.

"Maybe. So what? I'm not allowed?"

"I like having you here," he says.

"I like being here." She edges her seat closer to him.

"Look," he says. He puts his hand on her leg. The one thing he'd never done was apologize. He had, for so long, believed somehow that because he'd slept with the girl, that it meant something was wrong with his relationship with Catherine, that he loved her less than he should have. "What I did to you back then—"

"Don't even start," she says, her eyes wide. "Let's not even get into it."

He watches the good cheer rush out of her, all the energetic optimism he saw in her when she stepped off the train in Westwood. "I can't even believe I did it," he says.

123

"Please stop."

He takes his hand back. Beneath his hand, her leg had begun to quiver. "I think it's the worst thing I've ever done to another person."

Pointedly, she's turned away from him, and is facing the front window, black now with night.

"Let's have more to drink," he says, finally. "Do you want to take it outside? Into the orchard?"

"No," she says, her voice cool.

"Come on," he says. "It's a nice night."

"I said no, Henry."

"Fine, then," he says. "I guess we'll sit here and listen to Rod Stewart." They sit silent at the table before he says, "Your bedroom is up the stairs."

She plays with the used wine cork, rolling it against her fingers. "Thank you."

"It's good to see you," he says, finding her eyes.

She stands up from the table. "You know, I missed you forever. But you are still a motherfucker."

She wanted to confess to him that night in their apartment two years ago. When she didn't, her secret became lodged inside her like some surgical instrument left behind in her body, her skin sewn shut with a scalpel in her chest cavity. Often she found herself consumed with the anxiety that somehow Henry would find out what she and Minnie had done. And what would happen then? To sleep with a whore was one thing, but to lure your boyfriend with a whore seemed, over time, to be so much worse. Now she isn't sure she can confess at all. He'd tried to be kind to her in the kitchen, to apologize, and she'd rebuffed him, and now, under his roof, the guilt she expected has been replaced by her anger, old by now, a constant presence.

She can't sleep in his home. The smell of him is everywhere and it drives her crazy. She still likes the sight of him even though the skin near his eyes has wrinkled, has turned downward toward the floor as if he had fought gravity and lost, the spin of the earth grabbing his face and tugging on it. The two years between twenty-seven and twenty-nine have turned him into a frown.

She pulls his sheets up around her body and takes a deep breath.

She hasn't met another man since Henry, can't even go to coffee without thinking that the man across from her, whoever it is, however good the suit or the shoes or the watch, will eventually come home with the smell of another woman on him. His infidelity has bothered her much more than she imagined it would. The sin, she is surprised to learn, grows with time.

She climbs out of bed, looks in the mirror at her new smile; she's paid for it in installments, ten dollars a week. Henry was the first boy who did not call her a horse. Vincent, her first boyfriend in Madison, whom she'd met in her ninth-grade French class, had called her *mon petit cheval,* and at night, while he slept, she would go to the bathroom, hoping to train her lips to hide her teeth when she smiled.

Out the window, the moon hangs white and yellow over the fields. Thin clouds move straight across the sky like railroad tracks. Below her, the dog sleeps on the porch, his tail banging against the wood as he dreams. She looks at the apple trees. They turn into old women if she squints. As a girl, she liked to find hidden pictures in clouds, or trees, or in the knot on a piece of wood.

She goes to the top of the stairs, sits down, covers her bare legs with a sweater. Although there are many rooms to sleep in, he is asleep on the couch. He is fat like a Buddha now, and for a moment she has the funny notion that she will go and rub his belly for good luck. She is tired from the trip to see him, the three-hour train ride that snaked through Connecticut, and thinking of rubbing his belly makes her laugh.

He wakes for a moment, looks up at her. His eyes are green in the dark. He leans back down on the couch and smiles.

"Was I snoring? I'm sorry."

She comes down the stairs, climbs onto the sofa with him. He puts his arms around her. "Can I?" she asks, putting her hand on his belly, lying down, smelling his unwashed skin, his body odor, kissing the smallest, nearest part of his shoulder. She puts her head on his shoulder and thinks of the first time he kissed her, how they were outside the Angelika, waiting in line, how Henry grabbed her, pressed her into a brick wall on Houston Street.

"All right," he says in his sleepy voice.

For a moment, when he wakes next to her, his arms around her body, he doesn't remember how she got there. She is turned inward, her mouth against his neck, her lips formed almost like a kiss. For five minutes he is still, staring at the spot on her forehead where her hair starts, where the smooth part of her skin begins. He has gone to sleep, as he often does, on the couch in the living room—a room that opens up onto the southern view of the orchard, marked now at dawn with fog, steam rising from the hills. He has become able to tell the time by the character of this view. After his father died, he became unable to sleep in his boyhood bedroom, and chose instead to sleep here, where every morning the first flash of sunlight, urgent or modest or obscured with mist, woke him. The workers arrive near six in the morning. Later in the morning a flock of black turkeys often comes to graze on the flat landing near the house. A few minutes before eight, the fleet of mustard-yellow school buses rides along the county road toward the high school, each one affixed with a ribbony tail of silver exhaust. He hopes she might wake to see some of this. This is his town. If she is surprised by the sight of an apple still connected to a tree, then the sight of so many turkeys, still feathered and alive and pecking at the ground, might shock her.

Catherine has gone to bed in a boy's T-shirt, just as she did when they lived together in Brooklyn. Losing her has proved to be the biggest mistake of his life. He knew this before, but holding her, feeling her breath against his skin, coming and going, he realizes how badly he's missed her.

When she stirs, she regards him with a bemused smile, as if she, too, has forgotten for a moment where she is, or how exactly she has come to be here with him. She seems first to realize that he has become aroused. He sees this in her eyes before he feels it himself. It embarrasses him, his body betraying his desire like this: he has thought of it, of course, but his attraction to her is marked now with shame. He looks to see a glimmer of affirmation in Catherine's eyes, to see if she might be willing. She laughs at him, an exhausted laugh, and she puts her head down against his chest. He went to sleep without a shirt, and to have her head against him like this, her cheek against his skin, feels good after so long. Then, with her hand against him, she sits up, and smiles.

"I couldn't sleep," she says, after a moment.

He takes hold of her hand. "Do you want to?" he asks.

She laughs at the question, and so quickly, he lets go of her. Squinting across the room to the digital clock on his microwave oven, she sighs. "I have my train to catch."

"There are other trains."

She puts her hand on his leg and squeezes. "I have to go to New Hampshire," she says. "My cousin."

She goes upstairs and walks mistakenly into a room that she knows at once to be Henry's studio. In many ways it looks very much like her kitchen had looked for years. On a flat table, she sees watercolors, and everywhere there are glasses filled with brushes, like so many pincushions, all of them in a haphazard mess. Stacks of canvases, half a dozen deep, rest in a line against a far wall. She is without her glasses, and farther than an arm's length, her vision is blurry. Henry, she can hear, is in the kitchen, making coffee, unloading the dishwasher. She thinks of how it will be to go back downstairs and make love to him.

A mirror hangs on a wall across from her, a tool for self-portraiture, and standing in front of it, her right hand on her clavicle, frozen in an expression of surprise, or shock, she thinks of him waiting for her one story below. She has on just a T-shirt and a pair of panties she bought especially for this visit. That is what she came for, after all, and she tries, despite the temptation in this room, to refuse her curiosity.

She goes to the stack of his work, crouching at first, and then sitting on the floor. Because of her vision, she needs to bring each painting very close to her face, her eyes working over the smallest details of each canvas until it occurs to her what exactly she is looking at: the steep green slope at the entrance to the orchard; the antique cider press he showed her yesterday, the light against the wood done with such exquisite care; a bowl of McIntosh apples. She is looking for a painting of herself, evidence that Henry still thinks of her.

She doesn't look long before she finds what she is searching for: a large closet with paintings stacked along the floor, clearly hidden from her. She crouches and flips and sees many different versions of herself. It is an odd experience, like looking at pictures of sisters she has never had the opportunity to meet.

She holds the smallest canvas in her hands. In the painting she is facing forward, standing in front of a black background. Her eyes are wrong, her forehead is too short, her lips are thin, too long. She holds the painting in her hand and then, moving quickly, goes into the guest room and puts it into her suitcase. Smiddy runs into the room, startling her. She crouches to rub his head and ears. She whispers into one of his floppy ears. "Don't tell, okay?"

After a half hour, he goes to check on her. She's turned on the shower, but has, he sees, gone into his studio. The door is open in the studio, as is the window, and the wind through the screen has blown the bathroom door ajar. A small storm moving through. From where he stands he can see her in the tub, her body behind a sheer white shower curtain. Steam from the shower seeps out into the room. He has a cup of coffee for her in his hand, warm against his skin. She cuts the water then and steps out of the shower. He pauses to watch her comb her hair with just a towel around her waist. She looks like a Gauguin painting, her breasts flush against her skin, her nipples tight in the air. It would take just a small daub of black paint to get perfectly the shape of her navel, he thinks. Take a picture, he says to himself, blinking, trying to make his eyes a camera.

He carries her suitcase out to the platform. When he was younger, he caught the train to New York at this station. His father would drive him, drop him off. He stands beside Catherine, watches the ends of her hair blowing out from a knit cap she's pulled down over her head. They didn't speak on the ride from his house. The country passed out the window, all of the hills, the shuttered factories, the cranberry bogs and rail yards. He thinks of the long ride she has to New Hampshire. She looks bothered by this visit, by the night they spent on the couch. He wanted to take her clothes off. He wishes he had.

"What did you come up here for?" he asks.

"To see you," she says, small bursts of white air coming from her lips. She does not turn to look at him. "I miss you."

She juts out her bottom lip and shakes her head. When they lived together, she did this, shook her head as if she was trying to dislodge some water in her ears. The motion prevented her from crying, she claimed, but left her looking like a child throwing a tantrum.

"I miss you, too," he says. "I already told you that."

"No you didn't," she says.

"Of course I did," he says.

"I would remember," she says. "I thought it wasn't true."

"In my head I said it."

"Next time, you should try saying it out loud."

Where the right and the left of Catherine's lips meet there is a dimple as if a child has pressed his thumb into her, leaving a tiny imprint. At the corners of her eyes, there are five wrinkles that go in different directions. Where her old, big teeth rested for years, there are twin indentations on her bottom lip. The dentist did not fix these two creases. At the tip of her small nose, the thin spindle of a capillary runs beneath the skin like a child's scribble. This is new, and is probably covered with makeup every morning.

He had her memorized once, and had forgotten everything.

The headlight of the train in the distance, one bright eye.

He kisses her cheek.

"It's my fault," she says, grabbing her suitcase.

At first he isn't sure what she's said, but she repeats it, saying the words over and over. By the time she's finished, she is sobbing.

"What was?" he says, trying to hug her. "How could it be your fault? I'm sorry, Catherine. I'm sorry. Nothing's your fault. What can I do to make it up? I'm sorry for everything! I'm sorry!"

Our Portion, Our Rock

The year I turned thirty my father was dying slowly, and I was living in a fourth-floor walkup in Back Bay that was too large and too empty. I'd lived there for three years, and aside from Jenny McFee, who helped me pick the place, and who at one time was supposed to be my wife, the only other woman I'd brought home was my friend Susan, who said once that I kept the company of women the way a bishop would. I remember asking her to repeat the joke. Her attempts at humor were always unfunny or too close to the bone, but she was one of the few people in my life who kept me honest.

Despite a bank of windows on the eastern wall, I'd always thought the apartment was too dark. My building was sandwiched between two taller buildings, and most of the day it seemed as if someone had opened a giant umbrella overhead. At the moment when the light was best, flooding everything, I was usually at work, struggling to keep my job as an associate at the law firm where I'd worked for my first three years out of school. It was a large firm, supposedly one of the oldest and most prestigious in the city, a fact that pleased my father, who counted Louis Brandeis as one of his personal heroes and who had forever dreamed that I might someday be added to the list of Jewish Supreme Court justices. From the start, I'd never fit in well with my colleagues, and after a brief period where I tried to fix this, I was now content just to bill my hours, and spurn the social pressures of the senior partners. They were always on me to come with them for drinks, or dinners, and because I already saw so much of them, I never took up their offers.

I fully expected that by the end of winter, I'd be out of a job.

I was born on the last day of December, and because of this, I'd long stopped expecting anyone to cancel their New Year's plans for me. Susan was the exception. Two days after my birthday, she came to the firm to take me to lunch, bearing a wrapped present and a bouquet of flowers. I was in a meeting when she arrived, and while she waited at my desk, she sent me a text message: *This is the last year you struggle. Let's get some lunch. Happy birthday, Eric.*

I could see her through the interoffice window. She sat on the edge of my desk, dressed casually in jeans and a worsted-wool blazer. Her husband, Brian, worked across town as a radiologist, and although she'd been perhaps the sharpest person in our law school class, because of him she was now a wealthy full-time mother, and every time I saw her, I couldn't contain my jealousy. She had a sense of order in her life that I wanted for myself. From my seat, I saw her begin to walk around the floor, poking her head into cubicles, searching for me. My desk sat amid a cluster of these cubicles in an area called the pen. In other firms, the word might have brought to mind a bullpen full of relief pitchers eagerly awaiting their shot to save the game; at our firm, the word made me think of a pigpen full of condemned animals, silly enough to keep eating despite the constant specter of the ax.

I was in a meeting with one of our biggest clients, helping their company execute a reverse triangular merger. Although I could diagram for you what a transaction like this looks like—a diagram that depicts, in its circular transfer of funds, something like the flow of blood through the human heart—I understood little of the intricacies of what we were doing, and during these meetings I labored to avoid offering my opinion. I was the low man on the team, and I did nothing but agree forcefully with whatever my superiors said. Susan, having finally spotted me, waved in my direction, and I waved back and stood up from the conference table, drawing the attention of my boss.

The senior partner on the case was a former staff sergeant in the U.S. army named Jeff Savitsky. On the very first day I worked for him, he made it clear that he saw something in me that bothered him—a lack of fire, an aversion to the obscene hours required of us, an affinity for the wrong baseball team or the wrong kind of women or the wrong kind of Central American cigars. I'd never figured it out, and no amount of effort on my part ever rectified this.

"Horowitz, is something the matter?"

"I need to excuse myself for a moment," I said.

He leaned over to me, took my arm at the elbow, and whispered, "Sit back down, Eric."

The other partners and associates at the table eyed me with the same measured expressions of confusion and disappointment that I got every day. Our client owned half of the fiber-optic technology in the former eastern bloc, and he leaned back in his chair with a terrific grin on his face. He was Latvian and there was something in my show of insubordination that he found amusing.

"I really need to excuse myself."

"Are you sick?" Savitsky asked.

"No," I said. "I just need a moment."

He lowered his voice. "We're in the middle of a consult." He held up a pad of paper filled with his indecipherable handwriting.

I shrugged my shoulders. Somewhere around the conference table, one of my associates laughed too loudly.

Savitsky stood up and spoke directly into my ear. "If you don't sit down right now, we're going to have a big problem, you and me."

"It's my birthday, sir," I said.

For a long moment he stared blankly at me. Insurrection among junior associates was, I knew, the rarest of occurrences, like a solar eclipse right there above the pen.

"I'm sorry," I said.

Savitsky lowered his head, and did a tiny motion with his pen, waving it toward the door.

I figured that I had sixty days left, at best.

Jenny was three months pregnant when I graduated law school. By then, I'd already taken the job at the firm, and, for the first time, I had some money to take her back to New York to celebrate Passover with my father. Jenny came from a family of lapsed Catholics who took infrequent communion at an Episcopalian church in one of the smaller towns on the Charles. When I asked her once what she thought about the

Eucharist—metaphor or fact—she made a face at me, as if I'd asked her a question about her taxes. "It's just a stale cracker, I guess."

She took to her first seder nervously, not wanting to say anything that might upset my father, sitting politely through the hours of Hebrew but refusing to eat that sandwich of horseradish and matzo that is supposed to symbolize the bricks and mortar of the Ancient Egyptian cities, built for centuries upon the backs of the Jews. She held it in her hand, turned to regard me with a cockeyed glance, and indiscreetly wrapped it up with her napkin. "That's our suffering right there," I said, watching her.

"You're telling me," she said.

After the seder, Jenny told my father about the baby and he got up from his seat to rub his hand against her belly. He was drunk on wine, his lips stained red, and he proclaimed that she was carrying low, which was impossible to discern since she had not yet begun to show. "A boy," my father said, hoisting his glass into the air, spinning on his heels, taking Jenny's face into his hands and kissing her cheek. Together the both of them whirled around in a circle, my father singing and chanting and laughing. "Another Horowitz man! Another Horowitz man!"

Jenny was a musician, playing clarinet in one of the city's minor orchestras. She was younger than I was by four years, and aside from her very serious brilliance on the clarinet— she played for me one night the entirety of Mozart's Clarinet Concerto in A Major, and I wept for its beauty, right there on her living-room couch—she was, in many ways, still a girl. Her father called her every night, wired her money twice a month, and came south from Portsmouth when he could, taking her to Macy's for shoes and coats and to the Top of the Hub for the occasional chocolate martini. The pregnancy was a mistake, and Jenny, for all of the consoling conversations she'd had with her father, was not handling the situation well. The obvious truth was that she was terrified to become a mother. An hour after the seder, we took a train into Manhattan to see the park at night and to walk down Fifth Avenue. We were crossing Fifty-ninth Street when she told me that she didn't want to marry me. I didn't bother to remind her that I hadn't asked.

"It's not that I don't want to, eventually," she said.

Because of the baby, I'd stopped smoking, and when she said this to me, I wanted a cigarette. I'd had too much wine to drink at dinner, and had forgotten to take my kippah off my head.

"I'll try not to act too flattered," I said.

"I'm sorry, Eric. You're not upset, are you?"

It was night, and the avenue was empty of tourists and shoppers, and for the first time in years I found the peace and quiet of Fifth Avenue quite beautiful. I ran my hand across my head, trying to smooth down any stubborn strands of hair my yarmulke had covered. As we waited to cross the street, I looked west toward the Hudson, and I watched the storefront flags blowing in a headwind. Beside me, Jenny sighed loudly, and grabbed me at the hands so that we were face to face.

"Well, what are we going to call the kid?" she asked. "Is he going to be a Horowitz?"

"I don't know. I could care less. Do you want him to be a McFee? Is that what you're getting at?"

"Don't you want to give it your name?"

"I haven't thought about it," I said. "This is all very new."

"We don't have answers for any of these questions. Where are we going to live? Are we going to live here, in New York? I can't be that far away from my parents. But you want to come back here, don't you? I can see it. You want to be near your father."

I tried to get her to calm down. Her anxiety was, I knew, terrible for the baby.

"I don't know," Jenny said, walking off a little bit so that she was standing alone on the corner of Fifty-eighth Street. I will never forget the sight of her there, with the city behind her, the slow slope of the avenue. She turned to me and let out a tiny incredulous laugh.

"What?" I asked.

"Do you really think I could be a mother? I mean, really?"

Susan took me to a bar near the train station that she claimed made the perfect diamond fizz. She'd always had an old-fashioned taste in liquor. Her youngest girl had been born only eight weeks earlier, and she was enjoying her freedom to drink.

When we were seated, she handed me both the bouquet of flowers and a small wrapped gift. "I can't believe you just ran out of that meeting," she said, watching me unwrap my present. "You're going to get yourself fired. I thought you'd at least wait until it got out."

"I'm just expediting the process. They can't stand me anyway." The gift was a small box, too small for a necktie, but too large for a wallet. Other than my father, she was the only person who ever got me anything for my birthday.

"You're thirty," she said. "How about that?"

I ran my hand across my head. "I don't even remember

turning twenty-eight. I think I've had three days off since then."

"Try having a baby."

"Oh, please. You have a nanny. Don't complain. And besides, I'd love to have a baby. Do you know anybody that's interested?" I smiled at her, and then I saw her pout at me, so I tried to change the subject. I hated more than anything receiving the pity of my friends. "I still have all of my hair. It could be worse."

She took a long, large sip from her drink, reached out, and put her fingers in my hair. "Brian doesn't."

"That's true," I said, thinking of my friend's newly bald head, and his newly large ears, and I was glad to feel her hands on me. "But he can afford to buy somebody else's hair."

"If he wanted to he could, but he's confident and bald, which basically means that he's going to be bald forever." She frowned slightly and kept drinking.

I held the gift in my hand, one corner of the wrapping paper torn open, staring instead at the happy face of my old friend. Once, when we'd first met, I thought I wanted to fall in love with her. In photographs that I have from law school, she has a seriousness to her expressions, a thin mouth and a heavy brow, and although I'd never known her to be unconfident, I saw now what motherhood and money had done to her. She seemed relaxed, like her skin fit her better, as if she'd gone shopping for it at Saks. I had no family left but my father, and, in a way, I'd always considered her part of my family, but without any of the guilt or the trouble.

"Open it!" she said to me.

"You and your gifts," I said, tearing away the paper to find a black box.

"You don't get out enough," she said, as I lifted the top and removed two tickets to the Boston Symphony Orchestra.

"The symphony? I think you've got the wrong guy."

"We can go," she said. "The two of us. It's this week."

"Are you sure you brought the right gift? Usually you get me a wallet."

She smiled and playfully smacked me on the cheek.

"Do you listen to this sort of music?" I asked.

"No. But neither do you. That's the point."

"This is very fancy of you," I said, standing up to hug her. She put both hands around me and kissed the corner of my mouth. She'd gone for my cheek and missed.

"Brian's not cultured enough to go to the symphony," she said.

She lingered for a moment, one hand on my ear. I was close enough to her to see that she'd missed when applying her lipstick, and that a thin, deep red stripe ran across her front two teeth.

"You look pretty," I said, putting the tickets down on the table.

She looked away from me and pretended, it seemed, to look for our waiter. "Let's drink more," she said before turning back to me. "I see what you're doing. Don't flirt with me. I'm a mother."

I put my hands up in front of my face, a sign of innocence.

"My husband could kick your ass."

"I don't know about that," I said.

We sat for another hour, long past the point when my absence at the firm would have been tolerated. I'd spent so much time there that I believed I could sense somehow the anger that the senior partners had toward me, like a full-body ringing in the ears.

Afterward, out in the wind on Congress Street, both of us too drunk to do much but hold on to the twin humps of a parking meter, she motioned with her free hand over toward the taxi stand at South Station. "They go to the suburbs, right?"

"I don't know."

"You planned it, right? You told me to come over in the middle of the day. You knew you were going to walk out on work, didn't you?"

I didn't answer her. Instead, I watched the people across the street come out of the train station and climb into the waiting cars, everyone in black coats and good shoes. I'd been one of them for three years, but I'd never gotten comfortable in the uniform. In my mind I was still a kid from Brooklyn, my pocket loaded down with tokens for the train; I never thought I'd be a suit. Out across the harbor, two freighters were still in the water. So much of me wanted to be out there somewhere, riding the ferry out to the islands, or walking the length of the piers in the cold.

Susan sat down atop one of the sidewalk planters and tried to cross her legs. "You're getting more handsome," she said. "Do you know that? When you were young, you were awkward and too skinny. It was cute, sort of, like I always wanted to just hug you and feed you sandwiches. Now you're filling out. You're aging well."

I put my hand on Susan's arm and said, "Do you think I could come back home with you right now?"

* * *

Jenny waited until the start of my second month at the firm to get rid of the baby, and when I came back to my desk after lunch one afternoon in May of that year, a secretary had left a pink message slip on my telephone that read simply, "Jenny called. Re: Baby." When I'd left her that morning, she was sitting up in bed, normal as anything, flipping through a catalog full of baby furniture—white maple cribs, hanging mobiles, changing tables, rocking chairs, bassinets. I had to leave very early in the morning in those days so that I could be at my desk when Savitsky came to the office, and I did what I always did that day, which was to kiss Jenny on the top of the head, and then to kiss her on her stomach. She was four months pregnant, and I'd thought that we were finished with her apprehension. I took the pink message slip off my desk, and knew without calling her what she'd done, and for a very long moment I had to dig my fingernails into my thigh to keep myself from crying.

The firm felt to me at that moment like some cell I'd been forced into, and because I'd worked nearly two months without a day off, sitting at this same desk, cycling through the four neckties I owned, I couldn't shake the awful sensation that they were paying me to be a prisoner. We had several glass partitions in the pen, but no windows that looked out on the world, a strategy the original partners had devised to keep distractions to a minimum. The real windows were reserved for the places that clients visited—the offices of the senior partners, the conference rooms, the lounge. I stood up and I had the urge to look out a window. I had a memo in front of me that read: "Reminder: In order to boost billing, cots and showers are available for new associates."

I went to the far edge of the floor, where those junior

associates who were about to make partner had their desks, and I put my face directly against the wall. I knew that there were windows in the building. I'd gone out onto the street and found my floor and made sure of that fact. It'd taken me a month of sleeplessness and caffeine and delirium to walk outside and check, but they were there. Someone walked by, someone older and higher up than me, and he stopped to watch me cup my hands over my eyes, trying to see to the outside.

"It won't work," he said.

I turned around, refusing to be embarrassed. "What did they do?"

"They boarded up the windows with drywall. You'd have to kick the wall in."

I threw my hands up in the air.

"I know," he said. "Just keep working." He pointed to one of the offices the partners kept. The door was open and I could see a small slice of the window the man had behind his desk. "Then you get a window."

"Really," I said, and I turned around and began to kick at the wall. I'd played striker on my high school soccer squad, and had tried to be the placekicker on the football team. I could kick a ball a fucking mile, I kept thinking, but I couldn't kick a hole in the wall.

I sat down on the floor. Two partners came out into the hallway to see what was happening. I took a cigarette from my shirt pocket and lit it and closed my eyes. I thought of the apartment I had just bought, the room I had forbade myself to decorate for just this reason, and I remembered how it was when I was very young, in the old apartment on Grand Street, when I thought that the world disappeared when I closed my eyes. A moment later, Jeff Savitsky crouched down beside me.

"Horowitz, are you okay?"

"No, sir."

He took the cigarette from my hand and stubbed it out on the heel of his shoe.

"Horowitz," he said. "You want to tell me what the fuck is going on?"

"Not really, sir."

Savitsky sat down beside me. "I shouldn't have said it like it was a question, Horowitz."

I looked at him, eye to eye, even though I knew I was crying. "My wife just ended my baby, sir."

On the ride out from the city, I'd sobered a bit, but Susan hadn't, and it occurred to her that since she'd left her car in a parking garage by the firm, she'd also left her house keys in the parking garage, and that we had no way of getting in the house. "We'll have to break in," she said. "Or find the hidden key. One of the two. Whichever seems more fun."

She and Brian had built a home in a town fifteen miles west of the city, on a plot of land big enough for a guesthouse but small enough, she complained, so that they couldn't have both a swimming pool and a tennis court. She said this while leading me around the perimeter of the house, a walk that served as an ostensible history of its design and construction but was really just a search for the key that Brian had stashed somewhere beneath a fake rock. In one hand she held both of her shoes, and with the other she held hard onto my wrist, pulling me along like I was her little red Radio Flyer.

"But you don't play tennis," I said.

"It's an investment, Eric," she said, stopping to place her hand on my elbow. "The market is weak right now. When that happens, you build tennis courts. That way, when it's up, everything is worth more. And people who actually play tennis come and buy the house and you get to do it all over again, only with more cash."

I was put off by how priggish she sounded and I told her so, and in response she stopped, bent down, and rooted through the mulch in a flower bed. "I know how I sound," she said. "It's part of the problem."

"I didn't know there was a problem."

"What time is it, Eric?"

"It's two in the afternoon."

"And how many drinks have I had?"

She stood up and dangled the key in front of me. Her hair had come undone from her barrette and I reached out to take a piece of hair from her eyes.

"There you go," I said. "I didn't want you to hurt yourself. You look better with two eyes."

"You're sweet," she said, stepping close to me so that I could feel her breath on my face. I thought she was going to kiss me, and I closed my eyes in anticipation. Then she shook the keys again. "Let's go inside."

About my father: eighteen months ago, I went to New York to see him for the weekend. While we were walking home from breakfast, a beautiful Saturday morning near the wrecked river's edge in Greenpoint, he began to roll his arm over and over the way a pitcher might after going a complete game. Something, he claimed, had begun to happen to the muscles in his arm, and when I asked, he described the sensation as a sort of freezing. "It's as if this one tiny spot in here, this one little muscle, it's like it's been frozen." He pointed to a spot on his shoulder. "It doesn't even hurt, but it's hard to lift my arm." Not long after, he called to tell me that his other shoulder had begun to suffer the same problem, and then it was the entirety of both arms, and then in a month it was both of his legs, so that he could move just his torso comfortably. In four months, it began to spread toward his face, leaving his mouth partially paralyzed so that when he spoke it was as if someone were holding down his tongue.

I learned that it would go in one of two ways: either it would strike his brain first, that immaculate trap of his, capable of rattling off the names of each of the First Ladies of the U.S. or the metric length of each major river in California. This would eliminate his body's unconscious reflexes and he'd eventually stop breathing. Or it would claim his heart, and he'd go into cardiac arrest. Before the disease, my dad owned a hardware shop on Orchard Street that my great-grandfather had started at the turn of the last century, fresh off the boat from Kiev. Although my dad did well enough to buy a small one-bedroom in a neighborhood full of Black Hats, he had little in the way of a retirement fund, and when he became too ill to stay at home, I bought him a place in an assisted-living facility three blocks from my apartment. I arranged to have a portion of my pay automatically routed to the facility, and at the end of the workday, whenever that was, a pitch-black Tuesday two hours after midnight, or a Saturday afternoon in August, carrying a yard-high stack of briefs under my arm, I went to visit him.

The only person with whom I could talk about this was Susan's husband, Brian. He'd known my father about as long as I had. We'd been neighbors as kids, and we'd practiced throwing Hail Marys in McCarren Park. At the time, we didn't get the irony, two Jews yelling the words *Hail Mary* as we chucked a flattened ball as far as we could, counting down loudly to the last seconds of our imaginary game. If one of us missed the ball, or if one of us threw the ball into the bushes, we just began the countdown again, and chalked it up as a do-over.

When things got bad, or I felt scared, I called Brian. The last time we spoke, two weeks before my birthday, I'd caught him at the end of a long day on call.

He'd lost all traces of the old neighborhood, the accent, the swagger, the toughness. He'd become a sensitive doctor and he spoke in a voice that made me think that he'd seen far too many terrible things—people dying too young, a man with a bullet in his brain, children with incurable tumors in their bodies—and I suppose he had.

"The very worst part of this disease is that nobody lives long enough for us to research it," he said.

I wrote that down onto a piece of stationery and said, "I keep hoping that there's some antivenom."

"It's not a snake bite, Eric. It's a neurological disease."

"I know," I said, sighing into the telephone.

"I don't know what I'd do if something like this happened to Susan."

I was at my desk in the pen. It was the middle of the night, and two of my fellow associates were beside me, asleep soundlessly in their chairs, pencils in their hands, their computer screens flickering. Tacked onto the wall above the desk was a photograph I'd taken once of Susan and Brian at a holiday party. Four years ago, he took me to dinner at a steak house to ask if it'd be all right if he took her to dinner. He had the idea that we were together, or that I had feelings for her, and at the time I laughed it off, and nervously cut into my porter-house. The truth was that I'd been too afraid to ask her to dinner myself. I had the urge, nearly alone in my office at the most ungodly of hours, to tell him that I wanted to take back what I'd done, that I wanted a do-over.

"I don't know what I'd do, either," I said. "Susan is so full of life."

"She is," he said. "So full of life. It'd drive me crazy."

"I know."

"Fucking Lou Gehrig," he said. "More reason to like the Sox."

This was disingenuous, I knew. He was a Mets fan. For whatever inane reason. But I laughed anyway.

"There's really nothing we can do? There's no clinic some-where in the Netherlands or in India?"

He breathed into the receiver. "I'm really sorry, buddy. I really am."

Susan wanted to show me all of the dresses that Brian had bought for her. He was trying to become the head of his de-partment at the hospital and they constantly had to go to benefit dinners where she had to look good and play the part of the dutiful wife.

"I got pregnant and my body changed," she said, opening her closet doors to show me a row of black and red dresses. "And he wanted me to have a dress for whatever shape I was. Isn't that nice?"

I didn't know what to say. What can a man say about the body of a woman he's not allowed to touch? She had poured herself another drink. I wanted to ask where the kids were, but she'd put music on the stereo, and then she led me by the hand to her bedroom. Although it was becoming more and more difficult to make a good living as a doctor—partly because of medical malpractice suits, which my firm gladly took on, and which we gladly profited from—Brian did very well, and I saw evidence of this everywhere in his house. I'd grown up in a hardware store, and I knew how to spot quality. The wainscoting on the walls was maple, as were the hardwood floors that Brian had put down everywhere. The blades of the ceiling fans were inlaid with mother-of-pearl, and when they were spinning, it was like watching the neck of a guitar whirl around. Their closet doors were teak, which I knew was environmentally disastrous but undeniably beautiful. I sat back in an armchair near Brian's side of the bed. He had a copy of the King James Bible on the nightstand, and as I picked it up, I laughed quietly to myself.

Brian's father's name was Mordechai, and his mother's name was Esther, and when I was a kid they had run a luncheonette on the corner of Nassau and Monitor. There was nothing about his appearance that announced him as Jew. He had straight, improbably red hair and a flat nose. Susan told me once that he let everyone at the hospital know that he came from a long line of Presbyterian doctors in Scotland.

"Does Brian go to church with you?" I asked.

She was taking all of the dresses out of the closet and stacking them up on the bed. "He sings in the goddamned choir," she said.

"Really?"

"It's an awful sound," she said. "He claims to be a baritone."

"I can see that. He does have a deep voice."

"Have you ever stepped on a bullfrog?"

She'd completely emptied her closet, and she turned around to look at me, a dress in one hand and her glass of vodka in the other.

"I grew up in Brooklyn," I said. "If I wanted to see a frog I had to go to the museum."

"That's too bad. Because that's what he sounds like when he takes his solo," she said, performing for me an imitation of him singing. She croaked out the words to "O Come, All Ye Faithful" while walking over to me. She straddled my legs.

"What are you doing?" I asked.

"Have you seen my babies?" she said.

"Danny and Patty?" I asked, wondering whether she was resorting to some sort of innuendo. "Are they supposed to be here?"

"They're with the nanny. Have you seen them? Aren't they pretty?"

"They are."

She was very close to me.

"I should have waited, though. Just a few years. I didn't wait. Should I have waited?"

"Maybe."

"They'd be different babies then. Don't you think? That's how genetics works, right?"

I shifted in my seat. I wanted to say that it was her husband who was the doctor, and the one who knew about genetics, and that I was just a bad lawyer who was about to be fired.

"You haven't had enough to drink," she said, handing me her glass.

"For what?"

"You're an idiot," she said, getting off me, turning around and taking off her shirt. Then she pointed at the bed. "How many signals do I need to send you? Get out of the fucking chair, Eric."

I stayed where I was for a moment.

"I know you want to," she said. "Don't you?"

"Would it be terrible if I said yes?"

By the time I got out of work that day, Jenny was no longer in the hospital, and she was no longer at home in our apartment. I knew that she'd gone to Portsmouth to see her father, and I sat in my car, the radio going, trying to decide whether to go after her, or whether to let her be.

Her father had liked me fine, but we'd never moved beyond the sort of uncomfortable pleasantries I'd expected in the first month or two. After a year with his daughter, I'd hoped the acrimony would pass. When I got to their house, making the ninety-mile drive in under an hour, I was determined to level with the guy, to let him know that I wasn't some loudmouthed Jew lawyer without a spine. Whether or not he believed this about me I have no idea, but I was determined to change his mind.

"Look," he said to me when I finally got the courage to ring the doorbell. He was in a plaid shirt and a pair of corduroys. "She's upstairs. She's all broken up over this. So why don't you just get a room in a hotel and come back tomorrow morning."

"Why didn't she tell me?"

"What were you gonna do about it? Talk her out of it?"

"I'd have gone with her and helped her."

He looked at me like he wanted to hit me. "We don't believe that to be the case."

"*We* don't?"

"You heard me."

"That's bullshit, Kevin."

I took a step back, and then turned around. I thought I heard him scoff behind me, a rush of wind through his teeth, as if his suspicions about me were confirmed. They lived on a small plot of pasture west of the Spaulding Turnpike, and as I stood there in front of the house, a cool night in May with geese on the lawn and a teenager throttling the engine of his dirt bike somewhere, I looked out across the dark grass and Kevin's attempt at a vegetable garden, and I decided to try and get inside the house. I rushed at him like I was a fullback and he was a middle linebacker, my hand out in a perfect stiff-arm. He slipped his right hand beneath mine, flat against my chest, and pushed me down. I fell backward onto the ground. He stood over me.

"What're you thinking? Are you losing it?"

I was surprised to hear a note of kindness in his voice. "I just want to see her."

"I know you do, kid, but she feels differently. Like I said."

"What am I supposed to do?" I stayed on my back for a while, and tried to focus my eyes on the dark sky above me. Finally, I closed my eyes and said, "I have an extra room for the baby."

He paused for a moment, and then offered me a hand. When I was on my feet, he shook out a cigarette from a pack he kept in his front shirt pocket.

"I think you should find yourself another girl."

We stood there smoking. The geese were honking. I turned to him and opened my mouth and he put his hand up to stop me.

"That's the honest-to-God fucking truth right there, Horowitz. The honest-to-God truth."

* * *

The morning after I slept with Susan, I went to work early, and hadn't hung up my coat before Savitsky called me into his office. I walked the short distance across the pen believing I was about to be fired. In the beginning, I made an effort to try to impress Savitsky. He seemed to me at first to be the sort of tough guy I grew up with in Brooklyn, the sort who made a show of his strength but who secretly had a soft streak of empathy running through him. After the first month at the firm, I decided I was wrong about him.

"Sit down," he said, pointing to a chair across from him. He exercised before he came to work, showered in the staff bathroom, and when I sat down he was tying his necktie into a fat, preposterous Windsor knot. His office was meticulously organized, and had a window that opened up onto North Station and to the new Boston Garden. Susan had driven me into work, and sitting there across from Savitsky, I could still smell her on me; Brian had been on call at the hospital and I'd stayed there all night, sneaking out before the kids were awake.

"Listen," I said to Savitsky. "Before we start—"

Jeff was a big guy, broad in the shoulders, possessed with a square head and a small mouth. When he spoke, he made motions with his hands, like a pantomime. I wanted it to be over as quickly as possible.

"No," he said. "You do the listening."

"Okay, sir."

"You're a disaster, Horowitz."

I nodded my head.

"The list is fucking endless."

"I know."

"Endless."

"Can I speak?"

He stood up, turned around, went to a filing cabinet, and removed a fat manila folder. I had a mark on my neck from Susan's teeth, and the worst hangover sloshing around in the pit of my stomach. I hoped that Savitsky wouldn't notice.

"This is your file," he said, dropping it on the desk. "Most of it leaves something to be desired."

"If you're going to fire me, can we just get it over with?"

He leaned forward across his desk, his elbows on the wood. He had a crook in his nose, like someone had put a fist into it. "I saw that you've been having a portion of your pay routed to a nursing home around the corner."

"My father, sir."

"I know. I made a phone call. We do work for them, you know."

"I didn't know that."

"I'm not surprised."

I leaned back in my chair, sighed, and threw my hands in the air. I didn't talk to anybody but Brian about my dad, and it unnerved me to hear Savitsky talking about him. "What's this about?"

"Your dad's got ALS."

"Yeah, I know."

"It's similar in a way to Gulf War syndrome. Did you know that?"

"I think I may have read something."

"It's not as bad as ALS, mind you, but in the worst cases it's similar. A quarter of my squad has some of the symptoms. The government says they're healthy, that there's nothing wrong with them, that they're fucked in the head. Do you believe that?"

I wasn't sure whether he wanted me to talk about the sclerosis in my father's body or whether he was goading me into one of his famous discussions about war. He sat back in his seat, and I saw his face take on a serious, pensive stillness that I'd never seen on him.

"Sir?"

"It breaks me up," he said. "It really does, and it's not right."

"Nobody lives long enough for them to do any research," I said.

"That's right," he said, and he looked down at his hands. "That's exactly what happens. Look, I like what you're doing for your father. But you've got to do a better job here. All right? I'm giving you a pass for the last six months."

"A do-over?"

"Whatever you want to call it. But do me favor and get your ass in gear. I'm covering for you."

Jenny came to get her things two months later. When she came, she brought her father, whom I expected would come, and also her mother, who had showed me no amount of preference or disdain and whom I instinctively felt bad for because of her quiet voice and her skinny frame. She'd married a bear of a man and I had the awful thought that Kevin could probably back over her with his Jeep and she'd still get right up off the driveway to bake him a tray of muffins. She was the only one who spoke to me while Jenny and her father cleaned out her things. We were both sitting at my kitchen table. I'd made a pot of peppermint tea for her. She was wearing a long floral-print housedress and a pair of Mary Janes with white socks.

"You're not upset because of your religion, are you?" she asked.

"I don't think religion has anything to do with it, Mrs. McFee."

"It just seems that you got unnaturally upset about this. And I figured it had to be because of your religion."

"I'm not religious," I said.

I watched Jenny take her gym clothes out of the bottom dresser drawer. She had piles of colorful spandex that she'd never worn.

"I thought you were Jewish."

"It's not a one-size-fits-all sort of thing, Mrs. McFee. We come in all shapes."

"You don't have to joke."

"I didn't mean for it to be funny."

"We're Episcopalians now."

"Jenny said something."

"Our priest at Trinity wanted to tell us how to vote and we didn't appreciate that. A lot of people didn't appreciate that. But Kevin and I try to be understanding about things like this. That was the difference between us and them. They weren't willing to understand and we were."

I nodded my head. She seemed like a sweet woman, but also like the complete opposite of her daughter. Jenny was immature and curt, as if she'd grown up alone with her father without another woman around for miles; her mother was thoughtful and serious and, I felt, genuinely interested in what I had to say.

"So I guess what I'm saying is that I just want to know what made you so upset."

"She never told me," I said, turning to her. "That's why I'm upset. I'd have been there with her."

"Oh, that's not true." She put her hand on my wrist. "Of course she told you. She told us that she told you."

"She didn't. I got up and went to work and then she left me a message on the phone," I said, as Jenny carried a box into the room. I was speaking very softly, trying my best to be kind. "She went alone, without me, and that's why I was upset. It's not because I'm Jewish, Mrs. McFee. It's got nothing to do with it. I'm not even sure I know what being Jewish means, anyhow."

At this, Jenny looked up from the box she was packing. She walked over to where I was sitting with her mother. "This is painful enough, Mom," she said, and then she looked up at me for the briefest moment. She could only keep me in her focus for a moment before she started to cry. "I know you think I'm horrible. But I just got scared. I'm not ready. That's all. It had nothing to do with you."

That's when I tried to hug her, to do what I thought I would always do, but by then she was really crying, and both of her parents had come to take her away.

I went to see my father after work. It'd been nearly two weeks since I'd been to see him. This was the longest, by far, I'd ever gone without visiting. Even though I knew that he had trouble eating, I brought a bag of fast food with me. He'd always taken good care of his body, getting up early to run the length of the park near our house, but he'd had a secret weakness for a greasy burger. I stood by the door to his room. He was far kinder than I was, and he never tried to guilt me, but still, I was afraid of the sadness I expected to see in his face. My mother had been gone for twenty years. I was all he had and he was all I had, and that, as he used to say, was a tough god-damned chain to break.

I held up the bag of burgers and smiled. For a long while after the diagnosis, I could still make out the faint traces of the musculature of his legs beneath the bedsheets. He'd always been in action, always going somewhere, always carrying some ancient ladder across the floor of his shop to fetch a box of shelving or jigs or dowels for a customer. Now his body had atrophied after so much time in bed, and he looked impossibly tiny to me.

"Eric," he said.

"Hey, Dad."

"Hi."

He sounded awful. When I was younger, my father used to show off his ability to curse at me in Yiddish. Just as the Eskimos have hundreds of words for snow, he liked to say, Jews have hundreds of ways of calling someone an asshole. Now he got out only one word at a time when he tried to speak. Whatever he said, he tried to make it count.

"I'm sorry, Dad. I'm sorry I've been away." I sat down beside him. "I brought burgers."

"Excuses."

He couldn't turn his head to look at me, and he seemed to have no response to the food I brought. I set it down on the nightstand.

"Look," he said.

"What?"

"Look," he said, louder.

I turned in my chair and looked. His room had a window with a good view of the Esplanade, which now, at the beginning of January, was filled with snow and the thin branches of bare elm trees and the occasional frozen jogger. Pushed into a corner was a machine to register his heart rate and his blood pressure. Tiny seismographic lines spanned the screen in monochrome. I'd asked Brian to find him a room in the best facility in the city. I was willing to mortgage my home for my dad.

"Look for what?"

"TV," he said.

Bolted onto the wall was a large flat-screen television. This was new and I'd missed it. The facility gave small televisions to patients who asked for one, but my father was of that certain generation of workaholics who thought the thing was a vice, and I'd never bothered to make the request.

"Who brought this here?" I asked.

"Boss," he said.

"My boss?"

My father tried to smile, a small flickering in his mouth. He had to work so hard to make his body move.

"Savitsky brought this here for you? Did you threaten to sue him or something?"

My father looked at me. His eyes were still perfect, green as the Hudson in summer.

"Work harder," he said, and I laughed.

"It's hard."

"It's work," he said, getting the words out slowly, as though he were lifting something too heavy for him. "It's supposed to be hard."

The remote control was beside him on the bed. I stood

there for a moment, not knowing what to do. We'd never been especially affectionate with each other, and these visits were so difficult because I had inside me all of the things that I wanted to tell him but felt strange to say aloud. So I turned on the TV and, although it was discouraged I got into bed with my dad and sat next to him. I put the Celtics game on and for a long time we just sat and watched.

Later, a nurse came into the room and sat with us. She smiled at me, and then gave me a pitiful expression of thanks that I tried to ignore. After a while she turned to me. "You know, your father told me yesterday that he hasn't been outside in a year."

"Really?" I asked, looking down at my dad. "How's that possible? Has it been that long?"

"Fourteen months," he said.

"That's more than a year, Dad."

And he looked at me again and gave me a tiny, imperceptible nod of his head. He opened his eyes as wide as he could. All he said was: "Sun."

Two days later, Susan came to the office to take me to the symphony. She wore all black, and had her hair pulled back off her head so that she looked very severe. I watched her come through the pen. As she came toward me, I pretended to look busy. We'd fallen asleep for a few moments after we'd finished, and when we awoke, she turned over to me, laughed once, cursed the Lord, and then pushed me out of her bed and onto the floor.

"Are you ready?" she asked, and before I could answer, she turned around and walked to the elevator bank.

I hurried after her, carrying my briefcase in my hand. She

pressed the call button for the elevator, turned to me, and frowned.

"I'm a fucking mess because of you," she said.

I took a deep breath. "Okay."

"You're not taking that with you, are you?" She was looking at the briefcase.

"I can drop it off at home. It's on the way."

"Leave it here."

"I can't do that." I had briefs with me that I needed to go over for a meeting the next day. I was trying to appease Savitsky and be a good lawyer. "I'll have to come back for it afterward, and they'll make me stay here all night and sleep in the cot room."

She looked at her watch, and made a sound with her teeth and tongue that I knew she made when she got impatient, a sound she'd given me the other night in her bed. The elevator door opened and we stepped in.

"I'm not coming inside your apartment with you," she said.

"I'm not dangerous," I said.

"I don't know about that."

"Look," I said. "You were the one who got drunk and naked—"

The elevator stopped just then and a small crowd of lawyers came aboard. I knew two of the men from school, and I suppose Susan did also, and as we rode down to the ground, one of them patted me on the shoulder. His name was Justin.

"Horowitz," he said, "I'm glad you two finally got it done."

He was talking about Susan and me, remembering us, I guess, from the seminars in law school when we sat together and exchanged inside jokes, and for a moment I felt buoyed by the idea of the two of us, and I had the foolish image of us both in her enormous house with her two children, and I picked her hand into mine, smiled, and kissed the finger that held the diamond Brian had bought for her. I'd gone with him that day, the two of us in a building on Tremont Street shopping for jewels, and I remember that he'd facetiously asked me to model the rings for him, teasing me about my thin fingers.

I let go of Susan's hand just then.

"Oh," she said, turning red. "We're not together." She looked me up and down, her eyes narrowing. "We just have lunch sometimes. That's all."

The weekend after Jenny came to clear her things from the apartment, I went by train to New York, meeting my father on the lower level of Penn Station. I saw him before he saw me. He was leaning against one of the support pillars that hold up the floor of Madison Square Garden. He had on a beige jacket and his black cap and he was reading the *Daily News,* and although I didn't know at the time, it was the last time I would ever see him completely healthy. He was the image of peace and vigor and comfort, like a photograph of Dresden in January of 1945, or those moments along the Tigris in March of 2003 before all of the shock and the awe. For whatever reason, I stood there in the station, below that harried big board, its mechanized placards flickering wildly with every arrival and departure, and I waited for my dad to look up from his paper and see me. Here was a man comfortable with the noise of Manhattan, able to block out the city and enjoy his paper. I was always searching for that sort of peace, and he had it in spades. When he looked up to find me, he knew something was wrong before I said anything. I wasn't crying, but I'd never been particularly good at disguising my emotions. He crossed the station, folding the paper under his arm.

"What happened to the kid?" he asked.

I shook my head, dropped my suitcase quietly, and shrugged my shoulders. "She had other things to do."

My dad smiled slightly, a comforting thing, without the slightest trace of the sarcasm that came to him so easily.

"Poor thing."

"The baby?" I asked.

"No," he said, putting his arm on my shoulder, and picking up my suitcase into his hand. "Not the baby."

We were walking outside toward Eighth when I told him that she left me. He turned to look at me. On his days off he didn't shave, and it'd been so long since I'd seen him this way that I was surprised to find that his beard had gone entirely white.

"Wait here," he said.

I stood on the sidewalk and watched him walk with my suitcase down to the corner, where he bought me a doughnut and a coffee—very light and very sweet—from one of the men on the avenue. Whenever I was sick as a kid, he'd bought me coffee and a doughnut. My mother died when I was too young, and he'd had absolutely no idea how to handle me, so he'd bought me what he liked. When he was walking back toward me, balancing everything in one hand, the food and the paper and the suitcase, he stopped, closed his eyes, and lifted his head up to the sky. I walked to him.

"What's going on, Dad?"

"The sun," he said. "Do you feel that?"

It was an hour to noon and the sun was beginning to edge itself over the lips of the buildings along the street. In New York, every avenue gets a half hour of good sun.

"I've been working so much," he said. "You forget that this is all here. All of it."

After a moment, he turned to me. "Do it. Close your eyes. You'll feel better."

And I did.

Susan refused to come up into my apartment, insisting instead that she wait outside on the sidewalk. We hadn't said a word since we'd left the office, and when I came back down so that we could go to the symphony, she was gone. I stood on the street for a moment, looking both ways down the long stretch of sidewalk to see if I could find a trace of her.

It had been a mistake to sleep with her, and I knew this, even as I got into my car and headed out to the suburbs, making the trip from my house to her house by memory. So much of my life seemed to exist on the terms of other people, and I wanted to act, to exist in the moment, to make a mistake. She'd been too willing, or perhaps I'd been too willing, and my undressing in her bedroom, hopping like a teenager to free my foot from my pant leg, was nothing but a sign of my own considerable weakness. I'd fucked the wife of my oldest friend, the mother of his babies, a woman I'd wanted to sleep with for years, and even though I knew this was something I'd need to atone for, I still felt glad I'd done it.

I'd met Jenny a week after I told Brian he could ask Susan to dinner. When Susan called to tell me that she'd had a great night with my friend, and when he called to tell me quite the same thing, I directed my attention to Jenny. I hadn't had a girlfriend since my sophomore year in college, and I didn't know what to do. I honestly thought that I could trade one set of feelings for another, like swapping a new car for an old one.

It took me a half hour to drive from the Back Bay into the suburbs. I drove the length of their street, turning into their long driveway, stopping by their front door, and I saw the two of them standing in the front kitchen window, just standing there, fighting about me, or just talking about what to make for dinner. I sat there for a good long while, long enough for Brian to notice me, and for him to come out onto the walkway. I knew that she'd told him, just by the way he crossed his arms across his chest as he came out to my car.

"What do you want me to do?" he said. "You fuck my wife and then you come and drive your car and park in front of my house."

"She just up and left."

He gave me an incredulous laugh, a sound he'd made since he was a kid, a sound I'd always hated to hear. "That's because she's got some stuff to take care of. Like our kids."

"We had plans," I said. "We were going to see some music."

"Eric, what are you doing here? What do you think is going to happen? You think you're going to trade places with me? Who are you fooling?"

It hurt me to hear that, and I got out of the car quickly. He took a step back, and I suppose he thought he was going to be hit. We'd beat the shit out of each other a few times when we were kids. I saw Susan in the window, her face to the glass, looking at both of us.

"Who am *I* fooling?" I said, and then I said it again. "I'm not the one pretending to be Scottish. Who the fuck are you fooling?"

"Don't give me your Jew guilt, Eric. I can do whatever I want to do and live however I want to live."

I leaned against the car and laughed.

"This isn't Brooklyn," he said. "Nobody cares about who my parents were, or how it used to be."

Susan looked at me from her living room, shook her head, and turned away. The thing was that I could punch Brian out, or he could punch me out, and we could both be bleeding, and we'd still love each other, even if we hated each other— he was, for better or worse, just like Susan, part of my family.

"She's worried she's going to be pregnant now," he said after a long while. He said it softly.

"I don't think that's possible," I said. "I was careful."

"I should kill you."

"Do it, then."

"She was going to get her tubes tied before she went to see you the other day. That's probably why she got so drunk."

"Just hit me if you want to hit me."

"She doesn't want to have any more babies," he said. "She didn't want to have any babies in the first place."

I turned to him.

"I wanted babies," he said. "I wanted them and she just wanted to give me what I wanted."

I leaned back against the car. "I wanted babies, too," I said.

"Eric, I don't think I should see you for a while."

I thought he was finally going to hit me. I took two steps backward.

"I'm sorry, Brian."

He put his hands in his pockets. "I'm not going to hit you." Then he started to walk in to the house.

"Brian," I called after him. "Can't I just talk to her for a second?"

Then he walked back to me. And for the first time in years I saw the old swagger in his steps, the old Flatbush Avenue walk, and I was glad to see that somewhere inside he was still the same kid I knew from McCarren Park. He hit me in the cheek with his right. I fell back into my car. I straightened myself and I let him hit me again. This time I didn't fall backward.

"You need to go away," he said.

"We fucked up."

"Get out of here."

"Try to forgive me."

"Okay," he said, walking away. And over his shoulder he yelled out to me. "Maybe I'll fast. Maybe we should all fucking fast. Why don't you call the rabbi over? Maybe we can all pray together. Maybe that'll fix things."

The last time I saw Jenny, I went to see her play the clarinet. This was a year or so after she moved out of the apartment. The concert was in a church near my home, where on Tuesdays at noon they performed a Bach Mass. When we were together, she played every week, and although I'd always promised to go see her, I never did. She'd told me once that Bach had never written any music for the clarinet, and that she always had to play the score for the oboe. "It never sounds the way it's supposed to," she said, but I couldn't tell. He was her favorite, and I could see the thrill on her face while she played the music. Some people only come alive once in a while, I remember thinking, and watching her play, her cheeks filling with air, her lips puckered in their embouchure, I had the thought that I'd never once seen her truly happy until now.

I suppose I wasn't surprised to see that she was pregnant— very pregnant—or that she'd become, if it were possible, an even better musician. I'd just come from the hospital, where

Susan had given birth to their first boy. Before I left, I asked Brian if he was planning on giving him a bris, and he'd laughed at me. I told him that I would arrange it for him, that I would find a moyel and a rabbi. He put his hand on my shoulder and laughed.

"This is the future, Eric. They get circumcised right away. By doctors. Not by some crazy guy with a steak knife."

But as I sat there in the church watching Jenny play her clarinet below the looming stained-glass image of Christ atop Mount Zion, I remembered witnessing the bris of a new baby boy one Rosh Hashanah; the infant had the fortuitous privilege of being circumcised at the moment the Book of Life was being opened for all of us. It was the boy's eighth day of life; his first seven days of life having formed the beginning of him, just as the earth was formed in Genesis. Atop the bimah, the father held his baby nervously while the boy was cut.

My father knew all of the prayers by heart, and I stood watching him pray silently to himself, first the Hebrew, and then the English: *May the father rejoice in his offspring, and his mother be glad with the fruit of her womb.*

I laughed and turned to him. "How do you know this so well?"

He smiled at me and turned back. "I've done this before," he said. "That's how."

After the Mass ended, I waited outside on Arlington Street for Jenny, and when she came out, walking beside the man who, I assumed, was the baby's father—she stopped for a moment to say hello.

"You came," she said.

"Of course," I said. "You were terrific. Just terrific."

For too long a moment I stood staring at her, and then at

her man, and then finally, before walking away, I touched my hand to her belly, just as I'd done when I used to leave her in my bed in the morning, and I smiled at her. She flinched a bit when I touched her, and I thought I saw her boyfriend flinch, thinking perhaps that I was doing something I shouldn't be doing.

"I'm happy for you," I said. "For both of you."

A week after my birthday, I went into Savitsky's office a half hour before noon. It was a sunny day. He was on the telephone with the Latvian, and it amused me, listening to the chain of employment, how my boss sounded when he spoke to his boss. It was exactly how I sounded when I spoke to him. I looked out the window while he spoke. When he was finished, he shook his head and rolled his eyes.

"What is it, Horowitz?"

"First off, I want to thank you for the television you bought for my dad."

"I asked him if he missed watching the games, and he said yes, so I just took care of it. No big deal." He took a cigar out of his pocket, pointed it at me as an offering, and I shrugged him off.

"Well, he told me that he hasn't been outside in fourteen months. And, well, I want to take him outside."

"Right now?" he asked.

"It's gonna be heavy. The whole bed and everything. I'm not sure I can do it myself."

He smiled at me, and he kept smiling at me, even while we were wheeling my dad along the sidewalk, around the corner from his room to my apartment. It was the middle of the day, and we were outside, and my father made the whole trip with his eyes closed and the wind rushing against his skin.

"I can't let you just sit outside," I said when we got to my apartment. "You might catch a cold or something. But I've got this great window with the best kind of light and we can sit there all day."

Savitsky went first, taking the hospital bed into the freight elevator. I took my father into my arms and I carried him up the stairs, all four flights, and then through the door to my apartment. I didn't know then that this would be the last week of my father's life, or that, in the very end, when he finally passed, Brian and Susan would come to sit shivah with me in my apartment, all of us trying for forgiveness in the way we do, without food from sunup to sundown, torn black ribbons on our shirts, our mirrors covered with cloth, not out of any deeply held belief but simply because this is the way our parents had mourned their parents. And I didn't know then that, as we took the cushions from the chairs and set them down on the floor, we would all fall silent as the bright light of the afternoon passed by us, moving west across the sky, west above my home, this home that had always been too large and too empty, the light filling the hardwood. And their two little children would sit with us, eating and laughing.

Visiting

He brought in his shirt pocket the last photograph he'd taken of his son, an Instamatic snapshot: the carousel in the park, wind in the boy's hair, chocolate ice cream staining his smile, a pair of impossibly tiny blue jeans, striped socks, and a Yale sweatshirt snug across his chest. Jonathan had stood in the grass waiting for Marc to come around. The December day was warm, winter with a fever. Marc smiled, gripped tight the reins of his white plastic horse. This was years ago. Then, the visits were easy. Jonathan took the picture with him in case Marc wanted to see proof, evidence of a time when they had been able to maintain peace. Jonathan was not above super-stition. His boy was a teenager now. They were separated by three miles, one river, one bridge, and two train transfers. The distance, he thought often, was far too great.

He stood on the street below the apartment, his head to the sky; he tried to find the eighteenth story, where Marc lived with his mother. Each window looked the same from the ground: the slotted vent of an air conditioner, ivy trained to the brick, small square glass panes in a grid. For nearly fifteen years, Julia had lived on this block, with its old ginkgo trees, its gas lanterns, and its wide sidewalks. Steps away, in Central Park, children skated to Tchaikovsky on Wollman Rink, and through the trees he could hear the violins and the piano and the cymbals. This was, in every way, a better place than where he lived.

He'd rented a car for the afternoon. Parking had been difficult. He had lived too long in the city. From the sidewalk, he saw in the passenger-side window the reflection of his face and neck, streaked with the harsh winter sun, unflattering and bright. He had turned, at some point, into every man in his family. His mother had hoped that such a thing would not happen. She had said this, touching her hand to him, many years ago.

When he stepped into the lobby, he was met with a wall of warm air. He nodded at the doorman and cleared his throat. "Could you let Marc know that I'm here for him?"

Jonathan waited on a small white banquette, and rested his hands on the tops of his knees.

The doorman pushed two buttons. "Mr. Morris," the man said. "Your father is here for you."

The name *Morris* still sounded inaccurate. He'd fought over nothing but the name, and just to hear it here, in an empty lobby, spoken by a stranger, the softness of those last two letters, like something easy off the tongue, caused him to grimace. He'd wanted to leave his boy with some unalterable part of him, something concrete. Julia worked so hard to mold their son in her image. When they were married, she had done the same to him. "Few parts of you are truly unimpeachable," she'd said.

He didn't know his son well. He blamed this on Marc, who had always been quiet and distant, and on Julia, who did her best to inject their son with a subtle hatred for him. These were the clichéd, well-documented symptoms of divorce, and he'd expected them. What he hadn't expected, though, was how much they would bother him. Twenty-four times a year they ate pizza in silence and then sat in the back row of a Times Square movie theater.

The elevator doors opened, and his son walked out into the lobby. "Jonny Cohen," Marc called out. He never called him Dad. Marc made an overconfident swivel with his hips that to Jonathan looked vaguely sexual. He spoke too loudly, and in short bursts, as if he were screaming across a football field. He had headphones in his ears. "I'm. Like. Hungry. As. A. Horse."

He wanted to give his son a hug. They had done this when Marc was younger, but not for years. He wondered whether his son could hear anything or whether his music disallowed, in its volume, any other noise.

"You look good," he said.

Marc went out onto the street without stopping, pushing through the twin glass doors. When Jonathan followed him, he saw his boy's handprint as it remained on the glass. Marc had small hands with fat fingers, as if the rest of his body had grown out of infancy and his hands had been left behind. Out on the street, Marc stood shaking his hips to the music in his ears. He wore tight black jeans that clung to the skin of his legs, white canvas sneakers, and a red hooded sweatshirt. Jonathan inspected his son for evidence of change. He was pained by how much about Marc seemed different every time they were together.

"Are those new?" he asked, pointing to Marc's sneakers. "I used to have a pair of those."

"Where are we going?" Marc asked, yelling over the clamor of his headphones. "I'm hungry for pizza."

"We're not getting pizza," Jonathan said, walking to his rented car. He put the key into the door.

"What's this?"

"It's a car, Marc."

"I know it's a car."

"Get in."

"Fuck that."

"I've told you not to talk to me like that."

"So," Marc said, tilting his head, putting a hand on the hood of the car. "Did you steal this? Because I thought you didn't have any money."

"Who says I have no money?"

"Mom says."

"Well, I might not have the sort of money your mother has," he said. "But I have some money. Now get in the fucking car, Marc."

Jonathan drove north up the West Side Highway. The river glistened to his left. To his right, the city stretched out clean and blue. He had always loved Manhattan, its constant energies, the first day of spring in Union Square, nighttime below Canal Street; he only wished that he could afford to live there. His apartment in Brooklyn sat across from a middle school, and twice a day, at seven-thirty in the morning and at three in the afternoon, a rush of noise surrounded his house.

He tried to listen to the high treble coming from his son's headphones. Marc shifted in the passenger seat, his weight on one side. He could see only the back of his boy's head; he wondered what kind of music his son enjoyed. He couldn't hear well enough to tell what Marc was listening to. As they passed 125th Street, he saw, in the reflected glare of the window, that Marc was wearing black eyeliner.

"When I met your mother," he said, pointing at his son's eyes, "she used to do that."

"What was that?" Marc said, touching a button, pausing the music.

"I said that your mother used to wear her makeup like that."

"Maybe Mom was a homo."

"Are you a homo?" he asked.

"You shouldn't use that kind of language, Cohen."

He had become used to the way Marc turned questions around. His son was like Superman in that way, catching bullets in his hand and redirecting them. His own father had never answered his questions, had let them dangle in the air and disappear. He wasn't sure which was worse, to be mocked or to be ignored.

The song in Marc's ears ended, and for a brief moment the headphones were silent. When the music started again, another burst of noise, Jonathan reached out and grabbed the headphones from Marc's ears.

"How about we give the music a rest?"

"Fine," Marc said. He took a pack of cigarettes from the pocket of his sweatshirt. "Can I smoke at least?"

He saw that Marc smoked the same brand of cigarettes he had smoked when he was fifteen. They were cheap, and terrible, and he wondered whether children could unconsciously sense these things about their parents, a taste for nicotine, a particular way of applying eyeliner. Marc had been an infant the last time Jonathan had owned a pack of cigarettes.

"Of course you can't smoke."

"You smoke."

"I do not," he said. Years ago, he'd coughed strange black junk from his lungs for two weeks. Julia had come up behind him in the bathroom, looked into the sink, and whispered into his ear. "That's your lung, buddy." They were living then in the Village, on East Thirteenth Street, above a bakery. They woke to the smell of confectioners' sugar. Marc slept in a crib at the foot of the bed.

"Mom says you smoke."

"I used to smoke," he said. "Just like her. But I quit. I'm glad I did."

"Whatever."

His son sank into his seat. Before Marc was born, Jonathan was entirely confident that he possessed a paternal instinct, but after the birth he felt terribly unsure of how to hold his child, how to speak to him, how much food to give him. Child care had never become any easier. When Marc was a toddler, Jonathan had no idea how to quell the boy's tantrums. Now that Marc was a teenager, Jonathan felt as if he were in the company of a ticking bomb. He was never sure how much time was left on the bomb, but he knew, sooner or later, that it would go off.

He turned off the parkway and headed toward New England. From here, he could see the entirety of Manhattan. The sight was gorgeous from this angle, the city from head to toe, water everywhere. While Jonathan took notice, Marc was staring at his sneakers.

"We're going on a trip," Jonathan said.

"I see that we're going on a trip," Marc said. "I'm not, like, blind, Cohen."

"You having fun?"

Marc shrugged his shoulders. "I don't like cars."

"That's because you grew up here. If you grew up anywhere else, you'd love them."

"Cars are for taxi drivers. Is that how you make your money these days? As a taxi driver?"

They drove the next five miles in silence. Marc fiddled with the tiny black box that produced his music. Jonathan glanced at the thing and remembered the enormous turntable he'd owned at fifteen. In his backyard, he'd built a solid oak cabinet to house the record player. He'd needed help moving it to his bedroom. It was a piece of furniture. Marc's music player was smaller than a baseball card.

When they left the city, driving through the wooded, green stretch between the Bronx and Connecticut, Marc began to chew his fingernails. Jonathan turned the radio on. The Jets were playing the Patriots. The game came across the air.

"Turn it off," Marc said.

"You don't like football?"

"Where are we going, Jon?"

"Rhode Island."

"What the fuck is in Rhode Island?"

"Why do you have to curse like that?"

"I'm cursing because you're driving me out of the state."

"We're going to Rhode Island so you can meet someone."

"Meet who?" Marc asked.

"Your grandfather."

"Grandpa's dead. He died last year. You went to the funeral.

Remember? Biggest heart attack in medical history? Mom cried for, like, ten weeks."

"Not Grandpa Joe," he said. "We're going to see my father."

"I thought he was dead, too."

"Well," he said, squeezing the steering wheel very tight. "He's not."

Tucked into his jacket was a letter from his father's lawyer. The old man was dying. After eighteen years of silence, Jonathan had received a letter in the mail. He'd always wondered how his father might die.

Marc turned in his seat and said, "Look, I have to be back by six. It's the law. If I'm not, then you're kidnapping me."

Two hours later they were in New Haven, passing by the long blue stretch of Long Island Sound. A slow rain started to fall. Marc pressed his nose to the window as fat wet drops came down against the glass. Jonathan had done his graduate work in this city but hadn't been through in years. He felt warm in his body as he drove by the water.

"Is that the East River?" Marc asked, pointing at the water.

"No, Marc. That's not the East River."

"Well, what is it?"

"When you get home, why don't you look it up?" he said, unapologetically cribbing a line from his own father. He knew that Marc would never look it up.

His son sat back and huffed. "We're far away."

"Not really."

He wondered whether Julia ever took Marc out of Manhattan. The city had a way of trapping people; it was a true island.

"So," Marc said. "How is your painting going?"

Jonathan didn't answer for a while. He watched the wipers clean the glass. The rain came down fast and then it came down slow. Marc had never asked him a genuine question before. As a little boy, Marc had asked none of the confounding questions that children tended to ask. Jonathan hated to feel sentimental about such things. A question is a question.

"I'm not a painter," he said, finally. "I'm a sculptor."

"It's all the same shit, Jonny. How is your sculpting going?"

In profile, his son looked much the same as Jonathan had at fifteen: terrified, pimpled, and unmistakably Jewish. He wanted to tell him these things.

"It's difficult," he said. "It's hard because there's no real market anymore for what I do."

"What is it you do?"

"Figurative sculpture."

"Like people?"

"Exactly."

"Do you do naked women?"

With his hands, Marc made an approximation of the female form that looked disproportionately top-heavy.

"Sometimes I do."

"And they just come to your place and they take their clothes off and you sculpt them?"

"Not exactly," he said. "I take their pictures. Then I sculpt them."

"You know," Marc said, turning to him, nodding his head. "I think I want to be a sculptor when I grow up."

Jonathan felt improper laughing. He wondered whether his son had ever kissed a girl, and, if he had, what kind of girl liked kissing the sort of boy who wore eyeliner. Just then, they passed the exit to Yale. "This is where I went to grad school," he said, pointing to the sign. He had put himself into debt to go to school there, a fact that had caused trouble in his marriage.

Marc made a grunting noise that Jonathan took to be a sign of affirmation. Then, clearing his throat, Marc swatted his hair out of his face and said, "If you're so smart, then how come you have no money?"

"Do you think that one thing has anything to do with the other?"

"I'm not sure."

The city passed behind them. In the rearview mirror, the water looked cold. Marc had told him once, as a toddler, that he wanted to go to Yale: "Just like you." Then, hearing that had meant a good deal.

"This is the longest conversation we've ever had," Jonathan said.

"You think?" Marc asked.

"Yeah."

"I guess."

Jonathan drove into Warwick an hour later. The rain had stopped. Rhode Island, gray and old. Colonial homes, black shutters, elm trees like skeletons. He took the road by the water. The fishermen were out in the bay. His dad had hauled fish for years and had come home stinking of scallops and lobster. The ocean came in and out, swelling, releasing. Above the sea, the white thumbnail of the moon hung in the daylight. Marc rolled the windows down and let some rain in. They drove for a block, past the shuttered boardwalk and a Ferris wheel that hadn't worked, as far as Jonathan knew, for decades.

"I just wanted to smell it," Marc said, rolling up the window. "It smells better than Coney Island."

Two old men walked the beach, swinging metal detectors over the sand. A flock of dirty gulls swooped over the seacoast road. One bird had a paper soda cup trapped in its talons. In a parking lot beside a liquor store, teenagers stood around in the cold, smoking and begging for drinks. The restaurant at Divinity Place was open for lunch, its neon sign alternately blinking the words *Divinity* and *Lobster*. Jonathan had worked there for a summer when he was Marc's age. He'd lost his virginity in the stockroom with Marie Scarcella. She was ten years older and smelled like Pert shampoo and Old Bay seasoning. Within a half hour everyone knew that he wasn't a virgin any longer.

"So what is this place?" Marc asked.

"Warwick, Rhode Island."

"This is where you're from, huh?" Marc asked.

Jonathan thought he detected a note of satisfaction in the boy's voice, as if Marc had finally learned something that he had never considered. He was pleased that Marc would finally know that he hadn't always existed in a dark, cold apartment in Brooklyn, but that he had lived here, near the ocean.

"Do you still know people here?" Marc asked.

"I used to," Jonathan said. "But not anymore."

"Besides your dad."

"I don't know anyone here. Certainly not my father."

"Girls, I bet," Marc said, laughing. "I bet you had lots of girls here."

"Not really," Jonathan said, thinking of Marie. He had no idea what had happened to her. "I left and I didn't come back."

He drove inland through the beachside neighborhoods. The sun was dull in his rearview mirror. He pressed his hand to the window, felt how cold the air had become. Strong winds pushed the car from left to right. The smell of the ocean came through the heating vents. Close to the road, each house they passed had a square yard, one tree, a breezeway.

He took the old roads; he still knew the way. His house looked just as it had when he left. A large maple stood in the front yard. When he was young, he'd used its enormous system of bulging roots as the base of a fort. His father had hated this, the imaginary life he created with that tree, had pulled him inside by the ears. The same lace curtains his mother had hung forty years ago were still in the window. She had been dead since he was a boy.

"What are we doing?" Marc asked. He sat forward in his seat.

"We're gonna park here," Jonathan said.

In his head, he'd imagined that he'd feel very different parking in front of his old home. Now his palms were sweating. This had always been a problem for him. It made shaking hands difficult. He wiped his hands against his jeans and then through his thin hair. He wondered what his father would look like, whether his shoulders would still be stooped the way they were the last time Jonathan had seen him. He wondered whether his father's stark white hair had lasted another eighteen years, and whether his Polish accent would still be so pronounced.

"He's not dead," Marc said, fiddling now with his box of cigarettes. "You said he was dead."

"He's not dead," he said, wondering whether bumming a

cigarette from his son would be inappropriate. "Obviously. That's his car."

He pointed at a blue car. His father took pride in never buying a new car. He'd always claimed the ones others abandoned, put them on blocks, fixed them himself. Anything broken can be fixed. Buying new is a convenience for the lazy. That was his mantra. Their driveway was always stained with oil. This car looked new. A garden rake leaned against the house. He couldn't imagine his father in the yard. He had done the math in his head for years, keeping track of his father's age with each passing March. He would be eighty.

"Does Mom know?" Marc asked.

"No."

"He must be some son of a bitch for you to pretend like he's been dead this whole time."

"Yeah."

"What'd he do that was so bad?"

Jonathan pulled his sleeve up to show Marc three long scars stretching along the inside of his arm from his wrist to his elbow.

"Ouch."

"He did it with a fork," he said.

He'd told Julia that he'd injured himself while shaving down a slab of marble. By the time he'd met her, he was in the habit of pretending his father was dead. Marc ran his finger along the scar.

"It was a long time ago," Jonathan said.

"That's it?" Marc said. "He beat you up and you tell everybody that he's dead?"

"Once you stop talking to somebody, to start talking to them again gets harder," Jonathan said. "Momentum."

For the ten years after his mother's death, he and his father had lived alone in this small house. He had long forgotten the circumstances that surrounded their fights. They all blended together in his head. He did, though, remember his father holding his arm against the kitchen counter as he dragged the fork across his skin. His father had spit on the wound. Jonathan was eighteen; he left the next morning.

"Are you sure that you don't smoke?" Marc asked, taking a cigarette out of his pack. "Because this is stressing me out."

Jonathan looked at the cigarette. "No," he said. "If I have one then I'll have another, and then I'll be fucked forever."

"Sounds like you're already kind of fucked," Marc said, lighting the cigarette.

They sat for a while. Since the divorce, he hadn't spent a Christmas with Marc, an evening of Hanukkah, a Thanksgiving dinner, a Passover seder. He sent a card to Marc on his birthday, and a small gift. His mother had so much, gave their son so much, that he never felt he could compete.

Marc held his cigarette like a woman, between the tips of his fingers. Jonathan reached out, took the cigarette, and pushed it between Marc's knuckles.

"If you're gonna do it," he said, "do it like this."

"Look at you," Marc said. He possessed a perfectly sarcastic sense of humor. "Mr. Expert Smoker."

"He's dying," Jonathan said.

He stared at the maple tree and saw that it looked sick. He'd read years ago about a beetle infestation in Rhode Island. The bugs got inside the bark and devoured its insides. He was always searching for news about home.

"I got a letter from my father's lawyer saying that he was sick and that I was his beneficiary."

"What does that mean?" Marc asked.

He watched his son breathe in the smoke. Marc didn't look like he enjoyed the taste. "That means I'm going to inherit his money."

"Can't be much," Marc said. "This place isn't exactly the Waldorf."

"Hey," Jonathan said, taking the cigarette out of Marc's hand. "Watch it. He worked hard to get here."

Defending his father felt strange. Hidden somewhere inside him was a faint trace of loyalty. That's what had brought him here today, he knew. Death demanded company. He knew that he couldn't leave the car and walk the short distance to the doorbell. Whatever certainty he'd possessed about this, about the short walk, about the few moments of reunion on the old doorstep, had gone. The cherry of Marc's cigarette burned between his knuckles, and for a moment he considered putting it in his mouth. Then he tossed it out the window. The lights were off in the front room of the house. He could picture the inside of that room, the table lamp that sat on a tall slab of oak, the fake Persian rug, the framed photograph of the Temple Mount. Nothing would have changed. His father might have finally bought a new car, but he would never have moved the furniture.

The way Jonathan imagined the moment, they would sit in the kitchen, three generations of Cohen men, all beneath the hanging fluorescent lamp with their coffee cups, their cigarettes, their brusque dispositions. His father would look at Marc, squint his eyes, and say, "You look like us, kid." Marc would laugh, touch his nose, and shift nervously in his chair. Jonathan's father would pour a glass of vodka, light his pipe. For a half hour, Jonathan would feel as though he'd done the right thing, bringing his boy to meet his father. Then they would leave, and perhaps, possibly, he'd feel some of the guilt lift off him.

"Why don't we let him know that we're here?" Marc said, reaching out and pushing down on the horn.

"Don't," Jonathan said, trying with his hands to stop Marc. The horn was louder than he thought it would be, and sounded to him like one long blow from a trombone. Jonathan shook his head. "Why'd you do that?"

"Why'd we come if you were just gonna sit in the car?" Marc said. "That's stupid."

"I thought I'd want to see him," he said. "That's why."

He felt foolish having rented this car, having driven Marc all the way to Rhode Island for something that he didn't have the confidence to go through with.

A moment later, the curtains opened, and he saw his father: he didn't look ill. He'd expected to find his father gaunt, the skin on his face wrapped tight around his skull. His father peered out, his hands over his eyes to block the sun; he'd always had great eyes. Jonathan felt sick in his stomach. His father shifted his weight from foot to foot. Jonathan hadn't heard what his father was dying from. The letter hadn't said so much.

"That's him?" Marc asked.

"Yeah."

"You think he can see us?"

"I think he can."

"You look terrible, Cohen," Marc said.

"I don't want to do this," Jonathan said. "This was a mistake."

"Well," Marc said, unbuckling his seat belt. "I'm going to say hello."

"You don't have to," Jonathan said, wanting to put his hands on Marc's legs to hold him in his seat.

"Hey," Marc said. "My grandfather came back to life."

Marc stepped out into the yard. Jonathan watched him walk to the front door. Children from New York had a confidence that he didn't understand. The front door opened. His father had on the same work pants he'd always worn, and a long blue button-down with the sleeves rolled up to his elbows. On his head, he wore a wool watch cap. He still dressed like a fisherman. Marc stood on the front steps, shaking hands. His father had always tried to crush people's hands when he shook them. One needed to prepare in advance to shake Isaac Cohen's hand. He should have warned Marc.

He saw his father glaring over Marc's shoulder and squinting at the rental car. He felt like waving. Then, at nearly the same time, he thought of driving away. The car's engine was still running. Behind him, a thin stream of exhaust went up into the sky. He could tell that his father was staring at him. He had those bright Polish blue eyes that dug into people. In some ways, those eyes had never stopped looking at him, despite the distance and the silence and the separation. He tried to imagine the conversation that was occurring on the front step. He'd never felt like such a coward. He looked away, out across the street, concentrated on a knot in an oak tree.

After two minutes, Marc came back to the car, pulled the door shut, and touched him on the forehead.

"You're sweating."

"Am I?" Jonathan dabbed his fingers to his skin. "I feel freezing."

"Turn the heat up."

"Is he still looking?"

"No," Marc said. "He went inside."

"Are you sure?"

"I'm hungry," Marc said, buckling his seat belt. "You never fed me."

Inside Divinity Seafood, Jonathan took a seat by the window. He ordered a beer and a whiskey and drank them quickly. He had never been a good drinker, couldn't stomach the taste of liquor. The drinks warmed him and calmed his nerves for a moment. Out the window, he saw a police cruiser idling in the parking lot. He watched a traffic light swinging high above the street. The cars on the shore road idled. He waited for his father's car. Marc sat laughing on the opposite side of the table.

"I guess I'm driving home," Marc said.

"I'm fine," Jonathan said, looking around. "It's just one drink."

"I don't want to die," Marc said. "And you've had two drinks."

"You don't know how to drive."

"I don't know if you were paying much attention on the way up here," Marc said, smiling widely, "but neither do you."

The neon sign flashed beside Marc. His son's face went red and white and red again. In the light, Jonathan saw that he was wrong: Marc didn't look anything like him, or like his father. Marc was a good-looking kid, or at least he possessed the ingredients that would make him later, in his twenties, a good-looking kid.

"I'm ordering lobster," Marc said.

"It's good here," Jonathan said. "Or at least it was twenty years ago."

"I've never had it before."

"Really?" Jonathan asked. "How is that?"

"Mom says that they're nothing but big bugs," Marc said. "Aren't they?"

"Kind of," Jonathan said. "I'm not really sure. I'm a sculptor, Marc. Not a scientist."

The inside of Divinity Seafood was just as he remembered it. On the table there were plastic bibs to tack to your clothing. Marc pinned one onto his red hooded sweatshirt. Lobster traps hung from the ceiling as decoration.

Marc put his hands on the table and then cleared his throat. "You're Jewish, right?"

Jonathan smiled. "Yes, Marc. So are you, sort of."

"Then isn't lobster against the law?"

"Well," Jonathan said. "Not an actual law."

"You know what I mean," Marc said. "That kosher stuff. I got Jews for friends, you know. I do live in Manhattan."

Jonathan saw that his son didn't have any evidence of facial hair, not even the faintest trace of the peach fuzz that had invaded his own face during puberty. He thought, watching his son fidget with a lobster-claw cracker, that Marc was a young fifteen.

"Your father—" Marc said.

"I don't want to hear about it," Jonathan said. "I'm sorry we came, really."

"He had the numbers," Marc said, rolling up his sleeve and running his hand across the skin on the inside of his arm.

"Yeah," Jonathan said.

"They're in the same place as the marks on your arm."

Jonathan nodded his head. "That's true."

He reached across the table and took a fresh cigarette from Marc's pack. Those numbers. Marc furrowed his thin, black eyebrows; he looked like Julia when he did this. Jonathan turned the cigarette in his fingers. Flakes of tobacco came off onto the table.

"I went to the door," Marc said. "And I said that I was his grandson."

Jonathan put the cigarette in his mouth. He stared at its tip, hoping not to hear what Marc was saying. Out the window, gulls were diving into the water. He never understood why sometimes you could see the moon in the daytime and sometimes you couldn't. His father had tried to explain the reason when he was young, but he couldn't remember what he'd said. His father had left Poland after the war. He knew things about science. Fishing was a way to make money. Their long silence, like radiation on a tumor, might have eradicated the good memories along with the bad.

"And he shook my hand and said he was glad to meet me," Marc went on.

Jonathan didn't want to listen. On the table was a basket of matchbooks. He took one, removed a match, and struck it. He watched the flame shoot upward. He wondered if his father had crushed Marc's hand. He saw that Marc was looking directly at him.

"You're not listening."

"Marc," he said, sucking smoke into his mouth and lungs. "Please don't. This is bothering me."

"I told him that you were in the car. And that you wanted me to say hello."

Jonathan looked over the edge of his cigarette. He felt angry with his son. How could he do this, just sit here so calmly, filled with so much confidence, so much strength for so young a person?

"And he told me to tell you that he said hello," Marc said, reaching out and grabbing the cigarette from Jonathan's mouth and then snuffing it out in the ashtray.

Jonathan watched the restaurant's front door every time it opened. Three bells were strung along the hinge, a short, slight melody.

"What are you looking for?" Marc asked.

"Nothing."

"He's not going to come in," Marc said. "You can relax."

After a long moment, Jonathan let out a loud sigh. He hadn't realized that he was holding his breath.

White foam from the water sprayed the road. The traffic passed. The neon sign flashed onto the street. People walked along the barrier wall. Jonathan had done that with his father when he was young. It was the only way he could be as tall as his father, standing on that wall, trying not to lose his balance, and still, even up there, so high that he could see the tide and the waves and the shells of the hermit crabs left on the sand and even the crown of the old lighthouse out in the bay at Narragansett, he was still not as tall as his father. He never had been.

Beyond Any Blessing

A week after my grandfather was fired, I came to see him at his home near the city. He had been a rabbi at the same synagogue for six decades, and although I had expected for years that he would be fired, the news still came as a surprise. A member of the board of directors drafted a letter of termination, and had a copy delivered both to my grandfather and to me. They assumed, I suppose, that he was becoming too old to bear the news himself.

I had my own set of keys, and when I came that afternoon in September, two days removed from the end of the Jewish calendar year, and a week from the end of the baseball season, I could hear the clamor of my grandfather's radio from the doorstep. He never missed a ball game, even though his hearing had been nearly gone for most of my life. In the front hallway, the woman who cooked his meals met me and smiled. Her name was Marlena, and although we had passed each other in this way for years, we spoke very little. She stopped when she saw me, refusing, as always, to make eye contact;

she backed up against the wall, a stack of folded linens in her hand.

"He's in there," she said. She was Trinidadian and had, when I heard it, a lovely, lilting accent.

"How is he?" I asked.

She shrugged her shoulders. "He is the usual."

My grandfather was seated in his armchair, a blanket across his lap. I stood in the doorway, listening along with him. He had his eyes closed, and if it were not for the nervous twiddling of his fingers, I would have thought he was asleep. He was ninety years old.

"Grandpa," I said, trying to time my greeting with the pauses in the announcer's call. "Grandpa Sy."

He put one hand up in the air, as if he were a crossing guard. "Wait one more moment, Danny," he said, leaning forward in his seat, clenching his fists. He had about him all of the strained evidence of a lifetime of rooting for the Red Sox. "I have a feeling this is the pitch."

I cleared from the couch a stack of books, a bin of loose-leaf paper, his unopened mail, a box of illegal Churchills, a week's worth of the *Globe* still bound by elastics, and his ancient baseball mitt. He had lived most of his adult life here, a three-story wood-and-brick building adjacent to the synagogue. It was a home too large for one man—my grandmother had been dead for thirty years, and I had long since moved out—but my grandpa Sy wore its space well, cluttering every room, complicating Marlena's plans to clean, and smoking his cigars in the hallways. His study was the only room he deigned to keep in order, although it was terribly dark, lit only by a green desk lamp and a bank of west-facing windows.

"Here it comes," he said as the announcer called the

pitcher's delivery and then the batter's swinging and missing. As the game ended, my grandfather opened his eyes and laughed. It was a great hissing sound, his laugh, like air escaping a tire. I'd heard it my whole life, that serpentine sound, his tongue behind his teeth.

His chair turned on a pivot. It was a useful feature when he counseled his congregants. I was sitting where they normally sat, and for a short moment, as the game ended and he turned his attention to me, smiling, sliding his eyeglasses down to the tip of his nose, I felt as if I were about to be interrogated.

"Well, that was good fun," he said. "Did you think they would pull it out?"

"I haven't been following," I said. "I didn't know what to expect."

"Really? It's been so exciting. What else could you have been doing?"

However much it bothered him, I did not share his love for baseball, or his boundless faith, and not for the first time in my life, I had the realization that it was only a coincidence of blood that we ever spent time together. I shrugged my shoulders and we sat in silence, something he was quite skilled at but that I was uncomfortable with. To him, life was a series of silences punctuated by prayer, song, and laughter.

"I just wanted to check on you," I said, trying to speak with confidence. "I got the letter."

"What letter?"

"They sent me a copy of your termination letter."

He shifted in his seat. "Just the one letter?"

"Was there more than one?"

He opened the long desk drawer nearest to his chair. He was the most disorganized man I had ever known, and I watched with half a smile as he rummaged through his things, removing after a long moment an ordinary white envelope embossed with the name of his congregation.

"Take a moment and read it," he said.

"Are you sure?"

"It involves you. I suppose they didn't think so, but I do."

The letter was short, and was addressed to my grandfather by the same committee that decided his termination. It said, in six sentences, that he was to vacate his home some time before the end of the year. A date had not yet been determined, but was coming forthwith. If he wished, the congregation would fund his stay in a Jewish retirement home of his choosing.

"*Forthwith*," he said. "You'd think they have a Middle English scholar on the board now."

I'd just started my second year of law school, and as I sat in his study staring at that letter, I tried to remember the salient aspects of my last semester's class in contracts. My grandfather had not wanted me to become a lawyer. He knew that it was a move I was making out of desperation and a lack of other options. My memory of that class consisted of little else but the young people who sat in front me, all of whom typed their notes into a computer and had immaculate recall.

"Grandpa?" I said, holding the letter up. "Can they do this?"

"They sure can," he said, beginning the slow process of getting to his feet. "Middle English scholars come in all shapes and sizes these days. Even Jews."

"You're making jokes?"

"The line between humor and sadness is especially thin."

"What are you going to do?"

"I'm going to feel terrible. And then, I'm going to feel horrible. And then, I suppose, I'm going to move."

I watched him get to his feet. He had green eyes, which, even at ninety, seemed healthy and clear, and when he focused them on me, as he did now, I nearly always felt uncomfortable.

"I might be new to the law," I started. "But I think—"

He put his hand on my shoulder. "Your false confidence is not necessary, Daniel."

He had always been able to disarm me. I took a deep breath. "How does this involve me?" I asked.

"Well, it seems that they really do want me to leave. And I haven't lifted a box in three decades. You get the picture, don't you?"

He did not stop to get my response.

"I'm hungry," he said. "Let's get some dinner."

In the hallway, he took his overcoat off a hook. Marlena stood off to the side, holding another pile of folded linens. He smiled at her, and I followed him out to the street, walking two paces behind, close enough so that if he fell, I could catch him. I slid the letter into my jacket pocket. He walked with his head high, waving to his neighbors. This was Brookline, Massachusetts, three miles from Boston. My grandfather took from his pocket a rumpled Red Sox cap. It had once belonged to me, and although it did not look good on him, he was happy.

He'd parked his car by the front door of the synagogue's administrative offices. A light on the second floor of the building was still on, glowing softly behind a pair of sheer blue curtains I knew well. I took the letter from my jacket.

* * *

The year I turned seven, my parents took me from our home outside of Boston to a house they rented for the summer in Truro, a small town on the far end of Cape Cod. It was a Sunday evening. We went every July to this house, a small bungalow near the National Seashore, and I can remember looking forward to eating fried clams in the seafood shacks near our home, watching the buzzards and the beetles and the bullfinches, and to reading my favorite mystery novels on the stiff wicker couch we kept on the porch. "I'm not sure why they call it a commonwealth," my father said as we drove. "It's a very old place, Massachusetts. They like to emphasize that. We could look it up, though."

He turned in his seat so that he was facing me when he said this last thought, and our car was struck head-on by a red Jeep that had crossed the median. My parents never wore their seat belts, and when we crashed they were thrust through the windshield and into the swampy brush on the shoulder of Route 6. I was wearing my seat belt, a fact I was informed of when I woke later that day in a Barnstable hospital, attended to by a staff of three nurses. Of the six people involved in the crash—three in our car, three in the Jeep—I was the one person to survive.

I would be a liar if I said that I remember very much about growing up with my parents. There is little about a memory that stays accurate and true after so long. Certain foods remind me of my mother, who was the cook of the family, especially a well-seasoned lamb chop—she had a recipe with mint and mustard that has stayed with me. The voices of the old play-by-play men for the Sox remind me of my father, but only if I'm driving with the windows down. I remember the perfumes they owned, and I remember the thick terry-cloth bathrobes they liked to wear, and I remember their broad, old-fashioned accents—part Brahmin, part London, part Dorchester—and I remember the way their laughter sounded in our car, all three of us driving out to the Cape that Sunday, the windows down; the laughter rolling over the car upholstery, over the stereo, over their matching suitcases, and, if it can be said without sounding coy, over my head.

When I woke that day in the hospital in Barnstable, the only person there to see me was Grandpa Sy. Until that day, I'd never had a real conversation with him. He had always frightened me—his beard, his age, his enormous house, his polygraphic ability to tell when I was lying. I wasn't sure whom I expected to be there in the room with me—there was no one else, despite my wishes, no uncles or aunts, no cousins in Boston or Brooklyn or Montreal, but still, I wanted somebody other than him to come and claim me. He was sitting in a chair at the back of my hospital room. In his hands, he had a small radio. He came over to me, put his hands on my head.

"We'll listen to the games together while you get better," he said. "And then, when you're ready, we'll go home."

"Home where?"

"Home to my place."

"I don't like baseball."

He smiled at me. "That's quite all right."

"Is it true?" I asked, looking at the line of nurses standing at the foot of my bed, all of them staring at their shoes.

He patted the radio and placed it beside me on the bed. "A game is going to come on in a moment."

* * *

I stood at the door to Shari Levinson's office, my grandfather's eviction letter in my left hand, attempting to silently reassure myself. Although my wife didn't know it, Shari was the last woman I made love to before my wedding. This was eighteen months earlier, in a humid airport hotel room in Baltimore. I'd asked her to come there from Boston, paid for her ticket, registered under an assumed name. Despite whatever maturity I might have gained between then and now, I still suffered from the same problem I did when I met her, at ten years old, during a mandated summer-camp social, standing lakeside and bug-bitten beneath a flickering fluorescent lightbulb out on the recreation-hall deck. The best love affairs, I'd learned, die with an incredible slowness.

Shari worked as the administrative secretary for my grandfather's congregation, her office occupying the great bulkhead room that overlooked Beacon Street. She organized the synagogue's social outreach—the fund-raising for Israel, the planting of trees in the Negev, the periodic singles mixers held on Christian holidays, when the rest of the world shut down and there was nothing for a Jew to do. It did not surprise me that Shari was successful at her job. I knew, perhaps better than anybody, that she had a way of gaining the confidence of those around her, especially my grandfather.

The air conditioner was off and I could smell a hint of her sweat in the air. I knocked on the door frame, waited a moment, and went inside. It was eight in the evening, but this was summer, and it was still as bright as afternoon outside. The back of her head—black curls, the same butterfly barrette I recognized from the mid-nineties—was marked by the sunlight.

"I knew you'd be coming," she said, walking to a file cabinet, opening a long drawer, standing on her toes.

"You did?" I said. "Can you see the future now?"

"No," she said, still on her toes, flipping through the files with the tips of her fingernails. "I just know you and your grandfather too well."

"Really," I said, trying to see what she was looking for. "What're you doing, looking for the bottle of Scotch you keep hidden in there? I've got my grandfather waiting in the car. I'm not looking for a party."

"You've known me, what? Twenty years? And you think I drink Scotch?"

Shari turned around on her heels and put a stack of papers into my hand.

"I really wish you hadn't married that woman," she said.

"What is all this?" The stack of paper was an inch thick.

"Those are all the eviction notices," she said, flicking the paper I was holding with her index finger. "This little thing is just the tip of the iceberg."

I flipped through the pages. "Some of these go back twenty years."

She stood very close to me, but we did not touch. "Does she make you happy?"

"You might need to explain this to me."

"I miss you," she said. "When are we going to go to Baltimore again?"

I stepped away. "How has he stayed on?"

"They've been trying to get him out for twenty years," she said, rolling her eyes at me. "But he's good at what he does. He manages to keep his house. I'm relatively new to this charade and I don't have all the answers."

She looked expectantly at me.

"We're trying to get pregnant," I whispered.

"That's terrible news."

"Can you help me?"

"Do you really not know why they're getting rid of him?"

"No."

"Don't you see him often?"

"Twice a month."

She went to her desk and stood with her back to me. "And you still don't know why?"

"What are you getting at?"

"I have nothing to do with this. That's all I want you to know."

"With what?" I asked, growing impatient.

"Change is hard," she said, and then I thought she might begin to take off her sweater or that she might really reach for a bottle of something. She'd had a flair for the dramatic when we were young together. Instead, she turned to me. "Come back tomorrow morning and we'll talk."

"You'll tell me what's going on tomorrow?"

She nodded her head. I went to the door. She called after me.

"Dan," she said, smiling.

I turned around.

"I'm glad you came to see me."

Two weeks after the accident that killed my parents, my grandfather arrived at the hospital to bring me home. As a parting gift, my team of nurses gave me a rumpled Red Sox cap, and I went through the process of discharge with it on my head. I'd broken my left femur, and I had to be wheeled out into the parking lot, my grandfather with his hands on the back of my chair. A team of nurses assisted him, walking behind me. Outside, there was the smell of the ocean and a ring of white gulls circling over the hospital roof. My grandfather was in his seventies, and, although he tried, he could not lift me into the car.

"It's all right," he said, after trying and failing to get me inside. "Let me take a break for a moment."

"It's okay, Grandpa."

One of the nurses rubbed my head, mussed my hair. I had been perpetually frightened in the two weeks between my accident and that moment in the parking lot, but nothing caused me to worry so much as seeing my grandfather wiping sweat off of his forehead on a cool summer morning in Cape Cod. I closed my eyes and hoped that everything would not be this difficult. I needed my grandfather alive. He didn't seem up to the job.

"Why don't you let us take care of this, sir?" one of the nurses said. "Watch how we do it. You don't have to exert yourself so much."

One of the nurses took me from my chair and held me as if she were giving me a hug. The other took my chair, folded it, and put it in the trunk of my grandfather's car.

"That wasn't that bad," my grandfather said.

"You don't want to lift with your back," a nurse said.

"You can really hurt yourself," the other said.

"You wouldn't hurt me?" my grandfather asked. "Would you?"

I didn't answer.

"He wouldn't hurt me," my grandfather said to the nurses.

I did not want to leave the hospital. Inside my room, in

my bed, I had people who came for me when I called, and although none of them was my mother, who always doted on me, or even my father, who was the busier of the two but perhaps kinder than my mother, I knew that life in my grandfather's house was going to be different. I looked out the window as we drove away, waving to my nurses, one hand to the glass.

Out on the road, I kept my eyes closed. "Can you drive slow?"

"Of course," my grandfather said.

When we were close to the city I could see the twin spires of Boston in the distance, the Prudential and the Hancock towers, piercing the sky. I had been able to see these buildings from a high point of the town where I'd lived with my parents, and I had forever been told that my grandfather lived below those buildings. That was the first moment of comfort in my new life, and it came as a relief.

Moments later my grandfather, absently trying to adjust the radio, searching for the baseball game, had to slam on his brakes to avoid bumping the car ahead of us.

"Grandpa!"

"It's fine," he said. "It's fine. There's no accident. Don't worry."

"I can't believe you did that," I said, and I started to cry.

My grandfather pulled the car into the breakdown lane, and we sat there for a few minutes. "Until you calm down," he said, patting my knee with his hand.

Whenever we went to dinner we went to Sidman's, a small neighborhood steak place run by a pair of brothers my grandfather had known for years. It was a short drive from the house, and even though the Lincoln was my grandfather's car, I drove. He was a nervous passenger, fiddling with the radio dials, the climate controls, the buttons on his coat.

"Did you speak with Shari?" he asked, running his fingers along the insignia on his ball cap.

"I did."

"You've got a good girl at home," he said, patting my knee. "Don't you forget that."

"Why do you feel the need to say that?"

"I hear things," he said.

"Don't believe the gossip," I said.

"So it's not true?"

"Why the guilt trip? You've never liked my wife."

"She's misguided when it comes to the Messiah."

"Spare me the sermon."

"That's my job."

"Not any longer it isn't."

I regretted saying it as soon as I did. Ever since I was a boy I feared saying something cruel to Grandpa Sy, believing that he might die at any moment. It was a great worry of mine that I'd be stuck, eternally, with the guilt of whatever insult I last uttered to him, however harmless my true intentions.

"I didn't mean that," I said.

"No," he said, and then he let the silence linger in the car for too long a moment before saying, "You did, you meant it, and you're right."

"No. It's just a thing people say."

"I know," he said. "I know what people say."

We drove through a tunnel, a jewelry string of yellow lamplights bolted above us on the barrier wall.

"How am I going to get used to all of this?" he said, wringing his hands. "After all this time."

I wasn't sure if he wanted an answer or not. So much of my life with him went this way. I turned on the radio. There was incessant talk about the Red Sox. I wanted to talk about my grandfather's plans should he really be forced to move, but when I began to speak he waved his hands, scowled at me, and pointed at the radio. When we arrived outside the restaurant, my grandfather put his hand on mine.

"Don't turn off the car just yet," he said.

"Why not?"

"They're going to do a trivia contest at the end of the show," he said. "It's something they do. The winner gets tickets to the next game."

"You have bigger things to worry about," I said.

"Listen to you," he said. "You are so concerned and anxious. If I'm not worried, you shouldn't be worried. I'd like to try to go to a game before I die."

"I'm talking to Shari tomorrow," I said. "We're going to work something out."

"I'm no longer wanted. They've made that clear."

He spoke so softly. I put my hand on his shoulder.

"It's true," he said, turning away from me. "They've made that abundantly clear."

In profile, my grandfather looked exactly as I looked, and although I did not remember my mother very well, I knew from photographs that he looked the way she had. He had a kind face, round features, long lashes for a man. I could not imagine what he might have done to have earned such a steady threat of expulsion. He leaned forward and turned up the volume on the radio. His hands were terribly thin, pocked with liver spots and keratosis and thick black hair. I looked at my own hands. The mystery of my old age had, in some way, always been gone from me: I needed only to look to him to see what would happen to me.

Ari, one of the two brothers who owned the restaurant, came to the car door. Although there was no valet parking at their restaurant, the Sidman brothers extended this courtesy for my grandfather. I had known Ari and his brother, Jacob, since I was a boy, and I had never gotten along well with either of them. They were boorish in ways I was incapable of, and in ways, sadly, that my grandfather found amusing. My grandfather rolled down the window.

"Ari," he said. "I'm just waiting for the big contest."

"Sure thing, boss," Ari said, nodding to me. He never smiled at me. There was only this—the nodding—as if he and I were the drummer and bassist in a rock band. In many ways, the Sidman brothers considered my grandfather as their own, a sentiment my grandfather returned and that I chose to ignore.

"Playoff seats," my grandfather said.

"If you get through, you take me," Ari said.

"Yeah," I said. "I don't think so."

"You'd have to learn the rules first, Danielle," Ari said. This was his pet name for me.

My grandfather gave me his telephone. I'd bought it for him a year earlier on his birthday, and I was fairly sure that he didn't know how to use it.

"Get your telephone ready," he said. "When I say go, you push whatever you need to push."

"I'm sorry," I said. "I'm not doing this. I'm not calling in to a radio contest. Not tonight. Not with everything that's happening."

"Just do it," he said.

"Don't be a jerk, Danny," Ari said to me. "Make the old man happy."

"Stay out of it, Ari," I said.

"It's a small pleasure," my grandfather said. "Do what he said. Make me happy."

"I'm not doing it," I said calmly. I turned off the car and gave my grandfather back his telephone. "You're getting evicted. You're not going to have a place to live. Your congregation is going to get a new rabbi. Get serious and get your mind off baseball for a minute."

My broken leg itched beneath the heavy cast. When we arrived at his house, he left the car running and disappeared into the synagogue to retrieve two men to help carry me inside. He wasn't going to try and fail again. The radio played the baseball game, and I tried to listen to the call for a few minutes. My father had never enjoyed sports, and I had the beginnings of that predisposed aversion to ball games that I recognized later in friends of mine. I grew bored quickly. Baseball on the radio requires a certain patience that I didn't possess at seven. I saw out the car window the children of my grandfather's congregants playing hopscotch on the sidewalk. In the absence of something else to do, I made faces at them, and they made faces at me, and rather than return the favor again, I pretended that I had some very important business to take care of on the control panel of the car. I began to turn the radio dials, finding a station with a split signal, half violin music and half traffic report, and I turned the volume up as loud as I could. When my grandfather did not come after a few minutes, I turned the windshield wipers on, and listened as they skipped and skidded across the dry glass. He owned a used Cadillac then, and there were more dials and knobs to play with: climate control; the seat incline; and the emergency brake, which, when activated, I learned, caused the car to slightly bump the car in front of ours. This bit of contact did not frighten me, and the neighborhood children loved it. I figured that once my grandfather found out how badly I'd treated his car, he'd never allow me into the house.

His reaction, however, was just as it always had been, measured, patient, with a hint of a small grin. "Look at you," he said. "Ever the troublemaker. Just like your mother."

Before I could respond, two men picked me up into their arms. They worked for my grandfather in the office, typing, filing, doing odd jobs. The children on the block stopped their game to watch me.

"These are some friends," my grandfather said, patting the shoulder of the man who was holding my broken leg. "They're going to carry you."

They took me into the house and up the stairs. The lights were off. It was a Friday afternoon, and one of the men told me that the lights would come back on at sundown, on a timer. It had suddenly become the Sabbath. My grandfather walked behind us. The air conditioner was off, and both men began to sweat. There were books stacked on every step, and a thick sheet of dust covered the banister and the hardwood.

"Bring him in there, the first door on the left," my grandfather said. "Put him on the bed."

They put me on a cold stiff bed in a darkened room that had one window and yellow walls. My grandfather dismissed his two friends. When we were alone, my grandfather sat on the bed beside me.

"This is your mother's room."

"This was her room when she was a kid?"

"It wasn't that long ago."

"These are her things?" I asked, picking up a stuffed bird.

"All of them."

"It's dark."

He stood up and went to the window and opened the curtains.

"How's that?"

"Better."

He sat back down beside me. "She used to sneak out through that window."

"Why did she do that?"

"That's a good question," he said.

"I don't understand."

"That's a good thing," he said, resting his hand on the bed beside me.

"What happens now?"

"I have to go and lead a service in the temple. Would you like to join me?"

I closed my eyes. "I don't like going to temple."

"Very well," my grandfather said.

When he was gone, I realized that I was stuck in my mother's bedroom, and that until I healed I wasn't going anywhere unless someone was carrying me. There was an alarm clock on the bedside table, blinking the time. I ripped it from the wall, held it in my hands for a moment, and then hurled it against the window, shattering the glass.

At a large round table, I watched the Sidman brothers and my grandfather eat their steaks and smoke, each of them, a

Romeo y Julieta while raising their glasses of prosecco and toasting to life and then to the beautiful women they hoped to meet and then finally, as usual, to the impending victory of the Red Sox over the Yankees. My grandfather's disappointment with me seemed to disappear between his first and second drink, but my guilt, however, did as it always did—it mounted with considerable strength as time went on.

"I'm sorry for not calling the station," I said, my hand on his shoulder, whispering to him. "I should have. It's the least I could do for you."

"Daniel," he said, speaking at full voice, for he was unable to whisper. "I can't be sore about something I can't control."

I was the poorest sort of drinker, possessing a low tolerance and a surging garrulousness whenever I had a glass of liquor, and so I drank as slowly as possible. "Still," I said, feeling, after half a glass, already finished for the evening. "I want to make it up to you."

He sat back in his seat. "I love surprises," he said. "I really do. But I'd rather you just enjoy our dinner."

"I'm going to work everything out," I said.

"Just eat your steak, Daniel."

"No," I said. "I'm going to fix things for you."

I excused myself from the table and went out the front door onto the sidewalk. I called my wife. When I married Denise, we'd known each other for fourteen months, a length of time long enough to know someone well, surely, but not long enough to have discovered even their slightest secrets. I'd been on a break from Shari then, a break that lasted fourteen months, and until that evening in Baltimore, I had been terribly sure that I was doing the right thing by marrying Denise. In the video of the wedding ceremony, I look appropriately conflicted. Perhaps because an elderly man raised me, my sense of time differed from Denise's: fourteen months, I wanted desperately to convey to her, was a very short time for a life to change so drastically. A good part of me, the part of me that perhaps still belonged to Shari, had yet to catch up. It was as if I'd invited myself to a party and showed up realizing that I didn't want to be there.

When Denise came on the line, I lowered my voice, assuming the serious tone I knew she hated. "Something bad's happened," I said.

"Who died? Are you all right, Danny?"

"No one died," I said, pacing the block. "My grandfather's being evicted from his home."

"First they fire him, and then they evict him? Who'd do that?"

"I'm not sure what's going on," I said. "But I want to stick around tonight and help him sort this out."

"What are you going to do this late at night?"

"Nothing, obviously," I said. "But I'm going to wake up early and make some calls, see if I can work something out."

"Can't you do that from home?"

I thought about it. I was a poor liar. "I might have to go and see some of these people in person. They know me. It'll help if I stay in town."

I had no friends who existed both in my life with Shari and the life I shared with Denise, and even though Shari knew of Denise, the reverse was not true. We lived in a house sixty miles west of the city, close to the campus of my law school, far enough so that my life was safely split between my past and my present. In my mind, the Charles River, running west out of the city, divided my life into these two pieces, like the wall through Berlin.

"Where are you going to sleep?" she asked.

"In my old bedroom."

"Let me drive out and meet you," she said. "We don't sleep apart, remember?"

"That's too far to go tonight," I said, walking to the corner, standing beneath a streetlight. The neighborhood was quiet. "I'm gonna go to bed as soon as I get off the phone with you."

I did love her. This much I knew. She handled easily the parts of life I did not, and I suspected that there was something important about the calm and the peace I felt when I was with her. What I didn't know was whether there was a way to quantify the love I felt in my life. I wanted desperately to find some graph to plot my feelings upon, where I could find inarguable proof of where my heart belonged.

"It's just one night," I said.

I leaned my back against the darkened storefront window of a hardware shop. After I hung up, I took three deep breaths, looked to my left and then to my right, as if someone might see me, and then I called Shari.

Shari came through my window on a night in May when I was fourteen. She came every week to help me bear the boredom and the darkness of the Sabbath, turning a trash barrel upside down, standing on it, and hoisting herself up onto the sloping mansard roof, which led to my bedroom. My grandfather observed strictly, without electricity or automobiles, and she thought it was her duty to keep me entertained. That year, I earned money cleaning the banquet hall of the synagogue on Sunday afternoons, and with my savings I'd bought a tiny handheld television, which I surreptitiously watched beneath my bedcovers during the Sabbath. It got two stations clearly, and three others faintly, and when she came for me, I was watching the Red Sox play the Indians. However much base-ball bored me, I wanted something to talk to my grandfather about. She was in a black long-sleeved shirt and a pair of torn black jeans, her hair tied behind her head in a ponytail. Her fingernails were painted, alternately, with black and silver pol-ish. She smelled always of ripe peaches. She had not yet had her smile fixed by orthodontics and the twin slivers of her front teeth poked out from between her lips.

I helped her inside. She stood on my desk and I picked her up into my arms and dropped her on my bed. I loved kissing her more than I loved anything.

"We're going out tonight," she said.

"Where?"

"To do something."

"To do what?"

"Anything. We could go out to dinner. We could go to the Public Garden. We could go take a whale watch."

"A whale watch?"

She kissed me. I had always behaved nervously around her, too willing to do whatever she wanted.

"We're wasting our life celebrating the Sabbath," she said. "So let's go."

She pointed at the window.

"He'll kill me if he finds out."

She stood up on the bed. "'There is now no smooth road into the future: but we go 'round, or scramble over the ob-stacles. We've got to live, no matter how many skies have fallen.'"

"What is that?"

"D. H. Lawrence."

"Who?"

"It's the beginning of *Lady Chatterley's Lover*," she said, climbing up onto the desk. She had a memory for her favorite literature. It was something that alternately annoyed and fascinated me: an eidetic memory. The wind blew in, moved my mother's old curtains. Shari stood by the open window, waiting for me. I hesitated.

"Should I put a decoy in the bed?" I asked.

"That doesn't even work on television."

She reached out for me.

This was us at fourteen.

My grandfather was asleep in the seat beside me, his cap pulled down over his eyes, his lips fashioned into a slight grin. Boston was dark after midnight, the trains stopped and parked in the stations, the sidewalks filled with college students kissing against lampposts and smoking on the stoops of the tenement buildings. There was no moon, just the glowing hint of one, and a heavy cloud cover, and although it was dark, I could see as I drove along the unmoving Charles that the maples in Back Bay had begun to go red. It happened like this every September, a little earlier every year. In Kenmore Square, the lights at Fenway Park rose above the buildings.

I parked and walked around to his side of the car, opened the door, and tried to take him into my arms. He slapped my hands out of the way.

"I can do it," he said, his eyes closed.

"It's late and you've been drinking all night. Let me carry you."

"You can't carry me."

"You're tiny now," I said. "You couldn't weigh more than ninety pounds."

"You worry so much," he said. "Worry is negative prayer."

"I read that once on a fortune cookie."

I helped him out of the car. His hands were tiny and brittle in mine.

When we were at the steps to his house he looked me in the eyes and said, "You are so much like your mother."

As a teenager, I searched his face for signs of my mother when he said things like this. I was terrified when the memory of her began to slip away. Whenever I tried and failed to picture her, I looked to him for some trace of resemblance. There was only his insistence, his word, and as much as he had tried—and he did try—I was never somebody who could get by on faith alone.

I followed him through the door into the bedroom he kept off the parlor. The room was like the rest of his house. From his mattress, I cleared some hardbound books and a pile of newspapers. He was breathing heavily, and for a moment, I wondered if he was about to fall ill, or cry, or whether he wanted me to go so badly that it was making him angry.

"You're a good boy," he said, finally. "Don't listen to Ari."

"I don't."

"Good."

"You've had a long day. You should get some sleep."

"Sit down," he said.

"I've got to go," I said.

"Sit down," he said, speaking louder.

I did as I was told. We were side by side.

"Do you believe in God, Danny?"

"Let's not do this now," I said.

215

"I've had my doubts. Don't think I'm perfect."

"I'm going to talk to Shari tomorrow. We'll work it out. You don't need to pray."

"Did you hear me?" he asked.

"No one's perfect," I said, standing up once more. I took his cap off his head and kissed him on the forehead.

"I wouldn't want you to be disappointed."

"I'm gonna go home to my wife, Grandpa Sy."

I was out the door when he called out to me. I did not turn back.

"You're not a disappointment to me," he said. "Whether you believe or not."

The first time I had trouble with the police was at the harbor. I was fifteen. We used to go there on Friday nights because Shari had an uncle who had an apartment near Faneuil Hall, and although we never went to see him, if we were ever caught out so late at night, kissing on the wharf pier, we had a standing plan to say that we were on our way to visit her uncle Harlan. It was an easy ride by train. There was a T stop by my house, and from there it was twenty minutes underground. I always loved standing at the front window and watching as the car emerged from underground near Government Center, because, for a short moment, before the train turned a corner, I could see the ocean and the islands in the harbor and the boats docked in the pier.

We had tried to get into the New England Aquarium without paying. She dared me to try to duck under the turnstiles. I made a run for it and was caught before half of my body was in the building. In my defense, I told the officer that I was separated from my family. This was not, in a sense, a lie, and my eyes did not twitch, or blink, and my pulse did not quicken when I said it. The police officer who'd caught me interrogated me in the middle of the lobby. I knew Shari was waiting for me outside, watching.

"It's true," I said. "I don't know where they are."

"Your mother and father?"

"I'm all alone," I said.

"What happened to them?"

"They just left me."

He brought me to a bench. "Wait here," he said. "I'm going to drive you home."

"Okay," I said. Even then, I thought this was a rather amateurish move for a cop. He must have been new on the force.

"What's your name?" he had a notepad and a pen.

I looked out through the glass and saw Shari. She had her hands on her hips and was shaking her head at me. The image of her there, in the waterfront plaza, the wind at her back, her fifteen-year-old face scowling at me, is one of the most indelible memories of my childhood.

"Jeffrey Feldman," I said. It was my father's name.

"And your address?"

"Four twenty-nine Oak. Lexington." I said. It was the house where we had lived before they died. After the accident, I had never gone back. The house had sold to another family.

"Okay, Jeffrey Feldman." He started to write something down onto a pad of paper.

I watched him fill a sheet with his terrible handwriting before I made a run for it.

Shari lived two blocks away in an apartment that had once belonged to her mother. I walked there in the cold, my collar up, my head down to escape the wind. The traffic lights on Beacon Street blew back in the wind, their colors turned up into the sky on the breeze, the side of the buildings beside me painted with the red, yellow, and green. I was thirty-one years old. I had thought once about marrying Shari. At the time I believed it was a bad thing that we had just as much to quarrel about as we had to celebrate.

I rode up in the small elevator. In the reflection of the brushed-metal doors, I tried to fix my hair. I turned my telephone off. The last time I'd been here I'd told her that I needed a week to think things over. I met Denise two days later. At Shari's door, I rested my forehead against the wood, took two deep breaths, reached to feel my pulse.

She came to the door a few moments after I knocked. Behind her, she had the shades open and the city's two skyscrapers were lit and blinking. She wore jeans and a T-shirt, and had on the stereo the sort of soft guitar music that she loved. From the doorway, I could smell the familiar scent of her apartment—clove cigarettes and jasmine and bleach. I put my hands into my pockets.

"It's not Baltimore," she said.

"If I could climb up fifteen stories and sneak in, I'd do it."

"You're so nostalgic," she said, showing me the smallest of her smiles.

On Shari's sixteenth birthday, I attempted to break into Fenway Park with her so that we could walk across the freshly cut grass near the Green Monster. I was sixteen and hopelessly in love with her photographic memory and her confidence and her ability to make me feel like the most important person in her world. These were, at the time, sufficient reasons to do what I did. I wanted more than anything to impress her because she always impressed me, quoting the entire first chapter of *The Great Gatsby* while we were taking a city bus to the harbor; or going as Ophelia one Halloween, dragging me into a broom closet to kiss me and say, "'Could beauty, my lord, have better commerce than with honesty?'"

I'd planned my path of entry for weeks, discovering one night in January that under the right circumstances—with a healthy dose of fearlessness, and at an hour of the evening when there was no traffic on Van Ness Street—we might be able to make it over the brick boundary in right field. A drainpipe ran alongside a corner of the brick. I went first, the toes of my Chuck Taylors wedged in the tiny cracks that I thought were footholds. The wind grew stronger as I climbed and my fingers burned as I gripped the pipe. I looked down once, a poor idea, for I realized as I climbed that I did not have a taste for heights. She stood below me, her arms crossed against her chest, her hair blowing behind her. Every ten feet I passed a bracket on which I could rest my feet. After thirty feet, I turned back to see that I was about level with the second-story window of an apartment across the street. A young couple was standing in the window looking at me. The man had a telephone in his hand. He met my eyes and said something to me, which, although I could not hear, must have been something close to, "What the hell are you doing?" I turned back to the wall. I had thirty more feet to go. The couple across the street began to bang on their window. For a moment, I considered climbing down, and for another moment I considered praying that I wouldn't fall. My stomach began to quake and I could feel my heart beating in my fingers. I heard Shari scream a moment later. In quick succession, I saw three police cruisers below me, one growling German shepherd waiting for me to fall, and a Massachusetts state trooper with his hand on the butt of his pistol.

Shari had a complete photographic history of our life together aligned on her mantel, and for the first time in years I stood by the framed pictures and looked at myself as a boy. I had been coming to this apartment for the better part of my life, but I had never been comfortable looking at pictures of myself. In the earliest, we were eleven, and she was smiling like a starlet for the camera, one shoulder turned toward the lens, and I was laughing hysterically, caught in an honest reaction to a joke. This photograph was taken at the lake of our summer camp. I recognized, in the distance, the small lump of a rock poking from the water; it was the object of our afternoon swims, to reach that rock, touch it, and return to shore. I was happiest during the summer, at sleepaway camp. At least there was no pretense there; everyone was an orphan for the summer.

While I was standing there, holding the frame in my hands, she came up behind me. I could feel her breathing.

"Maybe we should start our own summer camp."

"Neither of us are the best examples for young children."

"Like that ever mattered," she said. "When I met you, our counselors were fifteen years old."

"You remember," I said.

"Yes, I remember. You never wanted to wear a yarmulke to services."

"I didn't believe, even then."

"No," she said. "I think that you said it ruined your hair."

"I was so vain as a boy," I said, laughing.

I put the frame down on the mantel. To see my life encased within a string of picture frames made me realize something that I suppose I had never thought of before: I'd known Shari longer than I'd known my parents.

"You want to go to bed?" I asked.

"You're married now."

I tried to turn my wedding band around on my finger. It was too snug and was hard to move. I was sure that Denise had sized it this way on purpose.

"I don't know what I'm doing here," I said. "I didn't plan any of this."

"You love me," she said, laughing, turning around, going into the kitchen. "That's why you're here."

"Do you think so?"

" 'Were I with thee,' " she said, standing at the sink, her back to me, " 'wild nights should be our luxury!' "

"What is that?"

"Emily Dickinson," she said, still at the sink. "Number two forty-nine."

"How do you do that?" I said, walking into the kitchen. I put my arms around her.

"I don't know," she said, stepping away from me. "But you're not allowed to touch me."

I'd been sitting on the floor of my cell for close to an hour before my grandfather came for me. I was given a metal bed, a toilet, and a view of a cement wall. There was a breeze coming from somewhere, and I was cold. There were no other prisoners around me that I could see or hear, and I imagined that I was being held in a part of the prison reserved for teenagers like me.

"What a daring plot you hatched," he said. "Not even your mother did anything like this. And she and your father were much more inclined to get into trouble than you."

"Are you going to get me out of here?"

One of the guards appeared, holding a chair for my grandfather. It was the same guard who had taken my mug shot. My grandfather thanked the officer and sat down.

"I'm going to sit with you," my grandfather said.

"I want to go home," I said.

"Me, too," he said, as the prison guard left us alone. "It's quite cold in here. I'm glad I brought my coat."

"Where is Shari?"

"Her parents came for her," he said. "This is no place for a young lady."

"What about me?"

"You're not a young lady, are you?"

"Grandpa. Please. I'm in prison. Get me out."

"This isn't prison," he said. "This is a holding cell."

"Same thing."

"No. If I don't bail you out, they will move you to a prison. This, they tell me, is much nicer than prison."

"Well, get me out then."

"I'm going to sit here with you all night," he said. "So you can talk to me about whatever's troubling you."

"Nothing's troubling me."

"Everyone is troubled by something."

I threw my hands into the air. "That might take forever."

"It's a good thing they have you locked up," he said, and then he laughed, and because we were in a closed space, with low cement ceilings, his laughter echoed.

* * *

Shari needed music to fall asleep, something I had forgotten. I wondered what else I had lost in the time we'd been apart. I envied Shari's memory, the trap of it. Shari put Mendelssohn on the stereo, her favorite, and I tried to fall asleep beside her while listening to the strains of one of his violin concertos. She wanted me as far from her as possible, on the far edge of her mattress, but as soon as we got into bed, she rolled over to face me. Behind her, a pair of sheer white curtains was billowing slightly from the baseboard heat.

"Do you ever think you're going to leave her?"

"I don't know."

"Yes, you do. You know. You've thought about it. I know you."

"Until tonight I hadn't given it any thought."

"That's not true," she said, and then she rolled over onto her back, and then she exhaled. "Baltimore, Maryland."

"It was a mistake."

"What was? Baltimore? Or your wedding?"

"I loved you when I was ten years old," I said, laughing. "What do you do with that? Where do you put that? It's like nuclear waste. I can't burn it. I can't bury it."

She rolled over toward me again. "Do you know about *Shomer Negiah*?"

"Are you going to give me a lesson?"

"There are some people who choose not be touched until they're married. Sometimes even after they're married. They make a pact with God. They'll only touch their spouse. I knew some girls like that when I was young."

"Poor things."

"It was a choice they made. But they always tried to find ways to circumvent it. They'd put a blanket between themselves and a boy and they'd hug or they'd hold hands with gloves on."

"That sounds horrible."

"It's a way of cheating the forbidden," she said, and then she sat up in bed, took a piece of her bedsheet, wrapped it around her hands, and softly, as if she were afraid that she might hurt me, she put her palm flat against my heart.

"See?" she said, whispering. "It's not that horrible."

"No," I said. "I guess it isn't."

In this way, we fell asleep.

My cell became even colder. At some point during the night, the police turned off whatever heat they'd been supplying. My coat was confiscated, and I had on only a T-shirt and a pair of jeans.

"I miss my parents," I said.

He was asleep in his chair. I was standing at the bars. I didn't think he could hear me. I'd never said it aloud to him.

"That's what's fucking bothering me, you dumb fucking old man. What the fuck did you think? You think I like being in jail or living in your fucking weird house with all of your books?"

I turned around and walked to the hard metal bed and kicked it. I sat down on the toilet and stared at the floor.

A few minutes later, my grandfather stood up, put his hands in his pockets, and rested his forehead against the bars.

I met his eyes. "What now? Did I break a Commandment? Do I have to fucking pray to God for forgiveness?"

"No," he said, lowering his head. "That won't be necessary."

* * *

In the morning, I woke first and stood in Shari's living room with the telephone cradled against my shoulder. A thin sheet of fog rolled in from the harbor and I couldn't see the tops of either skyscraper. Below me, the city traffic on Beacon Street started and halted. I closed my eyes and put my nose to the glass, and then, testing myself, I opened them. Even with a pane of glass between the outdoors and me I was uncomfortable with the height.

In my desperation, and in my guilt, I wanted to try to find tickets for my grandfather. I'd done nothing to help stop his imminent eviction. The least I could do was bring him to a ball game. I had, in my wallet, a credit card that my father-in-law had given me after my wedding. "Whenever my girl wants something," he told me, "you use this to give her whatever she needs." I held the card in my hand. It was imprinted both with his name and my name and there was something terrible about seeing the two of us juxtaposed this way, especially as I watched Shari walk from the bedroom to the bathroom, wearing just a knee-length baseball jersey I'd given her ten years ago. I heard the shower turn on.

"What are you doing?" she asked me, walking into the living room, groggy, her toothbrush in her mouth.

"I'm on hold with the Red Sox box office," I said. "I want to try and get Sy the tickets I cost him yesterday."

She took the toothbrush from her mouth. "At least that's a battle you might win."

"What does that mean?"

"It means," she said on her way back to the bathroom, "that there are some battles you can't win for him."

"Are you going to tell me what kind of trouble he's in?" I'd forgotten, in the past twelve hours, that she'd promised me that secret.

"I told you I would, didn't I?"

For a moment, I stood at the window and watched the people come and go from the buildings on Beacon. This, I thought, was how Shari saw the world most often, from a great height, and I wondered whether living so high in the air did something to her psyche, bestowing some wisdom on her that I, with my small house in the suburbs, my lawn, and the two empty bedrooms I was saving for my future babies, did not have.

I hung up the telephone and went into the bathroom. The shower was running and the mirror was fogged and I wrote my initials onto it. I did it on instinct. When I was young, I liked to write my initials into the fog of my parents' car windows, or onto the glass panes of my grandfather's study. I enjoyed how, days later, when I walked by, my initials would have reappeared when the windows fogged again, like ghost writing.

"Are you in here with me?" she asked.

"Yes," I said.

"I could hear your breathing."

I stood there at the shower curtain, and even though I thought for a moment that I could see the faint outline of her body through that thin piece of rubber, I could not. For as long as I could, I held my breath so that the moment would not pass.

"Did you get the tickets?"

"No. I gave up."

"That's too bad. I thought you'd make a go for it."

"I want to get inside."

For a long time, she did not say anything, and there was just the sound of the water hitting her body and running into the drain.

Finally, she said, "I know."

I exhaled. "The water probably isn't cold enough."

"I don't get it."

I took a deep breath.

"That's probably for the best," I said. "I'm going to wait outside."

Before I turned around to walk back into the kitchen, where I could both smell and hear the tiny percolations of a coffeemaker my grandfather had once given her, I saw that another pair of initials—hers: S.L.—had appeared on the mirror. Our initials were not next to each other, or even relatively close, and they didn't resemble any of the graffiti we'd left all over Boston a decade earlier, but I wondered, standing there, drawing a line down the middle of the fogged mirror, between her initials and mine, whether our old troubles arose because we were so similar.

We drove from the prison to the cemetery. I had not slept. It was February in New England—gray, unforgiving, without birds or leaves or football to watch. It had been years since I had gone to the graves. I didn't have a car, and they were buried in a part of the state that was hard to reach by bus. We stopped at the entrance, and my grandfather left the car running as he stepped out and walked to the gate that separated the cemetery from the street. I watched him kick his boot through the high brush, bend down, and take something into his hands. He brought back to the car two smooth red stones.

We drove. He gave me a rock.

"Do you know why we do this instead of flowers?" he asked.

"I don't care."

"Make a guess," he said, stopping the car again.

"Because rocks don't get blown away in the wind?"

"Smart boy."

It surprised me that he remembered where their graves were, and as we got out of the car, it occurred to me that although I had not visited my parents since that first year—that first week of shivah in my grandfather's house, pillows on the floor, the mirrors covered with sheets, my clothing torn at the chest, the unmarked graves, fresh grass grown over the top of both plots—he had been going, and the evidence was everywhere. Stones were arranged in a square around the perimeter of the grave marker.

He said the Mourner's Kaddish; I asked if he would say it in English. I watched him while he prayed. His eyes were closed. I had prayed before, but it had never looked the way it looked on my grandfather's face. At the end of the prayer he said, " 'He who makes peace in his heights, may he make peace.' "

When he was finished, he bent and put a stone upon the marker.

"We keep adding to the graves so we never stop missing them."

I wanted to tell him that I liked what he said.

He put his hand on my back. "Go ahead."

I put my stone down next to his, turned around, and walked back to the car.

* * *

Shari and I walked the two blocks from her apartment to the administrative office. From the front steps there, I could see the curtains of my grandfather's bedroom window, where in the spring and summer he hung flower boxes, and where, on the most sweltering days, he sat in a chair by the glass and called out to the neighborhood children playing on the sidewalk. It was terrible to think that he might have to move from this neighborhood, not only because he had lived here for so long, but because it had lived with him so long. He once told me that when he first moved here, his home and the synagogue were two of only six buildings for a quarter mile. When I asked him what the rest of the land was, he just laughed. "Why, we had a large park," he said, as if he'd forgotten. "We had owls. Isn't that something?"

I lingered on the doorstep with Shari and tried to grab hold of her hand.

"Remember what I said last night? *Shomer Negiah?*"

"I thought you were talking about girls you used to know."

She put her hands in her back pockets. "I just don't want you to touch me. I might cry. It might be horrible. I have eyeliner on."

"You're joking."

"Only partly joking."

"I'm glad I came to see you."

"If you go to your grandfather's now, I think you'll find out why he got fired."

I turned and looked back at the house. In my memories of living there, I had somehow lost track of how gorgeous a building it was.

"I'm gonna handle everything," I said.

"I'm sure you will."

"No," I said. "With Denise."

"You love her. You miss me. There's a difference," she said.

"Do you think so? Last night you said I loved you."

"What do *you* think?"

She went into her office and closed the door.

My grandfather's house was quiet. I went in the way I had when I was a teenager, stealthily, determined to avoid notice, turning back to the door to close it silently. When I turned back around I saw Marlena walking barefoot across the kitchen floor wearing just a dress shirt, her hair unfettered by her head wrap. The shirt was my grandfather's, a long blue-and-white striped shirt I recognized. The shirt was, in this way, just like the candles we used to light during those afternoons. She held two cups of coffee in her hands and when she saw me, I feared that the scare might cause her to drop them.

"I didn't see anything," I said, my hands in the air.

She still didn't move.

"Like I said, I didn't see a thing. We're okay. Don't worry."

Whenever I drove through the Back Bay, with its brownstone mansions and its flocks of dirty gulls landing on the wooden pylons of the boathouses on the Charles, and with its men selling bruised fruit on Beacon Street, and with its oil lanterns outside the Commonwealth Hotel, with its pretty Irish Catholic girls running drunk across Beacon with their white-blond hair and their windbreakers, I always had the fleeting hope that I would see my parents turning the corner onto Tremont or Boylston or riding like lovers inside the swan boats on the Public Garden pond, or taking their cappuccinos in a paper cup to walk through the Common. This was their city, and although they had been dead for twenty years, I still expected it to be theirs. I had suffered from this false hope for most of my life, whether I was alone or whether I was with company. Today was no different. I found it strange to discover that the neatly dressed couple lunching on a fresh green salad in the window of a Newbury Street café was not, despite my belief that it should be, my mom and my dad.

I had told my grandfather that I was prepared to scalp tickets from whomever was selling, and, although he had hesitated, I had succeeded in tempting his interest. When we parked, I stood on the corner beside the Lincoln, ran a hand through my hair, and took a deep breath of the city, of everything, the smell of fried food pouring from the windows of the apartments in the Fens, the smell of the fresh water from the Charles, the smell of car exhaust, the smell of a freshly hosed city sidewalk, the smell of the cigar my grandfather had lit.

I followed him toward the ballpark, walking two steps behind him. He moved quite well for a man of his age, and it made me very happy to see him pounding his right fist into his glove, ready at any moment for a wayward foul ball. I had not been to a game at Fenway since I was a boy, and had not been in the vicinity of the park since that night with Shari, and I found, as we grew closer, that much had changed. The team had come under new ownership, and they had transformed the narrow streets near the park into an outdoor shopping plaza of souvenirs and sketch artists and chefs. Men were frying sausage, and roasting lamb on a spit; two wire-thin women were steaming mussels and quahogs, shucking Wellfleet oysters by the crate, breading scrod, and simmering chowder in kerosene-powered vats. Tables for dining were set up along the concourse. My grandfather stopped amid the foot traffic.

"Let's try to get our tickets first," I said, having to yell. "And then we'll get what we need."

He stood there in the swell of people, turning in circles; he looked to me like a child who'd been brought to the ballpark for the first time.

"We don't need tickets," he said. "This is fine."

"Are you sure?"

He turned to me and put one hand on my shoulder. "I'm in street clothing," he said, running his hands over his chest. He was wearing a blue sweater.

"I know that."

"I haven't done this in ages," he said. "I was always in a suit."

"You're not going to be struck down."

"The ancient Greeks were struck down," he said.

"The Jewish God doesn't have a thunderbolt?" I asked. "What a disappointment."

He wandered over to the two women cooking seafood and peered into the vat of chowder. "Do you know that I've never once eaten clam chowder?" he said.

"How is that possible?"

"I've never eaten a shrimp."

"You never stole a bite?"

"I'm a very good rabbi," he said.

"You're a very deprived human," I said.

I heard, finally, the sound of his laughter when it was genuine, and realized that the sound I had always associated with my grandfather's amusement—that serpentine hissing, a knife into the rubber of a tire—was a fake.

I bought some chowder and a ring of shrimp cocktail and sat beside him on a bench.

"I can't do this," he said. "Be this close. It smells too good."

"Nobody's watching."

At this, he smiled.

"Just a little bit. I won't tell."

"Why don't I just watch you? And why don't you just hurry up?"

I nodded and began to eat.

"My family were all fishermen, and I have lived in New England my entire life, and I've never eaten a clam," he said.

"Look," I said. "If you want it, eat it."

He laughed. "Just eat quickly."

A moment later, I turned to see him sulking, his eyes closed.

"Are you okay?" I said.

His eyes were still closed.

I put my hand on his arm.

"Are you all right?"

"I've suddenly become profoundly sad," he said. "I never thought they'd win, Daniel."

We sat in silence for a moment. The crowd was beginning to thin in the plaza; the game was going to start soon.

"Shari showed me the eviction notices."

He laughed. "So you saw the stack?"

"It's quite impressive that you weren't homeless a decade ago."

"I'm strong," he said, grabbing hold of my arm. "It runs in us."

"I also saw Marlena this morning."

He turned to me, and for the very first time, I felt that we were on level ground.

"Is she the whole reason?"

"You can't help these sorts of things," he said.

"I'm well aware."

He laughed. "I know you are."

"Is it because she's not white? Or is it because she's a Christian?"

"Oh, it's got nothing to do with that. Shari thinks so. But she's wrong. It's because they want someone else," he said. "That's what it's always about. They got me fired finally. So they win. They get what they want."

I put my hand on his shoulder. "I have an extra bedroom."

"Oh, that's not going to work. You don't like baseball nearly enough," he said.

There is one last thing: at the end of his life, my grandfather confessed to me that even though he knew he was dying he was surprised to discover that he wasn't thinking very much about what might happen when he passed. I took this to mean that he wasn't thinking about heaven, or whatever he considered to be heaven. Instead, he told me that he often thought of something he had seen once, years earlier, when he was still a student. In fact, he told me, he thought of this so often that it sometimes seemed to him to be the only memory left in his mind.

In his memory it was summer, and he had, out of boredom, or out of sheer curiosity, borrowed a bicycle and gone out into the country alone, following the Charles. "I don't know what got into me," he said. "But I was from the city, you have to remember, and I'd never really considered what the

river looked like all the way out. I had heard stories about
the towns out there, and I'd seen pictures, of course, but I
wanted to see it all for myself. And so I went out ten miles or
so from the city. It was summer, a brutally hot day. Of course,
I was in my school uniform still. Even then, I couldn't bear
just to go out into the world dressed as I wanted. Eventually,
I stopped at a bridge, a simple one-lane crossing. I was far
too hot to keep going, and it was getting to be about midday.
Below me, in the water, I saw a couple swimming, a young
man and a young woman. The woman was in her underwear,
and the man was swimming in his blue jeans. This was before
the Second World War, when everyone believed we were going to join the fight. Periodically you would hear about young
men consumed with their emotions, doing something wild a
night or so before they shipped off. This is what I figured
I was watching, and I have to admit that I stood for a very
long time to watch them. I shouldn't have done it. But none-
theless, they began to kiss at a certain point. There was this
old rock jutting out of the water, covered in moss and river
weeds, and they were resting against it, and there were some
fish milling around them, and the sun was striking the trees
and all of it was hitting the water just so, making all these
flashing diamonds and shadows and shifting patterns of light.
They seemed very passionate about one another, this man and
woman. I was young and I didn't know very well what love
looked like, and so I kept watching. It was wrong of me, but
there was something about the two of them in the water,
with the sun and the wind and the light on the Charles. It all
seemed so wonderful to me. It was the first moment in which
I knew with certainty that God existed. Whatever certainty I'd
had previous to this I realized had been a simple assumption.

But then there was this. And whenever I had doubts in my life, and I had many of them, like any man does, I thought of that moment."

He closed his eyes.

"That's what you're thinking of?" I asked. "Right now?"

We were quiet for a while. Then he looked straight at me. "At this very moment."

"It must have been very nice," I said.

"Any man who has a doubt in God needs to see what I saw that afternoon, Danny. With the way the river looked. And those two people in love just swimming there in the middle of the afternoon. It was the most pure moment."

"Well," I said. "I'm not sure that's true."

Again, that laugh. He took my hand in his and squeezed. "Oh, you and your doubts."

Acknowledgments

This book was written with assistance from the Iowa Writers' Workshop, the Truman Capote Literary Trust, and the Institute for Creative Writing at the University of Wisconsin.

In addition, the author wishes to thank: Shamis Beckley, PJ Mark, Stephanie Koven, Andrea Walker, Ethan Canin, Reagan Arthur, Michael Pietsch, Marlena Bittner, Eve Atterman, Barbara Clark, Peggy Freudenthal, James Alan McPherson, Marilynne Robinson, Tony Eprile, Lan Samantha Chang, Connie Brothers, Deb West, Jan Zenisek, Carol Houck Smith, the Bread Loaf Writers' Conference, Jesse Lee Kercheval, Ron Wallace, Ron Kuka, Judy Mitchell, Andrew Milward, Emma Straub, Michael Fusco, C. Michael Curtis, Maria Steshinsky, Rachael Brown, Tod Lippy, Ted Thompson, the Beckley and Burant family, Robbie Sokolowsky, and Richard, Pamela, and Marissa Nadler.

The Book of Life

Stuart Nadler

A conversation with
Stuart Nadler

Tell me about your writing process. Where does a story begin for you—with an idea, or with an individual character, place, or mood?

I try not to have a lot of rules. That's the most important thing. In short fiction especially, what works for one story usually doesn't work for every story. The whole enterprise would be much easier if only there were some magic vein to tap. Updike once said that if a story "doesn't pour smooth from the start, it never will." I can't say that I haven't tried, for months sometimes, to fix an irreparably broken story, or tried for months just to write a story, like "The Moon Landing," which seemed, to use Updike's phrase, to pour fine, but to do so like maple syrup rather than wine, everything coming so slowly. But his general idea is a good one. Many of these stories were written quickly, usually in between other stories that I began and couldn't get right. "In the Book of Life" was written in one quick week. "Visiting" came to me nearly whole while I exercised on a treadmill during an Iowa ice storm. Others, however, took ages. I began "Catherine and Henry" two months before I started the Writers' Workshop in 2006, and I finished it four years afterward, long after I'd graduated, some thirty or forty drafts later. The rest is just habit: I write early and often, and I never leave myself a blank page to come back to.

Tell me about this collection as a whole—what are the thematic ties that unite these stories, and what was the process like in assembling the book?

I don't know if many writers plan to write story collections, or whether, as it happened to me, the collection just announces itself once the work is over. I wrote all but one of these stories while I was at the University of Iowa, and they all reflect what had become by then serious preoccupations with religious identity, cultural assimilation, morality and sin, and of course the enduring difficulties between fathers and sons. In the end, I imagine my process was like that of a lot of writers who have to try to piece together seemingly disparate stories into some sort of cohesive whole: you begin to realize the similarities, the common touchstones, the places where certain stories touch and where others diverge. Assembling the book was largely a matter of trial and error. I learned later that Cheever apparently had a strategy for sequencing a story collection. (Your best story first, next best last, everything else in the middle.) I think my first instincts were similar, although once you start showing your work around, you realize what you consider to be your best work is really just your favorite work. And your favorite stories aren't always your best stories. In fact, two of my favorite stories were cut from this book days before it was sold.

Speaking of Cheever and Updike, can you say a bit more about your influences and inspirations in terms of other writers?

I think if you love good writing then it's impossible not to have particular books or writers amaze you and then, subsequently, make you sadly reconsider everything you've ever tried to write and deem it a failure. Everybody has writers who do this, and the experience is always thrilling and terrifying and discouraging all at once. But there are still a few writers I keep coming back to, like Michael Chabon and Marilynne Robinson and Vladimir Nabokov. Chabon once wrote that reading Cheever before sitting down to work was like eating before swimming: you need to wait at least twenty minutes before jumping in. I feel that way about a lot of writers, those two included, but also Lorrie Moore and Alice Munro and David Mitchell and Ethan Canin (who mentored me while I worked on these stories).

You've said elsewhere that your main characters are not all religious, but they are all Jews. Can you say more about what being Jewish means in this context, as divorced from some form of daily spiritual practice?

I'm not sure I have a good answer to this question. And I'm not sure my characters would have an answer either. What they have, and what I have, is an awareness and an appreciation for the conflict between spiritual and cultural identity that exists in the diaspora. Part of the issue, of course, is that Judaism exists now for a lot of people as both a faith and a culture. So what you have is a big portion of the community, especially lately and especially in America, who seem to have chosen the culture while leaving the faith behind—in some instances entirely. Consider the new popularity of secular humanist congregations across the country, where every mention of God has been replaced by some benign substitution. Some of this is the fault of assimilation, and some of this is because of interfaith marriages, and some of this exists because people, as they have for millennia, struggle to negotiate their belief in God with the ever-quickening revelations of cosmology. But it's a peculiar secularism, one informed just as much by the pull of tradition as it is with a genuine love of the culture. People need community. But people are also terrified of upsetting tradition. What you find, I think, are whole groups of people who, as you say, live their lives divorced from daily religious practice, but whose very essence is wrapped up in being Jewish—the definition of which is largely self-imposed. There's a conflict there, obviously: depending on where you fall on the spectrum of piety, this very idea borders on the heretical. That's why this conversation endures. For my grandparents' generation it was about being a first-generation American and making those initial movements away from the mentality of the shtetl. For my parents' generation there was an even greater loosening. And now, in my generation, there's a certain part of the secular community who've looked at the way they understand their faith and found it unrecognizable or unfulfilling. This is how I can arrive at Lewis from "Winter on the Sawtooth," who, when we meet him, hasn't been to synagogue in almost forty years but who readily defines himself as Jewish. And also how I can arrive at his son, Josh, who maybe has studied a little more than his father and who realizes that the faith, as they've practiced it, is perhaps a little too relaxed.

These issues are not new, of course, and not unique to Judaism, and people far smarter than I am have written and spoken and preached and prayed over them. Anyone who has ever reinterpreted their faith in a way different from their parents, or altered a family tradition, or decided one year not to attend Mass on Easter, or not to keep kosher during Passover, understands how difficult issues of identity can be, and how strong and serious the urge can be to resist allowing the most stringent definitions of the culture to define you rather than the other way around. Assimilation and identity (racial, religious, sexual) are, at times, diametrically opposed cultural forces. Set ideas of identity are what tell us that there is a solid, unalterable definition of manhood or piety or goodliness or motherhood. And we're all aware of cultures that refuse to assimilate. What continues to compel me as a writer is the inevitable intersection of these two forces. There's a conflict that comes out of that collision. The conflict is where the stories come from.

Many of these stories feature a generational conflict. Sometimes this involves religion, but just as frequently it involves differing ideas about obligations to oneself versus family and community, or obligations to a romantic partner. Other stories feature this rivalry between siblings or friends. To what extent is this conflict necessary to your fiction?

As a reader, I tend to prefer fiction where the conflict is clear and palpable, and I tend also to shy away from fiction whose primary—and sometimes only—goal is to impart some subtle, glancing epiphany. Obviously these categories aren't always mutually exclusive, but the latter was, and maybe still is, in vogue among some short-story writers. I tend to agree with Charles Baxter when he writes that "radiance, after a while, gets routine." So part of the central design of these stories was to present the conflict up front, whatever it was— generational, familial, romantic—and to let the energy of that conflict drive the narrative. At the end of the day, these are the things that interest me as a person, even more than as a writer. Tolstoy had it right in those famous first lines of *Anna*

Karenina. Families build themselves up and tear themselves down.

In stories such as "In the Book of Life" and "Catherine and Henry," characters betray the people they love the most and are sometimes changed by this act, but sometimes not. How important is it that your characters be flawed in some way?

Everyone is flawed, obviously. But I suppose as a writer the big decision you're faced with making is exactly how flawed your characters are. I'm not sure I had a conscious value system in my head when I wrote these stories. Some of the people here are so flawed that, on the face of things or taken out of context, they're deplorable, and some of them are so flawed that they've reached some point of self-actualization by way of all their sins and errors. The job of the writer is to zero in on the flaws, find the narrative that explains them, and write that story. A lot has been written about the idea of a moral fiction—from Tolstoy's *What Is Art?* to John Gardner's book on the subject. The idea fascinates me. It's imperative to me that I address the humanity of my characters and resist the urge to degrade, dehumanize, or make a caricature out of their plight, or what might seem like the foolishness of their decisions. Understanding this makes it easier for me to write a character like Abe Rivkin from "In the Book of Life." The job is to treat him honestly, to portray the reality of his decisions the way *he* sees them rather than the way *I* see them. As for whatever journey these characters might be on, I will say that to my mind, redemption is a natural impulse, whether you seek it because someone asks you to, whether you feel compelled by your faith to seek it, or whether you stumble upon it by accident.

What are you working on next?

I've just finished a novel called *Wise Men*. Because it's still sort of a newborn, I'm reluctant to say too much about it. But it's a big book that takes place over fifty years, beginning when Harry Truman was president and ending in 2003. It opens with a plane crash and ends on the beach in Cape Cod. Writing the book was, as it usually is for me, an occasionally exhilarating experience and occasionally so frustrating that every few months I tore it all up and put it back together again. I can't wait for people to read it.

Questions and topics for discussion

1. In the collection's first story, "In the Book of Life," why does Abe begin an affair with Jane, in spite of knowing "he was not the sort of man to do such a thing"?

2. At the end of "In the Book of Life," we see a moment from Larry and Abe's past. What does this moment suggest about their future?

3. Why does the narrator of "Winter on the Sawtooth" allow his wife to take a lover? How are his and his wife's separate relationships with Josh changed over the course of the story?

4. Describe the differences between Charles's and David's personalities in "The Moon Landing." Why is David less upset about their parents' death?

5. "Catherine and Henry" is the only story that is narrated, in part, from a woman's perspective. How is Catherine different from the men in this collection? In what ways is she like them?

6. In "Our Portion, Our Rock," Eric wants desperately to be a father. In what way does this desire change after Jenny's sudden abortion?

7. Why, in the story "Visiting," is it Marc who insists on talking to his grandfather, despite the fact that it was Jonathan who forced him to go on the trip?

8. How would you describe the way the characters in these stories think about their faith?

Stories I love

Recommendations from Stuart Nadler

"In the Cemetery Where Al Jolson Is Buried" by Amy Hempel— It may be a crafty bit of apocrypha, but I read once that this was the first story she ever wrote. Which is enough to make even the most determined writers think of quitting. Possibly the most heartbreaking final line ever.

"Goodbye, My Brother" by John Cheever—The first story in his collected works, the first of his that I ever read, and the story, when pressed, I still say is my favorite. Sometimes I pick this up just to read the final two paragraphs, which he claims to have composed aloud while standing "under the canopy of a Fifty-ninth Street apartment house."

"Love and Honor and Pity and Pride and Compassion and Sacrifice" by Nam Le—A cunning commentary on the pressures of writing ethnic fiction, this is a brilliant story in a collection packed with great work. So smart and filled with beautiful, lean writing. The fire at the end kills me every time. Nam makes it look easy.

"Last Night" by James Salter—I saw Salter read this one night in Iowa City in front of a packed room at the Dey House. He had the crowd in his palm. Near the end, most of the people were weeping. I've never seen anything like it. A

gorgeous, riveting, clear-eyed look at lust and death and the impossible responsibilities of love.

"A Solo Song: For Doc" by James Alan McPherson—I'm lucky to have had Jim as a teacher, and even luckier to have had the opportunity just to sit with him in his office and talk about whatever he wanted to talk about. A member of the first class of MacArthur Fellows, Jim is a real genius—and this story of a Pullman porter trying to fight off retirement is a classic American masterpiece.

"A Real Doll" by A. M. Homes—Her collection *The Safety of Objects* is bookended with two amazing stories, the first being "Adults Alone," populated by the crack-smoking parents she later wrote about in *Music for Torching*. "A Real Doll" ends the collection on the same sinister, devious, perverted note. Not especially suitable for younger readers.

"Twin Beds in Rome" by John Updike—It's hard to pick just one story of his, but I've always loved his stories about the Maples—their courting, marrying, quarreling, cheating, divorcing, and reconnecting—and I was happy to see that the Everyman's Pocket Classics released them in hardcover not so long ago. Any of those stories would fit quite comfortably on this list, but this one is particularly good: sad, nasty, cunning, passionate. This is the story that has Richard saying to Joan, "You're such a nice woman. I can't understand why I'm so miserable with you." It's not difficult to imagine Updike hammering this story out in his office in Ipswich one afternoon and then driving the short distance home to his family.

"The Year of Getting to Know Us" by Ethan Canin—Canin is one of the best story writers in America, and this, written when he was so ridiculously young, is one of my favorites of his. I remember reading this for the first time one warm after-

noon in Union Square Park, delighted that the main character had stowed away in the trunk of his father's Cadillac. This was a decade before he became my teacher. I'm still impressed by the audacity of its structure, and of course by its beautiful, heartbreaking opening. A great read.

"Secrets and Surprises" by Ann Beattie—Another master of the form, Beattie is one of my very favorite writers. This is the title story from a great collection of hers published the year I was born. The whole book is filled with classics: "A Vintage Thunderbird," "Weekend," "Shifting." But this one is my favorite, and over the years I've kept coming back to it, happy each time to find some new secret in this story about impossible romance, piano playing, and old friends. It's a great development that so much of her work has just begun to be re-collected into big comprehensive volumes. She's one of the best.

"Trilobites" by Breece D'J Pancake—Breece D'J Pancake killed himself in 1979, when he was only twenty-six years old. The writing he left behind was published as an eponymous collection four years later by Little, Brown. The stories are astonishing, none more so than this one, the first in the collection and probably the single best piece of writing about West Virginia ever set to paper. Every line is a treasure.